Dedication

Dedicated to my mother

Arthur Carlyle is the pen name of an author from London, England. Having grown up in the East End of London, he studied at the University of London before beginning a career in Government.

Arthur Carlyle

ARSENIC PLACEBO

AUSTIN MACAULEY PUBLISHERS™

LONDON • CAMBRIDGE • NEW YORK • SHARJAH

A CIP catalogue record for this title is available from the British Library.

ISBN 9781788485364 (Paperback)
ISBN 9781788485371 (Hardback)
ISBN 9781788485388 (E-Book)

www.austinmacauley.com

First Published (2018)
Austin Macauley Publishers Ltd™
25 Canada Square
Canary Wharf
London
E14 5LQ

Chapter One

This is so annoying! Amber thought to herself, scanning the magazine stand with conveyor-belt accuracy. *The one time I'm actually looking for something and I can't see the stupid... Oh... At last!* Some unhelpful soul had stuffed it behind the motoring magazines. Despite working as an MP's intern and studying politics at university, Amber wasn't actually much of a political bookworm. But this month's special edition of *Political Engagement* was not to be missed. It was published to mark the fifth anniversary of the passing of Lady Victoria Hanley, the much-loved disability-rights campaigner. *Political Engagement's* editor, Sir Henry Jacob, was regarded as an intellectual heir to Lady Hanley, and thus for some time had wished to dedicate an issue of the magazine to her legacy and set out what needed to be done so that her vision for disabled people was not buried under nostalgic razzmatazz. In all honesty, none of that particularly mattered to Amber. What marked this issue out for special attention was that she was interning for the Shadow Employment and Welfare Secretary, Guy Freedman, the current darling of the Opposition and, by most educated accounts, future Prime Minister material. Freedman, as the opposition's chief spokesman on all things' disability, had been asked to throw his two pennies into the maelstrom of epiphanies and apologias that was the world of disability politics. The request from *Political Engagement* also came with the assurance that he would be the highest profile contributor, with no question of a minister or a pretentious upstart stealing his thunder.

Amber almost body-checked the gift card stand into the path of another customer as she rushed down the narrow walkway to pay for the magazine and then made a lumbering exit out the door. "Flippin' 'eck Amber! They reform tax laws quicker than this! Or did you forget the name of the magazine again?"

"Shut your face Tom!" retorted Amber, with a sense of laughter and acknowledgement. If politics didn't work out, postwoman or librarian would definitely not be next on the career list.

"Well, come on then! Let's have a look!" As a fellow intern, Tom Harrison also had a vested interest in the success of the article.

Amber flicked through the pages like a person who had used a winning lottery ticket as a bookmark but had then inexplicably lost sight of it. She finally found the article and began reading in a proud yet considered manner. "*A new agenda for disabled people: Guy Freedman tells Political Engagement the rules of the game must change in order for disabled people to fully participate in the world of work!*"

"Oh for...! Get to it woman! Is it all there?" Tom enquired, somewhat exasperated. "I don't give a toss if it was in the preview copies we were sent. Just bloody make sure it's all there now!"

"It's all here," reassured Amber. "Listen, here is the bit we helped with. *By providing smaller businesses with financial incentives to hire more disabled staff, a future Union government aims to put the accelerator on the lethargic pace of change currently being overseen by those populating the government benches. Our research indicates that striking a balance between financial sustainability and genuine social emancipation can reap enormous benefits for both disabled people and inclusively-minded employers.*"

"All that hard work and it boils down to one poxy paragraph," reflected Tom. "But still, we're on our way now, eh?"

"Yep," agreed Amber.

Tom glanced at his phone. "Shit. We better shift our backsides sharpish or else that numpty will turn around and say 'thanks for your help, now cheerio'!"

"Now now," replied Amber whimsically. "The Rt Hon Guy Freedman is a man who stands for impeccable moral qualities. He just needs to be reminded sometimes that's all." They both let out a giggle signalling their agreement to Guy Freedman's questionable personality traits. It was time to make a rapid dash across the road and make their way to the Parliamentary Private Offices.

Despite Guy Freedman's freakish obsession with time keeping, on this particular morning, Amber and Tom were actually quite keen on arriving on time, or possibly early if they could help it. It seemed illogical to ruin what had for them been a momentous morning by then walking into the office at two minutes past nine. That being the case, there was a pronounced intensity in their steps as they made their way through the Old House Street Market, still quiet at this relatively early hour. Unfortunately, walking briskly was not one of Amber's strong points. As they navigated their way through Old House and onto Greater Parliament Road, Amber was totally oblivious to a man in possession of a three-foot cane moving in her direction, on a speedy intercept course. Tom was already thinking ahead when he first noticed the man and instinctively moved to the side of the pavement with plenty of time to spare, avoiding any unintended awkwardness. Sadly on this occasion, such intuition was lost on Amber. In an attempt to divert herself at the last second, she left a trailing leg behind her. The man tripped forward but, thankfully, remained upright.

Dumbfounded and irritated, the accosted gentleman suddenly bent down and swung his cane a full three-hundred and sixty degrees, clobbering Amber's lower shin. For a second time in a matter of moments, Amber's internal radar could not re-adjust itself, but the shock of the situation was an adequate explanation on this occasion. "Not too good at hurdles yourself then, eh? Stupid girl!" jeered the man in obvious frustration.

"Oh! I am so…"

"Don't touch me! Freak!" he hissed, justifiably shoving Amber to the side as she tried to put her hand on his shoulder. With that, he hastily departed, leaving Amber and Tom looking forlorn in the middle of the street, with bemused pedestrians shaking their heads in disbelief as they scurried by.

"You need to sort that out Amber. Paraplegic goldfish have faster reaction times than you," said Tom, somehow trying to sound comforting and admonishing, yet falling short on both counts. Thanks to Amber's unfortunate mishap, any ideas about arriving early in the office had fallen by the wayside. Priority number one was to simply get there on time and avoid any pompous lecture from Guy Freedman.

The building housing the Private Offices, Portcullis House, was unquestionably an architectural gem. Most people agreed it possessed a bizarre propensity to generate a monotonous, sombre atmosphere around its immediate vicinity. The architects had surrendered to the cult of personality that insisted galactic-sized glass mortuaries must cover large swathes of the city. Yet the cocktail of ancient markets, cobbled streets and endless lines of tourists seemed to give the offices a peculiar romantic quality that many architects and town planners craved. Arriving at the offices with milliseconds to spare, Tom and Amber walked through the door to slightly more cheerful sounds than they were used to. Isabelle, the default Diary Manager, and Marcus, intern number four, were sharing their observations on the *Political Engagement* article.

"I actually think it's cracking stuff," enthused Isabelle as she turned the page. Marcus was about to speak when the meeting room door swung open and Guy Freedman steadily strode out whilst finishing off a conversation on his mobile phone.

"OK no worries James, The Sunflower it is… Yes, absolutely, as I said they have some private rooms there where we can actually have a proper chat… OK, cheers then." Upon termination of the call, Freedman immediately noticed the presence of Amber and Tom.

"Good morning gentleman and gentlewoman. Glad to see your new claim to fame hasn't eroded your time management skills. I assume you've read the published piece." commented Freedman, before asking, "Any thoughts?"

"A job well-done Guy," said Amber, trying to sound authoritative yet clearly intimidated by being put on the spot in front of her colleagues.

"Quite right," replied Freedman, sounding more relaxed than when he first spoke. "I'm having lunch tomorrow with Sir Henry, get a sense of the reception and so on and maybe have a chat about a few other things. Would have wanted to meet today but Giles wants us all in the House to vote on the Public Advertising Bill. Not entirely sure why. I think he's fallen for the media hype about it being a close one. It'll sail through I'm sure. And so it should. The Government isn't always wrong, you know! Anyway, can I have one of you there with me tomorrow to do the usual? I'll leave it to yourselves to decide who."

"The car is waiting downstairs for us Guy," said Isabelle, waiting long enough after he had finished speaking to guarantee she wouldn't interrupt him but not waiting too long and creating an awkward silence. "I've booked another car for later so that you and Giles will arrive at the House for half two." Isabelle was looking for some sort of signal that Freedman was in agreement with the arrangements.

"Very good, very good," he said contentedly, and with that, they were both out the door, the echo of their footsteps gradually dissipating. Getting a posting with a frontline MP, shadow or otherwise, intern or paid, was easier said than done. Amber wasn't entirely sure how she managed it but was pleased nonetheless. Guy Freedman's office was unique in that for a frontbench politician, he wasn't swamped with special advisers and an army of PR people. There were certainly enough of them, but the nature of his operations was that there were always three to four internship positions available, and as long as interns kept their superiors updated with their work, they were largely left to their own devices. The set up presented those fortunate enough to be successful in their applications and opportunity to do elements of valuable work among the truck loads of useless admin.

Mornings seemed to flash by whenever Guy Freedman wasn't there constantly interrupting conversations and asking for meetings to be arranged post-haste and then asking for them to be cancelled again. Add to that what can only be described as a tea-fetish addiction that needed constant feeding and his leniency for some amoral political stances, you had what some might say was an archetypal, frustratingly demanding Member of Parliament. It was only the self-evident reality that success or failure was inextricably linked to his personal patronage that stopped the level of his support staff's tolerance of him diminishing even further.

The swift elapsing of the morning meant the time had come for Amber and Tom to assemble themselves and make their way to Northborough Plaza for a much-anticipated lunchtime get together with two ex-interns who had been based in Guy Freedman's office but had since moved on to bigger and brighter things. Even a king of a village full of idiots would be well-aware that at this stage in their fledgling careers, networking was everything. They were young and enthusiastic and hadn't quite had the utopianism ground out of them yet. One of the ex-colleagues, Katrina, had managed to snap up a corporate communications role with Mortimer Brothers, one of the world's leading advertising houses, based only a few hundred yards away in Old City Central. Anthony, ex-intern number two and also ex-school friend acquaintance of Tom, had wriggled his way into Malone and Harper (M&H), one of the Magic Triangle law firms based a short train ride away at Queen Anne's Point. M&H and Mortimer Brothers is what it was all about as far as Amber and Tom were concerned, and their zest for getting on in life was, for now, compensating for any naïvety-bordering-delusion that the likes of Marcus would accuse them of suffering from.

Meeting at the entrance of Northborough Plaza, the four efficiently debated where they ought to go and eat before deciding on Grill of Malaysia, one of a number of new, energetic and cosmopolitan eateries that had sprung up in quick succession in the local area over the past few months. Although admittedly on this occasion, the decision was conveniently assisted by Anthony possessing a ten per cent group discount card that he had obtained from one of the plethora of daily deal websites he was subscribed to. Even if he and Katrina were now signed-up tax-payers, this was the city and it remained prudent for anyone with any sense of balance and self-restraint to keep one eye on personal expenditure.

There was minimal attention paid to eating, however, as the bulk of the lunch hour was consumed by frantic chatter and an exchange of stories and advice. Amber and Tom smartly summarised their *Political Engagement* escapade and had no inhibitions in engaging in what, for Katrina and Anthony, must have felt like at times a celebrity-style media interrogation. They were totally relaxed, however. They hadn't as yet acquired a snooty, downward-gazing mind-set now that they had entered what for them must have seemed like the corporate big-time. Moreover, being social science graduates, they were hardly immune to the inevitable muckraking and gossip that came with working in Parliamentary Affairs. If there was a chance of hearing about a future political hot potato, then they were all ears.

Katrina was particularly interested in the background to the *Political Engagement* article.

"Tell me, Guy Freedman isn't the sort of dude to write THAT kind of article about disability really, is he? Despite any number of omissions there may have been or whether he's the shadow Secretary of State. I mean, the actual SoS didn't even contribute and nobody is batting an eye-lid. And why would they for such a safe subject? Everyone agrees what needs to be done, don't they? So why did he do it?" she enquired.

Amber and Tom didn't want to look foolish twice in one day, regardless of whether Katrina not being the type to judge. "It's just politics." ventured Tom casually.

"And a bit of ego," added Amber, taking up the baton. "If he really is future Prime Minister material, then that's the sort of bish-bosh that he'll have to come out with of his own accord rather than acting like one of Giles' sycophants. I suspect as time goes on he'll be throwing his weight into every innocuous debate there is and let Giles & Co take any flack for any sensitive nonsense." After reflecting on her analysis, Amber was actually quite surprised by her own mental astuteness, regardless of whether how blindingly an obvious observation it was.

"Hmmm," murmured Katrina, "but still, I'm grateful for the article regardless. Even a small step is a step in the right direction."

"You're dyslexic aren't you, Katrina?" Tom suddenly interrupted, abruptly but innocently.

"I am indeedy," confirmed Katrina.

"So I guess you're quite pleased with the Political Engagement stuff then? On a personal level I mean... "

"Of course, why not? There will always be politics and business and whatever. That's life. But regardless, everybody needs a spokesman, and I happen to think Sir Henry is quite a good one," exclaimed Katrina, before revealing, "he was down here last week actually..."

"What? Sir Henry?" asked Amber with a subtle bemusement. She heard the first time perfectly well, as most people do when asking for a surprise revelation to be repeated. But the idea of Sir Henry Jacob meeting Howard Blackwood, a total sociopath, momentarily stirred her curiosity.

"Yep," confirmed Katrina. "I thought it was a bit random at first, but then, I figured even Howard Blackwood can see the brownie points to be gained, particularly for the company's rep, even though he's a bit of a crap bag."

Everyone leaned back for a few seconds, briefly contemplating this mismatch of a rendezvous.

"Any idea what they talked about?" questioned Anthony.

"Well I had a brief chat with Howard's PA, Rachel, poor thing, and she basically said they and the HR Director initially went over how recruitment was going on the grand scheme... vis-a-vis disabled graduates obviously. Then they asked to be left in private to talk about some nonsense or other. She didn't really say much else to be honest. I got my role through the grand scheme actually, so I'm not fussed really."

The lunch hour was zipping away, and all four knew they needed to be frugal with their use of time as well as their use of money. Anthony graciously offered to change the 10% discount into picking up the tab completely, a lovely gesture that any recent graduate would appreciate. The gesture did leave Tom feeling slightly guilty, as he had left half a steak to his imaginary friend…or the homeless person bound to search the bins afterward, whichever of the two got to it first. Farewells were hastily followed by a mad dash to their respective offices, with the depressing thought of burning the afternoon oil, an all too familiar occurrence. Perhaps they could lobby Guy Freedman to put down an early day motion expressing his fondness for siestas?

The bulk of the afternoon did in fact revolve around Guy Freedman. Any sense of exertion was abandoned, being replaced by farcical but incisive argument and counter-argument as to who ought to accompany Freedman on his afternoon shindig with Sir Henry the next day.

"I nominate you Amber," said an insistent Tom.

"Why?"

"You can speak English."

"Pardon?" replied Amber, with a quizzical look on her face, whilst actually knowing precisely what Tom was referring to.

"You know full well he reckons people with accents are some sort of illegal immigrant group! Remember he was describing meeting a group of constituents? What was it again? He said he was intrigued because one was a Liverpudlian, one was a Yorkshireman…and one guy was an Englishman!"

"Sod that!" maintained Amber, "It's Sir Henry who he's meeting, and if that man asks me where my grandparents are from, one more time, I'll let the tyres down on his wheelchair! Plus he can be SO impatient!"

"Next time he asks you about your heritage, tell him you're amphibious and that your parents and grandparents were exiled from Amphibia, then see how long it takes him to catch on to what the heck you're talking about!"

During their attempts to downplay their suitability for accompanying Guy Freedman, it dawned on them that they had overlooked the obvious in that Isabelle was also a candidate for the task and, more conveniently, the two of them were in a position to partake in a little office gerrymandering and nominate Isabelle to accompany Guy. Upon her return to the office that afternoon, Amber and Tom wasted no time in presenting their majority-decision to her as a fait accompli. Isabelle, as well as any right-minded observer who happened to take notice, couldn't help but be staggered that of the three of them, she was the de-facto Diary Manager and they the de-facto Policy Assistants. When it came to substance, for all their good intentions, Amber and Tom were muffins without the chocolate chip, whereas she was as refined as an ancient piece of calligraphy. She didn't possess the naïvety sometimes displayed by Tom and Amber. Yet, she also refused to display the more callous traits that the likes of Guy Freedman were receptive to. More commendable though, was her sense of self-worth, in contrast to the 'Yes Men' mentality that inhabited the office. This explained her relegation to administrative duties and her sometimes understandable annoyance at having to be dictated to by, in comparison to her, two blithering idiots. Nevertheless, Isabelle didn't bother protesting. She knew how to pick her battles. Note-taking was one she would happily concede, fully aware that Amber and Tom attached an illogical weighting to it that she could use to her advantage whenever they discussed the office workload.

**

Upon arriving home that evening, Amber was pleasantly surprised to find her close friend and neighbour, Clare, Clare's mother Kerry and her mother enjoying some gingersnaps and a brew of Kenyan tea.

"Greetings people! Hey Clare, how you doin'?"

"Squire-ess!"

"Hey hey! Can't have that sort of language in front of our mothers!"

Kerry turned to Amber's mother with a smile on her face and said, "Come on Jan, shall we go to your living room and leave these two alone? If Clare doesn't detox now, I'll get the brunt of it later!" And with that both mothers retired to the living room, leaving the kitchen to Amber and Clare.

Some might find it strange that Amber and Clare didn't venture straight to Amber's room, as per the supposed household etiquette, leaving parents to freely wander around the rest of the home. However, in this case Clare's restriction to a wheelchair meant manoeuvrability was at a premium. The situation was further aggravated by the incongruous layout of the home, barring any attempts at installing anything that resembled a stair lift.

Amber took a seat at the table next to Clare and poured a cup of tea for herself, taking care not to spill any on to the table. "So, how go things in the world of Clare Gwendoline Thomas? Shall I pop a film on or something? Actually let's see what's on the radio…ah! Classic rock…oh I like this bit, I like when he says crazy…*you can have a change of heart, if you would only change your mind, cause' I'm crazy about you baby, crazy… CRAZY!*"

"Nah, not up for watching anything, really. Turn that off please. Things are as crap as ever, I'm afraid. Remember that internship I told you about? The one at KL Energy?"

"Yes, I remember… I take it from your demeanour they've got back to you?"

"Yep. Thanks but no thanks. It's absolutely ridiculous. I told the interview panel I have a slight stutter. They said it wasn't a problem but you could *so* tell it was bothering them. The main guy was a proper idiot. It was as if he was just going through the motions."

"Did you call them to get feedback?"

"I called them this afternoon. Same old nonsense. Although to be fair, this time at least they were a bit more honest. The lady I spoke to basically told me in a coded way that they thought I might find it all a bit too much! How gracious of them to tell me!"

"This is probably of no use but the best thing you can do is keep on trying. They can't all be wankers." Amber was trying her utmost to sound comforting, whilst avoiding the trap of patronising idealism. "I met an old work colleague for lunch today. She is dyslexic but still got into Mortimer Brothers. So it's irritating but you just need to keep plugging away."

"*You're* irritating," said a frustrated Clare. "Tell me, what extra stuff they need to do for her to help her do her job properly?" she asked sharply.

"Not too much from memory. She sometimes needs things printed on different coloured paper and she sometimes needs reminding about bits of work and stuff, but nothing too drastic. If memory serves me correctly, she keeps a Dictaphone on her as well." Amber had an element of hesitancy in her voice.

"So basically nothing too intrusive then?"

Amber reflected upon the question and said, "I suppose not. Actually just speaking to her and being around her you'd never guess she was dyslexic."

"Well there you go then," said Clare with finality.

"I'm sorry... What do you mean mate?" retorted a puzzled Amber.

"What you just said. That explains why your buddy got into Mortimer Bros and I'm still faffing around with internship interviews five years after graduating."

"What?" Amber was looking for a pointer.

"They don't see her as a burden. The first thing they ask themselves is 'oh for goodness... Am I going to be this dude's carer?' Then on top of that she doesn't represent some sort of visual anomaly, does she?"

"How do you mean?" replied Amber, now all at sea trying to follow where Clare was going with her remarks.

"What I mean is, these companies, they sign up to this bollocks and that bollocks. And people say, oh wow these big corporates are starting to take us seriously and that sort of thing. But look at the sort of disabled people they hire. Look at how many they hire. People are stupid if they think these guys are gonna put an end to their old ways. They just cover themselves with the equality and diversity bullshit and hire one or two disabled people as a front for poster campaigns." Clare's voice grew sterner as she confronted Amber with her analysis. Amber paused for a moment, still not fully sure whether she had grasped the gist of what was being said.

"So you think people like Katrina are sort of... Useful idiots?"

"Well yea. But obviously it won't click with them coz they're in a job. But these companies won't ever recruit anyone who they think is a burden. Not in an equitable way anyway. They'll pick up one or two for the posters, and even then they'll try and make sure they're pretty faces, tick the disability box when HR do their annual sheep count and everybody's happy."

Clare's cynicism and apparent contempt for the world of big business caught Amber cold. It was a window into Clare's seemingly never-ending struggles, struggles that until then had been skilfully veiled away from the world outside but then appearing in a blink of an eye like some devilish conjuring trick. Characteristically not knowing precisely how to respond, Amber was acutely aware, however, that this sort of thinking could spiral into a cesspit of intense frustration. But at the same time, she couldn't help feel Clare's mindset was merely a product of her personal circumstances, and that if she hung on in there, things would work out in the end. For once, however, Amber had judged the mood in the room accurately. Clare was clearly on a downer, and offering impractical sound bites would almost certainly come across as being impertinent. In the research for the piece for *Political Engagement*, she had come across a myriad of statistics relating to employment, but their significance just didn't register, leaving her with nothing sensible to offer Clare.

"So what do you plan on doing next?" The only way to seem supportive was apparently to ask more questions, absolving Amber of the immediate need to think more deeply about Clare's predicament.

"I don't know. May need to take a step back. See if I can get any unpaid stuff. Might even do another qualification, at least that way I'd be keeping myself productive." For all her despondency, deep down Clare was adamant that she wouldn't give those who she thought had a benevolently backward view of where she belonged in the world, some sort of confirmation of their blinkered view. Amber got up from her seat and circled the room, ostensibly to put her cup on the side table, but really to take a moment to see if she could just suggest even the smallest positive idea. As she circled to the side table and back again, she felt like a distressed pilot, unable to find the correct flight path.

"Shall I try and put you in touch with Katrina?" she then said suddenly. Under the circumstances it sounded like an industrious idea. If networking worked for her, it could work for Clare, and thankfully, Clare was receptive.

"Actually that might be useful. Don't tell her what I said though! Like I was saying she hasn't done anything wrong obviously but she'll still rightly be offended. In the meantime, I'll drop my friend Veronica a line to see if she's come across any openings. She's normally quite good with stuff like that."

"Don't worry, I'm not silly. I appreciate what you're saying. I shall remain shtoom."

A day that appeared to be ending in the doldrums was pulled from the wreckage at the last moment, with an offshoot of cheerfulness still intact.

Clare and her mother left quite late, but Amber was a late sleeper so it didn't bother her. Amber was slumped in the corner sofa, flicking through the late night television. Her mother entered and sat in the opposite corner sofa.

"Oh hang on, leave it on that for a sec. It's *That Sketch Show*. You'll love this bit. All you need to know is that guy has turned up for a job interview. Just watch the next bit...!"

"Erm this is Craig Foster he's our next candidate... Erm, hello Craig, I'm Felix I'll be interviewing you along with my colleague whom you've already met. Erm, sorry can I just ask, who is this?... Ah, certainly. This is Mike... Erm, yes, sorry, have we missed something? I apologise if we have. Is Mike meant to be fulfilling a reasonable adjustment or something like that? I don't recall seeing anything on your application... Oh, no nothing like that, Mike will be answering all my interview questions that's all... Sorry, what do you mean...? Oh, I should explain. He's my avatar. Obviously they're my answers, he's just an avatar that's all (interview panel look at each other in bemusement)."

Amber's mum couldn't stop laughing, but Amber didn't seem in the mood.

"Is everything all right honey? You look shattered darling. How are things in the world of unpaid internships?"

"Well it's all good because you're the super mummy who's got two jobs!" and with that Amber's mood turned as she joined her mother in her chair and embraced her in a jubilant cuddle.

"But how is the work going?"

"It's all right you know. They sort of screwed us over with that magazine article I was telling you about. They only published bits. But I guess it's better than nothing. We were fortunate to be able to do anything. They normally get a media person to write it and then credit it to the MP or something like that."

"Well if that's the worst thing that happens then you've done all right. You already know what I think. You never know what those people will pull."

"Mum honestly. It's just like any other work place with a bad reputation. Everyone who actually works there says it's fine. Guy Freedman is a bit hit and miss but obviously I don't have that much contact with him." Amber wasn't as enthusiastic about the role as she made out, despite knowing how fortunate she was. She was more concerned about putting her mother's fears to rest.

"I don't know. You just hear stories. There was that girl who committed suicide because her MP boss was bullying her and harassing her. And what about that other boy—Christopher or whatever his name was."

"I read about that guy. He had issues or something, didn't he?"

"Just because somebody has issues, doesn't mean they straight disappear off the face of the earth, does it?"

"I think you're exaggerating. He hasn't actually disappeared. I mean, his family haven't said anything, have they? It's probably some sort of personal issue that everyone prefers to keep quiet. You can't be regarded as missing if your family say you're fine, right?"

"Yes, but there was an article I read by one of his friends saying they hadn't seen or heard from him. The article was actually about unpaid internships, and that sort of thing, and how it can link to depression. You shouldn't dismiss these people Amber. Who knows what's going through someone's head." Amber's mother was candid but caring.

"It's probably just an episode he's going through or something." Amber let out an extraordinary yawn. "Remember what granddad used to say—the people see conspiracy theories while the rulers rob them with their pants down. Clare always says there are enough real things out there for people to get mad about without needing to make things up. Anyway, I'm off to bed. Love you!" Amber embraced her mother a final time before retiring to her bedroom.

The story of Harry Christopher cast a spell over the media for nearly a fortnight, and then everything went dead, as if the two week circus never happened. Christopher was an intern working for a frontbench politician. Rumours of politicians overworking their unpaid employees were quite common. Christopher's ill-treatment was under the spotlight due to the drip-fed way details were being released. The politician in question regarded Christopher as a paid

p undercover reporter and had him sacked. The sacking left a sour taste in the minds of many following an appearance of Christopher's mother on a daytime chat show. She dissected the abuse done to her son as well as the ridiculous claims of links to newspapers. It was her disclosure of her son's psychological state that caused rage among viewers, and the offending politician was broadcast entering the family home in an apparent attempt to apologise. The story then dropped off without any public conclusion—most likely due to political pressure asking for some closure. Not a comment was heard from Christopher again. Upon enquiring, his family repeated the same line over and over that Christopher was dealing with personal issues and didn't wish to enter the public domain again. It seemed to be an acceptable explanation for everyone concerned and the matter was never looked into any further.

Chapter Two

Upon arriving at work the next morning, Amber was summoned to an impromptu meeting with Guy Freedman, along with Tom, Marcus and Isabelle. Although meetings were regularly scrambled together at a moment's notice, the additional presence of Alexander Hayes was a cause for anxiety for Amber. It definitely was not a normal occurrence. When Guy Freedman and Alexander Hayes usually met, it was rarely in Guy's parliamentary private office. For that matter they rarely met in the private offices building full stop. Hayes, like most MPs in the public eye, had always been conscious of privacy. Hundreds of MPs and interns, intermixed with a dizzying number of visitors and lobbyists was a perfect environment for stirring gossip. Yet that wasn't really the main source of his anxiety. There was a sense of predictability in holding meetings in the same old places. When one had grand plans for a nation's financial future, it made sense to shy away from prying eyes as often as possible. The intense levels of security that engulfed the private offices did little to ease his discomfort. For the sake of cordiality and government efficiency, most meetings needed a touch of confidentiality. And as far as Hayes was concerned that was that.

Amber and Marcus entered the private meeting room where Isabelle and Tom were already congregating. Also present were two of Hayes' aides, Samuel Bertrand and Rein Turner. Both were looking dolefully across the table at their colleagues, neither seeming to want to offer a word of a greeting. Tom half-opened his mouth to offer something, but the attempt turned into a mere murmur by the sudden jerking of the meeting room door. Any remote attempt at a quick-fire free-for-all as to why the meeting had been called was quickly eliminated by the entrance of Guy Freedman and Alexander Hayes. Freedman had an almost feverish look on his face as he began to speak. They were followed into the room by a company of spin doctors.

"We've called you in order to bring some important news to you. And before it breaks in the media we want to clear things and get our message straight with you so that you know what to say when some tabloid hack starts harassing you on the phone for information. The fact that Guy and I haven't delegated this task to the media team should show you how important we regard this and that it should be handled as professionally as possible so make sure you listen carefully." *What was coming?* Amber thought to herself. *Had somebody quit? Had somebody died? Had somebody been caught doing drugs?* Hayes, still standing, bent forward and rested his palms on the table. Expressionless, he began to talk. Whatever it was, they were all about to find out.

"Giles is standing down as Party leader."

"PAR..." Tom's attempt to vocalise his astonishment and bewilderment at the revelation was comprehensively nullified by a penetrative glance Hayes aimed in his direction. That set the tone for the rest of the meeting. Some meetings are for asking questions. Others are for maintaining a sense of docility. This one seemed to emphatically fall into the latter category.

"This is the situation: for a while now Giles has felt the Party needs to head in a new direction. Naturally, we all think he's done fantastically well to get us into a position where we have a bona fide chance of winning in eighteen months' time. Despite that, for some time now he's told us that he doesn't have the enthusiasm to carry us into the last leg of this Parliament. Up to now we've obviously managed to convince him to stay as long as possible, but he now feels the time is right." Hayes' force was so strong, those present could have been forgiven had they began to sweat intensely. "Now just to repeat the fact that Guy and I are here debriefing you personally demonstrates how sensitive we think the matter is. These are times when messaging and presentation are everything."

Hayes stopped talking, with Freedman seamlessly carrying on from where he left off.

"So, as far as we're concerned it's going to be business as usual. Just be clear on what you say to journalists who might phone up the office. If you're asked why, it's a simple matter of Giles wanting to move away from frontbench politics and out of the public eye. Just make your responses sound as conciliatory as possible and you'll be fine. Anybody unclear on anything?" Freedman's ever so slightly more placid body language brought a welcomed, if ephemeral, air of calmness to proceedings, allowing Amber and her co-workers to digest the bombshell.

"When did this first come out?" probed Isabelle gently.

"Giles broke the news publicly to senior staff early yesterday evening, though as I mentioned we've had indications it's been on the cards," responded Hayes. "Shadow Cabinet colleagues and special advisors have been working with the press and PR guys in order to brief as many people as possible since then, to make sure as many people as possible linked to the Party are on the same wavelength. We're very fortunate. This sort of thing usually gets out into the press in a heartbeat. Giles is leaving us on good terms and we've had time to sort things out, notwithstanding the precipitous nature of the situation."

Marcus was perceptive enough to fire an understandable follow-up question before the atmosphere turned claustrophobic again. "So what's the situation with the leadership?"

"In the past, we've held a number of off-the-record discussions to agree something mutually acceptable in the event Giles ever stood down," explained Guy Freedman intently. "We've always wanted to avoid the nonsense of leadership run-offs and contrived public-spats, so on that basis we eventually decided Alexander would be the next leader. Giles is due to announce his resignation officially and Alexander's ascension to the leadership in the same speech at 1pm. So, from now until the press lose interest, just make sure you stick to what we've told you." Freedman suddenly seemed disconcerted and eager to leave, and for that matter, so did Hayes.

"Anything else?" he asked decisively. Everyone knew not to rock the boat and remained silent. "Good. Well, Alexander and I will be tied up for the rest of morning with media stuff and so on. You know how to contact us if any emergencies pop up. But please try your utmost to make sure they don't. None of you are stupid." And with that Freedman and Hayes vacated the room, tailed by Bertrand and Turner.

Tom, Amber, Marcus and Isabelle were left in the room, all of them caught in a state of wonderment and began to deconstruct what had just happened.

"Flamin' 'eck!" gasped Tom. "Anybody see that coming?"

"Nope." responded Amber immediately.

"He's quite old, and we all know how vainglorious Freedman and Hayes are, but I am surprised he has decided to go so relatively close to the elections. Regardless of how big opinion poll leads are. He was a safe pair of hands image-wise. Even Hayes and Freedman knew that. So I guess he really did just want to go." Isabelle's prudent analysis of the situation seemed to find instant agreement among her colleagues. At the back of her mind, however, she did have the feeling that the timing of the announcement was just a little *too* unpredicted. There were no ostensible mutterings of discontent from shadow front-benchers, and Giles Gibbs was well-respected among the grassroots, even though he wasn't the most charismatic leader a political party could hoped to have. And, despite their shortcomings, Freedman and Hayes definitely knew the importance of continuity in the run-up to an election. Yes, the alacrity with which they seemed to accept Giles' resignation was quite puzzling.

"Do you think they're actually happy with Hayes taking over?" asked Tom speculatively. "I mean, a narcissist like that. Freedman is all sycophantic around him. I wouldn't be surprised if the two of them just laid the law down and the rest of them were terrified and just went along with it."

"Not sure," said a dispassionate Marcus. "Freedman wants to be leader at some point, that's for sure. I guess he is biding his time. Or maybe he isn't as confident as he makes out about the elections. Either way, I'm not that fussed, nor should you be. One is a slightly larger dickhead than the other. I think that neatly sums up any qualitative differences." Marcus left his half-finished cup of takeaway coffee on the meeting room table and went to his desk.

"What do you guys think?" Tom asked, turning to Isabelle and Amber, laudably attempting to postpone for as long as humanly possible, the inescapable return to the anaesthetising routine of office work that had been temporarily interrupted. Amber and Isabelle, however, had already absorbed the news and had no further gambits to put forward. Amber shrugged and went to sit down at her desk. Isabelle also seemed disinterested in continuing the conversation further, despite her slight misgivings as to the nature of the events that had taken place.

"They're both twats. Don't really care who takes over." With that frank statement, she stood up, collecting her notebook in one hand and her skinny latte in the other. "Anyway, I need to go and type some notes up quickly before I go do some more note-taking courtesy of you two." She wasn't rueful, but she did have that early morning feeling that commonly afflicts office folk across the country—*why did I agree to another stupid meeting?*

Amber joined the others in the main office. Portcullis House wasn't outrageously exquisite on the inside, but it was certainly more salubrious than most offices could hope to be and it was unquestionably the place to be as the winter began to settle in. The stratospheric sums needed to build and furnish the place caused a mini-political firestorm for the main parties. But it seems that when a number of MPs have their heart set on something, they suddenly develop a funny knack of riding out the most turbulent of storms, even if those storms were generated by dozens of protests, thousands of strongly-worded letters and ritual humiliation by television news presenters.

The office layout was open-plan, with the main seating consisting of a gigantic round table, designed in such a way as to incorporate a number of desks whilst having visibility of everybody who was seated. Whoever designed this set-up was clearly a paranoid lunatic or tormented at school or a control freak—or perhaps all of these things.

"So what was all this chat about the Public Advertising Bill yesterday afternoon?" asked Amber as she swung her chair around to face the others more comfortably. "I hear that some backbenchers were doing their nut about a rebellion that never was or something?"

"Not sure," said Marcus. "A lot of our guys didn't appreciate backing the government line obviously. But I hear that an off-the-record memo is no longer off-the-record. Though we'll never know if it's true or not. I haven't seen any random post-its or emails. In any case, it'll get buried under Giles' news now."

"Where? What memo?" asked Tom interrogatively.

"Piss off! How the heck am I supposed to know? I just told you I haven't seen or heard anything!" came a crabby response from Marcus. Thankfully, Isabelle came to everyone's rescue and filled in the tantalising gaps.

"Remember yesterday Guy was quietly confident that the Bill would go through despite all this hullabaloo in the press and so on? Well now we know why. Apparently, a note of some sort has been leaked, and it looks like a lot of staging has gone on with some backbenchers and possibly some tabloid hacks."

"Oooooooh!" enthused Amber. "Do we know what sort of staging?"

"Well it seems like Hayes and some of the others done some sort of deal with a group of our backbenchers. They wanted to take credit for the Public Advertising Bill even though it was a government initiative. But they knew it could only get through with opposition support. The government has a genuine backbench issue with the hard core libertarians. So it looks like our bastard guys have had a chat with a group of our bastard backbenchers who were always going to vote yes and have told them to throw their toys out of the pram."

"So go on..." said Marcus, not quite able to put two and two together.

"SO!" continued Isabelle, "Hayes, Giles and Co get to publicly 'win them over', the Bill goes through successfully, the Union Party gets the credit and Hayes and all those guys get all the prestige and bollocks from all those media and PR firms."

"Scheming shits!" exclaimed Marcus as he stood up to make a cup of tea.

"Do you know what the fallout is all about then?" asked Amber earnestly.

"Not sure, they can do what they like," said a detached Isabelle. "They'll probably have an All Party Members meeting at some point in the near future, today or tomorrow if they have the brains. They'll probably try and convince the people that didn't know about the deal that it'll all be worth it when they win the election. They can't do much about it anyway. Even our backbenchers won't do anything too drastic with an election not far away."

"What about the press guys? Do we know who it is and what they were asked to do?"

"Well I don't think they're that concerned about that side of things. My guess is that they've probably given people like Bob O'Hara a heads up on what was going on. They've only tipped off guys who support the Party already, as tipping anybody else off would obviously be suicide."

"Where the heck do you pick up on all this stuff Izzy?" asked a dazzled Amber.

"I pay attention. Now shut up. I need to get this crap typed up." Isabelle was now visibly peeved with providing answers to questions that people working in a MP's office ought to know already. Amber didn't disturb her for the rest of the morning.

The bulk of the morning was taken up with answering calls and exchanging superficial pleasantries with journalists from some media outfit or another. They weren't all bad, but some in particular were staggeringly sordid and self-absorbed. O'Hara was a prime example. Reading a selection of his articles appeared to suggest he had an encyclopaedia on his bedside table of things he hated and things he wanted to be banned or incinerated. The eclectic entry list so far included Australia, successful women, sugar, oranges, disabled people, the minimum wage, candy-floss, ketch-up and men who refuse to wear ties when in a suit. *The National* was a card-carrying supporter of the Union Party and was developing an aggressive, disreputable streak in its journalism since 'prizing' O'Hara away from *The British Tribune*. He had clearly become disenchanted with being the token ass-wipe at the more progressive *Tribune*, and everyone in the industry agreed that *The National* and O'Hara were perfect bedfellows. Everyone in the office constructed a sufficient brick wall when responding to queries, even when being driven round the bend by one of the resident know-it-alls from the *Tribune*. Annoyer-in-Chief was Henrietta Barnes, who possessed a penchant for misinterpreting misplaced commas as evidence of an alien invasion. Though, by and large, she was one who meant well, and so everyone in the office had considerably more time for her than the nincompoops at *The National*.

As the time moved torturously closer to lunch, Marcus suddenly adjusted his seat so that he was facing more of Amber and Tom and less of Isabelle.

"You two, The Communications Committee is meeting at half two over in Parliament House. Do you want to go along and check it out?" he asked invitingly. "But only one of you though—we still need someone to stay here and man the phones. There's bound to be some fallout from the Public Advertising Bill. But they only meet four or five times a year for some silly reason so it'll be a chance to catch-up on all the boring crap we don't normally pay attention to." For once Amber was first to the buzzer.

"I call it!" she screeched, putting her hand in the air as if she had been transported back to primary school, whilst turning to Tom with a merry smile on her face. Anything was better than spending the entire afternoon acting like a toilet roll.

"I most probably won't see either of you until tomorrow then," informed Isabelle. "I'm going straight to Guy and Sir Henry's chitchat immediately after lunch. Enjoy the boredom."

The spectacular windows in theory provided for a regal view of the ancient streets surrounding Portcullis House, however, during the grey, morbid autumn and winter months, they only served to reinforce the dreary mood lingering around the building. However, downcast weather might make for fickle moods, and fickle moods in a kingdom of skulduggery would make for fun committee viewing. The crashing of Marcus' PC conveniently signalled that it was worth packing up early and make a move to Parliament House.

"Come on let's go. If we leave now, we'll get some good seats. I don't like peeping over someone's shoulder." In a few ironically brisk movements, Amber had got her things together and the two of them were on their way to Parliament House.

Parliament House was for the most part a throwback to an altogether different era. With the exception of some re-built sections that were destroyed by fire, the building maintained a primordial, venerable expressiveness. Walking through the tangle of corridors, underneath the spectacular chandeliers and past an endless array of twenty-foot pieces of self-infatuated art, no reminders were needed as to the historic resonance of the building. Such splendour, however, had disadvantages stemming from the antiquated nature of the structure. Chief among them was the lighting. Being classified as 'A Building of Historic Significance' meant that the only changes that could be made were those that had to comply with the rigmarole of health and safety. But apparently, such is the nature of modern red tape, being killed by a falling piece of roof was most improper, but being killed as a result of not being able to see where you were going was totally acceptable. On a number of occasions, Amber and Marcus had seen unsuspecting visitors plummet down stairs. The dim lighting was more suited to breeding an exotic breed of plant.

A burley security officer stood outside the door of committee room 2. As Amber and Marcus approached the door, the Officer advanced forward in order to obstruct their entry. The way he was standing, it was as if he was waiting for one of them to dispense with a secret handshake in order to be let in.

"Excuse me, are you cleared to attend this meeting?"

"Cleared?" snarled Marcus. "It's a public meeting. Anyone who qualifies as human is cleared!"

"Not today. Due to expected high-turnout, only those pre-registered can attend."

"We're here on behalf of Guy Freedman. Will that do?" Amber and Marcus flashed their ID cards like well-trained detectives.

He turned his eyes down at his clipboard, whilst hideously managing not to move his body an inch.

"Fine. You can go in. Seats with a white sheet of paper are taken. You're free to sit anywhere else." Amber and Marcus entered the room to find the entire first four rows of seats with pieces of paper on them. Leaving early had been a waste of time.

"Just remind me, I know I don't come to these things too often, but it isn't normally like this, is it?" asked Amber with a befuddled look on her face. "I mean, even when you watch it on TV when they have the big Treasury and Security Committees, you can still see a couple of empty chairs. So what the heck is going on here?"

"They set it up like this when it suits them. Come on, let's get what's left of the few remaining seats."

The room began to fill up apace as MPs entered and took their seats at the grandiose table at the front of the room. A plethora of industry observers and journalists swapped the pieces of paper with their backsides, whilst a handful of members of the public were standing in a herd at the back. Amber leaned gently into Marcus.

"How do you think this will go? Are we due any fireworks?"

"Don't know. Samantha Barratt is the Chair and definitely competent enough. But if they get tongue-tied they normally just close ranks and ramble nonsense."

Star attraction at this committee hearing was blusterer-in-chief, Howard Blackwood of Mortimer Brothers. Mortimer seemed to be winning every government marketing and advertising contract going, and they had also been at the forefront in the lobbying campaign to pass the Public Advertising Bill. But how Blackwood was CEO of a major advertising and PR company and managing to stay there was the mother of conundrums. Discourteous and ill-mannered, he was a serial dropper of clangers. The committee encounter would have made for satirical viewing, had it not been for Blackwood being flanked by two of his legal heavies. Their presence riled Barratt, and a quick fire exchange of greetings soon descended into an intense face-off. The tit-for-tat eventually turned to the circumstances surrounding the passing of the Public Advertising Bill. Barratt was a Union MP, but more importantly had not been one of the opposition's backbench conspirators that had worked with the leadership behind closed doors. She was more than happy to ask the sticky questions. She was also a seasoned backbencher, with no inclination for a ministerial position in any future Union administration. She was though a second-generation MP, her father having entered Parliament shortly after the war. Mercifully for her, this was the only common denominator between her and Alexander Hayes, whose own father was ejected from the House in rancorous circumstances following the Kershal Wood Affair.

"Tell me Mr Blackwood... I'm going through these amendments that were tabled by the Member for Avonley Green, that you and your colleagues wished to incorporate into the Bill...and I was hoping you could enlighten me as to why you thought it so important that they be included?"

"Perhaps you should ask Mr Carley why he thought those particular amendments were so crucial."

"Mortimer Brothers were the chief architects of the amendments, were they not?"

"Not necessarily so. I think you'll find a number of other reputable firms voiced their approval to the amendments"

"Yes, yes, of course. But MB appear to be the ringleaders don't they...for want of a better word? Shall I read Mr Carley's contributions to the debate in the chamber?"

"No... I'm not denying. My organisation was in agreement with the changes, I'm merely saying there was wider industry satisfaction. I don't mind MB being singled out as a leader in that context..."

"Well in that case you're well-placed to explain the rationale to some of these ostensibly last-minute changes? I mean, asking for the withdrawal of clauses dealing with restricted advertising during children's shows, asking for a 'creativity' exemption from the Persons of Disability Act. You even had the impudence to ask for a softening of the Tobacco Advertising Regulations." A low-intensity undertone whizzed around the committee room. Clearly some industry-insiders had been paying more attention to the passage of the Bill than others. Amber shifted ever so slightly to her left once again.

"Is this guy on drugs? They didn't get all that in there, did they?"

"No, only the creativity exemption nonsense…and some other thing about a voluntary Code of Conduct rather than a legal one. And yes, he is almost certainly a consumer of some loathsome mixture…his left eye-brow is greyer than his right…he must be sucking it all through his left nostril…"

Notes were being frantically passed between Blackwood and his wingmen as he attempted to provide believable responses to Barratt's questions. He came across as doing an intentionally offensive impression of someone with Multiple Personality Disorder. He smiled at Barratt, then grimaced and then shuddered to his right to take in a whisper. Looking at an explanatory note given to him, he began talking as if was reading from a broken autocue, before easing into his flash PR man in a suite' routine.

It was at this stage, that Amber detected the racket coming from outside the window. It sounded like chanting of some variety, but she couldn't make out any of the words. There didn't appear to be any conspicuous crowds beyond the normal line of tourists when she and Marcus made their way over to Parliament House. Although, for Amber, more weird was the desired wish to start a ruckus in such dreadful weather. They could have picked a better day for it. Whoever it was, they clearly cared.

"What the heck is going on outside?" she whispered to Marcus.

"Probably some mob or other protesting about something. Don't remember reading about it though. I mean, meant to give three months' notice to protest around here after what happened last summer."

"Three months?"

"Yep."

Movement could now be heard outside the committee room door. The stifled sound of a radio exchange was just about detectible. Amber and Marcus concluded from the sounds that security staff was engaged in some toing and frowing, but they weren't sure whether it was related to what was going on outside or whether an incident had occurred somewhere in the main building. The door then opened as a member of the security team paced towards Samantha Barratt and handed her a note. She thanked him, before he retreated back out the door. As the minutes passed, the crowd outside was clearly getting larger. Charged voices were now clearly chanting in unison—but Amber, Marcus and probably everyone in the room still couldn't make out what was being said.

Perturbation and intrigue had now filled the room. Barratt then brought formality back to proceedings.

"Apologies everyone for the on-going disturbance. We appear to have an unauthorised demonstration outside by some disability campaigners. However, I do think it best that we continue with our discussions. I've been advised that room 10 is vacant and is thankfully on the inner perimeter of the House. So granted this is highly irregular, but can I ask you all to follow our security officers to room 10, where we can hopefully continue in relative peace." There was then one of those classic ludicrous pauses as nobody moved, despite Barratt's clear exhortation. That collective sense of disorientation that engulfs a group when knocked out of its comforting routine. Brains finally re-engaged as people began to follow the security staff out of the door and down the corridor. As he passed her, Amber was horrified to hear a crude remark from Blackwood to one of his associates made under his breath about the protesters outside. Blackwood laughed quietly, with his colleague forcing a smile. He clearly wasn't impressed, but he was getting paid a fortune all the same.

Amber decided she wasn't interested in the remaining shenanigans.

"This is nonsense. I'll see you back at the office."

"I'm not sure what exactly you were expecting. See you later on then." Marcus and Amber then left the room and began to walk in opposite directions. Marcus got on a little skip as he caught up with the crowd going to committee room 10, whilst Amber began the long walk to the security barriers. As she passed through the barriers, curiosity overcame her, and rather than crossing the road, she navigated around to where the demonstrators were. Parliament House was built to resemble two circles, one inside the other. The circular design had been impregnated at various junctures where the original structure needed to be replaced. This meant some parts, particularly the newly built committee corridors, were largely shielded from the streets outside. With a well-looked after garden, the space made an ideal location for holding small-scale demonstrations. It was here that around twenty-five demonstrators had set up a mini-camp, waving placards and chanting against the Public Advertising Bill. They were shepherded in by a few symbolic makeshift fences. Amber walked gingerly closer to read some of the placards. It came to her notice that the number of security offers present was greater than what she thought was reasonable. *Twenty or thirty? For about twenty or thirty people? Half of them in wheelchairs? Did they think the chairs were concealing RPGs?* Her eyes then promptly expanded as if she were a dragonfly on steroids as she spotted someone who looked uncannily like Clare in the midst of the group. *Was it her...?* Yes! It was! Amber looked on approvingly as she saw her pal successfully animate the crowd. It was a vivacious atmosphere, but a well-meaning and harmless one. A couple of information stands had been set up for adventurous passers-by. But it was some way from the street and members of the public didn't seem intrigued enough to see what was going on. Clare and a few fellow demonstrators began to lead a small section of the crowd slightly closer to the façade of the committee buildings. They had noticed Parliamentary staff gaping at the windows and wanted to unveil a stand that was close enough for them to read. The body-language of the security personnel then metamorphosed when they perceived the attempt to play to the gallery. Four or five officers bundled one demonstrator to the floor in order to get to Clare, who was in the midst of unravelling the stand. Without an intimation of warning, one of the buffoons put an arm lock on Clare and attempted to drag her away. She screeched to be let free, at which point a second security officer grabbed her other arm and they dragged her out of her wheelchair. Other wheelchair users attempted to obstruct them, pleading for them to let go. Amber then saw Clare's head bounce off the makeshift fence as the security staff tried to pull her to the side of the garden. Amber, looked around in a panic, but the world was continuing as normal. She ran towards the repugnant sight, and as she got closer, she screamed,

"Get off her you ruddy shits!"

But as she got closer she was mauled to the ground by three security staff. She yelped repeatedly,

"Get off! I'm from Guy Freedman's office! I'm from Guy Freedman's office!"

A growly voice interrupted.

"OK let the stupid cow stand up."

She was forcefully pulled to her feet, dazed and delirious. She was with it enough to see where Clare was. No longer on the floor, Clare had surreptitiously been put back into her wheelchair whilst Amber was being man-handled. Thankfully, blood pouring from her head was also being seen to. An additional twenty or so

Parliamentary security staff had appeared wearing high-visibility jackets. The protesters were slowly being ushered away. Still juddered, Amber was furiously tutting and groaning, trying to figure out what to do. Nothing was coming to her, and within minutes, the scene had been converted into an idyllic backdrop for an oil painting. The only vestige of the destruction was Amber's ringing ears vaguely picking-up a Security Officer saying 'LGW 1 all-clear' via his radio. Amber looked around again, now with most of her senses back in check. But the world still seemed to be rolling along tickity-boo. Up at the windows, no semblance of humanity, just row upon row of blinds and shutters.

Chapter Three

It was a Wednesday, and twenty-four hours had elapsed for Amber to recollect the events of the previous day. Amber was in no need of a cooling off period, however. Her bruises and the image of Clare's head bouncing off a steel fence going around in her mind like a carousel, were reminders that weren't about to subside; reminders that only served to infuriate her. She lay in her bed, fidgety, distressed and fuming. A small part of her had recovered from the actual events that had taken place. Another part of her was incandescent every time she reflected upon the circumstances. The inertia of the passers-by, the automatons standing at the window—it was baffling. In no mood to go in to work, she had called in first thing in the morning to tell Tom and Co not to expect her.

After having a couple of pieces of toast for breakfast, Amber assessed what she was going to do for the rest of the day. She knew at some point she would go to the hospital to see how Clare was doing. Clare was being kept under observation after suffering mild concussion. But what was Amber to do with her time until then? Watch a film? Write someone in power a strongly worded letter or email? No. Amber wasn't up for that at the current time. Besides, working in an MP's office, she was alert to the fact that expressions of disgust from members of the public fell on deaf ears more often than not. In Guy Freedman's office, at one stage they had even begun to use standard templates for responding to a large amount of mail. The wording was so vague and indecisive. Only once a couple of letters were sent to the *Tribune* and subsequent published did Freedman and the other senior party members pay more attention to their content. The practice had just been instituted, and so Freedman publicly placed the blame on what he described as a 'rogue intern'. Why not just set-up Out-of-Office auto-replies with the words 'piss off we're not interested'? It's the sort of thing you would associate with Freedman, were he given the choice. Rather than dance to the tune of her haughty superiors, Amber sat about determining what she might want to do. She was aghast as to the apparent non-existent reaction among the press following the previous day's events. On that basis, Amber logged-on to her computer and began undertaking news searches to see if anyone at all had registered the incident on their radar. Incidents of reports were not forthcoming, however. Amber went to the *Tribune's* website to see if anything had been posted. All she could find was a minor summary report of a disturbance at Parliament House, with a laughable final sentence claiming that "the incident was eventually resolved in a professional manner by parliamentary security staff." *How do they know? They weren't there!* One or two other news outlets did report that a demonstration had taken place, but the repetitive omission of the double-assault was now winding-up Amber so much it was beginning to give her a headache. Amber then came across an extraordinary explanation for the lack of coverage. She discovered that Parliament House only allowed what it described as 'authorised photographs', and there was no chance they were going to allow the house photographer to take pictures of security beating up disabled people. *How about the Disability Institute Website?* Amber asked herself. If they didn't mention it, then the entire world may as well just go home and fall asleep. The main site was in the style of a blog, so upon arriving on the homepage, Amber immediately saw pictures from the demonstration. Thinking that she was finally getting somewhere, she began to scroll through the pictures and the accompanying captions and comments. Something was definitely off here. Missing from the collection was any evidence of the altercation with the parliamentary security team. Amber wanted to smash the keyboard. Remaining composed, however, she continued to scroll down the page. Eventually, she came across a few brief paragraphs describing a 'minor disturbance'—but nothing more. Amber scrolled around the homepage to see what other content was available, before noticing the link for forums. Entering the section, with a single click she seemed to be transported to a different dimension.

Reading the various subject lines of the topics, there were plenty of people here who had definitely been made aware or had witnessed what had happened, and many were obviously livid. Amber saw one forum subject entitled, "another Disability Institute whitewash," and promptly entered to read what was being said.

Although it was the Disability Institute Website, there wasn't much love emanating from the various people putting up posts. The forum was awash with vexation, the general feeling being that the Institute had taken an inexplicably diplomatic line, when unambiguous condemnation was the order of the day. A contributor called Prosper44 appeared to be the most vocal, repeatedly saying that the Institute could no longer be trusted, and constantly asking every new contributor if they had photos of the events. It was time to enter the fray. Amber added a very short comment, "Hi, I was one of the people involved in the scuffle yesterday." then pressed 'Send'. A request to register first stopped her in her tracks. Amber entered her details as accurately as someone filling out a birth certificate. As far as she was concerned, the hardest part of the process was picking a screen name. Deliberating in her mind as to what was best, Amber settled for the not so imaginative Rebma10. The screen then returned her to the comment box, and she typed in her message again before clicking 'Send' for a second time.

Multiple exclamation marks began to bombard Amber's screen as the various posters began to react to her revelation. Prosper44 was at the front of the queue, hurrying Amber for more information, whilst questioning her authenticity.

"What? You were there? Do me a favour! Why haven't you been out there telling people what happened? Or are you just some troll taking the piss?"

"Piss off! I was there all right! That was my friend who got her head smashed on the fence. She's in hospital right now with concussion! I'm going to see her later on! I'll take a photo of her scar as proof if you like?"

"How do you know Clare?"

"I just told you I'm her friend. So why don't you tell me how YOU know her name? And why are you telling the world what her name is?"

"Because people need to know who she is! Clare is part of a small campaigning group a few of us started up about a year ago called Gold Front. It's just a bunch of young people getting together and trying to do something. If you're her friend, why don't you know she's a member?"

Amber ruminated for a moment before sending a response. She had no idea who this person was, but their question raised a good point. Why was this the first time she had heard about any of this?

"Well, she may have mentioned me to you. We are genuinely the best of friends. I'd rather not disclose my name right now, but it starts with 'A' and ends in 'R'—actually you've figured that out from my screen name I'm guessing!—my surname begins with 'W' and ends with 'S'." Some sensibility was finally returning to Amber, stopping her from unnecessarily revealing too much about herself—though admittedly giving away enough clues as to her identity. The drift of the conversation took a marked turn, however, as soon as Amber posted her last comment. Prosper44 used the 'private' messaging function to carry on the exchange.

"Sorry A. Didn't mean to startle you. Clare speaks very highly of you actually. Not sure what possessed you to go work for that asshole. But still, I suppose that's one less position taken by an enemy. Always good to have someone on the inside. I mean let's face it THEY seem to have people everywhere, don't they?"

"Erm, sorry mate, can you give me an inkling as to exactly who you are?"

"Well, like you I'd prefer not to put my name up. But to use your sorry excuse for Morse code, my name begins with 'V' and ends in 'A'. Ring any bells? Clare mentioned any names?"

Amber began to rack her brains, but nothing was springing to mind. She was having one of those mornings when one pulls out the car keys rather than the ticket at a train station. A light came on eventually though. *Veronica!* She doubted it could be anybody else. Clare rarely mentioned her though whenever the two of them were together, a situation which now seemed irregular considering the circumstances.

"Ah! Hi V. Yes, she has mentioned you. So have you gone to see her in hospital?"

"I would have done but I'm not sure where she is. Haven't had a proper chance to talk to her as a result. How about you?"

"I'm going to see her this evening actually. You're welcome to come along. Meet me outside the entrance of Greg Waters Hospital at 7."

"Excellent!"

"Now tell me, why are you hounding everyone for photos?"

"Don't you know what happened? As they were breaking up the demonstration yesterday, they confiscated everybody's phones and cameras. They said we could go pick them up later on. When I went to pick mine up all the pictures and videos were deleted. I've checked with some of the others and it's the same for them as well."

"That's outrageous! Are they even allowed to do that?"

"Well they were justifying it on security grounds which is a load of baloney obviously."

"This is insane! Have I missed something? Why isn't this being reported? Why aren't people going mad?"

"In short, nobody particularly cares; all the main parties backed the Public Advertising Bill. As for DI, well as far as they were concerned, we were part of an unauthorised demo so they aren't too interested either. Eventually, they'll close these forums too. They prefer us to stay in our wheelchairs at home and only come out when they tell us to. Bunch of patronising, paternalistic shits."

"Well, I can't help you I'm afraid. I was getting my internal organs rearranged by some fatso. I thought people might do something. But nothing."

"Well, we need o talk to someone quick. I think we should go and have a chat with Samantha Barratt."

"What? I was with her in one of the committee rooms when the demonstrations were happening. She couldn't give a toss."

"Ah, trust me, that woman has tact."

"I say we go have a chat with Sir Henry Jacob."

"Don't be ridiculous!" Veronica's dismissal of Sir Henry jolted Amber. Surely under the circumstances, he would be the ideal person to contact?

"What's wrong with Sir Henry?"

"When it comes to the bottom line, the man is a waste of space. He'll never do anything that rocks the boat."

"But still, he has friends in high places. No harm in having a chat with him as well as Barratt."

"Fine. If you insist."

"But what on earth are we supposed to tell them? Barratt at least would probably have heard by now."

"We're gonna ask them to do something about it. We need to get one of those gorillas who assaulted Clare charged or prosecuted or sacked or something. I'm not even talking about a mass rally or anything…but you know…it's proper out of order."

"Well, we can decide what we want to do when we go and see Clare later." They had been talking for so long, Amber couldn't even remember how they got started. Glancing up at the top right hand corner of the screen, the 'private' icon boosted her memory.

"How will I know who you are—we haven't met, remember?"

"I'll be wearing a black and purple coat. Main entrance. Greg Waters. 7. See you there!" Closing the browser in a jiffy without bothering to sign-out, the conversation ended as hastily as it had started, but it ended on good terms.

Having a look at the DI forums led to Amber deciding to scour the online world and see how it was reacting to other disability-related news. Maybe everyone had just conspired to miss the events of the previous day because something even more atrocious had happened? And the more Amber read, the more she realised that there was a tug of war going on. On one side was the moral world, and on the other side was a virtual pit of squalor, serenading every story that featured a disabled person with ceremonious hatred, while basking in self-congratulation. Those who inhabited this dismal sphere seemed to be unable to engage any mind-set other than paranoia, smugness and outright hatred. Amber had seen these parasites crawl through the tiny gaps of the collage of free speech and the right to express oneself and had seen them find a nest for themselves in the comment sections and opinion pieces of almost every website on the internet. Amber always wondered how on earth something as liberating and sophisticated as the internet ended by being synonymous with its polar opposites—comments and opinions that paid homage to intellectual oblivion. At first, the bile was largely refined to various celebrity websites. Websites that ran twenty-four hour commentaries on how big such and such a person's arse was or how much money such and such a person spent on a new toilet seat. Amber didn't like to generalise about people, but she thought she had a pretty good idea about the kind of person who visited those sites. As a result, she also thought she had a good idea about the type of person who would comment on the sites. In her eyes, there were two types of people who visited and commented. The first type was the delusional crowd who actually seemed to be interested in the nonsense that was being reported. On one level the commitment of these folks was actually strangely admirable. Amber concluded that these were people that were trying to see some sort of fantasy come to fruition. It was pure escapism designed to mitigate for the fact that in their real lives, there was little to nothing they could do to fix the downward spiral they were on. Insecure jobs, insecure housing and insecure families had led to insecure minds. It's not that these people were too ashamed to seek out some form of help or assistance—the truth was that the help was slowly being cut away by successive governments. Those who had immediate recourse to help were those smack at the very bottom and those smack at the very top. Anyone in between were holding on by their finger nails, dreading the drop below into the abyss that the Government said only scroungers inhabited, and so they were looking for anything of value to cling on to. The sort of comments that this group posted was pure banality—but it was in a sense harmless. The intellectual decay that some people thought it portrayed was something that could be discussed for ages. The second group of commentators were the real danger. There was no obvious source of enmity that Amber could see. This group seemed to start off poking fun and making derisory comments about various celebrities. When those comments were posted, nobody thought much of it as many people took the line that the targets had gone out of their way to put themselves in the line of fire by leading such hedonistic, public lifestyles, and so in actual fact, they were most likely half expecting the level of abuse they received. Even when it came to attacks on personal appearance, not many people fluttered an eye lid. At the end of the day, these were a bunch of tax dodging charlatans. Although Amber didn't fully agree with that line of thinking, she could at least see the basic elements of the argument. There was nothing, however, that justified the level of antagonism and loathing aimed at every other story that was about some form of real life incident that seemed to merit wider social attention. Amber was looking at a story about a young girl who had Down's syndrome. Her story had made the news as she had been a victim of cyber bullying, but the authorities had failed to do anything about it until it had gotten out of control. The reaction of the posters was anything other than sympathetic or appreciative of the girl's situation. Instead, there was a stream of comments *actually taking issue* with the fact that the girl had Down's syndrome. People were *actually* questioning the legitimacy of the condition, speculating how much benefit money she was on or just saying that the family should just grow up and get on with it. Amber refused to accept explanations that these were just people that were simply unhinged or that they were simply looking for a reaction—the so-called dark side of the 'Me' generation. That was all apologetic nonsense.

Amber wanted to know what the real thought process was that these scumbags were going through—for there definitely was a thought process going on—no matter how perverse it was. Amber was actually on the *Tribune* website. The moderators were working overtime to clean up comments, but Amber wasn't sure why they were bothering. She couldn't really see how a lot of the stuff left behind was fit for publishing. Being on the *Tribune* meant Amber could log on and directly engage with one of the lunatics. There were a number of candidates for her to choose from, settling on "ByronDoesTheSquats," Amber held her breath and went in.

"Can I ask you, have you taken something?"

"WTF are you on about?"

"I'm just trying to figure out what causes a rational human being to reach the levels of depravity that you've demonstrated on this website"

"WTF is your problem b*itch?"

"I feel touched that you've tried to sensor your insult but if you look carefully you'll see that you've actually spelt it out. It just looks like a typo now."

"Who made you the moral police? Do you want some as well?"

"What? Drugs? No, thank you. I just wanna know what makes you feel entitled to go off at people the way you do?"

"WTF is your problem? It's a free country B*TCH. She's probably a waster."

"Are you serious? Is that what it boils down to for you? You're allowed to and you think she deserves it? Please tell me there's more! Please tell me someone has paid you or this is part of a sick bet or someone is holding a gun to your temple as we speak or you've been diagnosed as being clinically insane or someone is blackmailing you."

"Cleaner to isle 3, major spill—clean up required. What is it, Sam? Someone's OD'd on their own morality!"

"CORRECTION SAM—some pathetic fool has voluntarily spat out his own heart and left it for a stray vulture to eat. The vulture swallowed it up but then, promptly dropped dead!"

Amber had had enough, but so too did the person she was talking to—mainly because of the hassle he was getting following Amber's instant retort. Amber wasn't sure why he had bothered. She knew beforehand that it was almost certainly going to be a waste of time, but something in her was holding out for someone with an ounce of common sense. Maybe she had chosen the wrong candidate, but either way, she was done.

Reading various newspaper and magazine articles, Amber began to struggle to keep her eyes open, and before she knew it, she had fallen asleep. Waking up a few hours later, the sparkling street lights outside sobered her up. Recalling that she needed to be somewhere, she looked around the room like an imposter, trying to locate a watch or a clock. Picking her phone up, it had just gone quarter past six. *Perfect timing,* she thought, even if unintended. Greg Waters was conveniently located opposite Harrington Road Tube Station. Harrington Road was an old-fashioned station that had no escalators and what felt like a gazillion staircases and lifts. The announcers on the underground network would often announce that the station was temporarily closed due to a 'passenger incident', which translated meant that some sorry commuter had fallen down the stairs. As her train pulled into the preceding station, Addison Square, the driver's voice came cracking through the announce system.

"Evening ladies and gentleman. Unfortunately, due to an incident at Harrington Road, this train will not be stopping there. The next stop for this train shall be Harding Park East. Those customers wishing to travel to Harrington Road should either alight here and continue at street level or stay on board and alight at Harding Park East."

Whoever the hopeless wonder was who had come a cropper at Harrington Road, it better at least be a broken leg, seeing as they've managed to ruin my plans and bring an entire station to a shutdown! Such negativity wasn't in Amber's DNA. It was simply an indication of her ongoing mental maelstrom. But where to get off, the walk was about the same if memory served her correctly, so it was a question of which station had the more confusing exit. On came the driver again,

"This train is ready to depart, please stand clear of the doors."

The announcement caused an instinctive reaction and Amber hurtled forward as the doors began to slide closed. Before she knew it, she had been violently sandwiched for a second successive day. She got herself free, but her bag was still stuck. On came the driver again, this time sounding fierce.

"Can the passenger is the fourth car stop obstructing the doors."

"I'm not obstructing the doors you stupid bastard! The doors are obstructing me!" She almost tore the straps off as she finally yanked the bag free on the fifth attempt. What should have been a relatively comfortable journey was now no better than the morning commute, as Amber hopped from escalator to escalator and out of the main exit. Reaching the main entrance of Greg Waters with five minutes to spare, she looked around to see if anybody was hanging around. A dark figure with a low centre of gravity could be detected coming closer, slaloming around some bollards. As the figure got closer, Amber could now see a very fashion-conscious wheelchair gleaming in the light of the hospital's main entrance. A yard or so separated them before a confident sounding voice pierced the howling wind.

"Amber?"

"Veronica! Hi! How are you doing?"

"I'll feel much better once we're out of this crummy weather. Shall we go in?"

"Absolutely. Non-family visitor's hours finish at eight, so we should have quite a bit of time to talk to her and see how she's doing."

Entering the building, upon reaching reception, they seemed to want to go in different directions, Veronica moving towards the lift and Amber falling behind, lingering around reception. Veronica pirouetted to face Amber.

"What's the problem?"

"Sorry mate, when I spoke to Clare I forgot to ask where the ward was."

Veronica shook her head, but was smiling, and came back to join Amber in the queue. Retrieving the necessary information, they began to make their way to bed number thirteen in the Alex Kemp ward. The lugubrious looks on the faces of every other person who went by, reminded Amber and Veronica why they disliked hospitals so much. Melancholy turned to felicity, however, as they saw a smiling Clare sitting up in bed, in conversation with her mother.

"Oh dear!" laughed Clare as she saw Amber and Veronica approach together. "Am I in trouble? I was supposed to introduce you to each other at some point! But you've found each other and saved me the trouble! Lovely!"

"Hey Clare!" Amber felt the weight of aggravation lift from her shoulders as she greeted Clare.

"How have you been doing?" asked Veronica, pulling up directly beside her.

"I'll leave you girls to catch up for a bit. Would you two like a cup of tea or anything?"

"No, thank you Mrs T," came the instant joint-response. Clare's mother picked up her handbag and popped out of the room.

"How have you been doing?" repeated Veronica, this time in a less high-pitched tone and sounding all together more poignant.

"I've been all right. Had a banging headache for a while but it's all calmed down now thankfully. They're only keeping me for observation to be honest. All being well, I can go home in the morning."

"Has anyone come to see you?" asked Amber searchingly. "Anyone? Police? Journalists? Even someone from Parliament to apologise?"

"Do me a favour! Only reason anyone from there would come down is to finish me off!"

The concern on Amber's face began to grow.

"Look, please can you start from the beginning? What were you doing there? Who were you with...? How you met Veronica? Sorry for so many questions, but you know me, I get bemused by decimal places... I just want to know what's going on here and what we can do about getting some payback for you!"

"I told you! Don't expect anyone to do anything about it!"

"Well are you two going to give the lowdown on the rest of it?" Amber's conflation of Clare and Veronica caused the latter to raise an eyebrow slightly.

"Why are you so obsessed with the fact that you don't know what I've been up to? I didn't realise you were keeping a register on me. We've all got friends that haven't met our other friends... Why should I be any different?" Though the situation was favourable to harsh words, Amber instantly knew Clare largely meant the tone she was taking. She didn't react, however, at what she regarded as a deeply unfair assessment of her intentions. Instilling tenderness into her voice, she carried on trying to get to the bottom of what had happened. In any case, Veronica wasn't about to come out and defend her.

"Look, I'm sorry. I just wanna know you're all right and if there's anything we can do..." Clare gently leaned back.

"Roni and I came across each other at this mentoring scheme a year or so ago. How did we bump into each other again?"

"You ran my mum over in the car park. Cow!" That revelation partially released the tension in what appeared to be heading for a fractured discussion.

"Ah yes, Roni's mum makes you look like a greyhound that's been slipped a laxative Amber…"

"Thanks!" exclaimed Veronica with wild sarcasm.

That was better, Clare was beginning to lighten up a bit more. Actually, *no wait, that wasn't better*. Amber had a strange epiphany.

"Erm, excuse me, I don't ever recall mocking you and your wheelchair. I can't help it if I'm a bit clumsy, it's not like I'm doing it on purpose. It's just one of those things."

Flummoxed and repudiated, Clare and Veronica were checked in their tracks. A brief interlude then followed. Clare didn't expressly apologise, but really, it wasn't necessary. The point was well-made, and Clare's glum exterior was soon re-jigged into something far more welcoming.

"So, really, it all started from there," continued Clare eventually. "We began to do a few things here and there, get petitions together that sort of thing. And, as time went on, we just, sort of, came across other peeps who were interested in the same things."

"So are you both members of DI?"

"Used to be," groaned Veronica. "But that lot are just a bunch of men in cheap suits."

"And women," added Clare.

"Not a fan of Mary Harper then I take it?"

"There are a couple of good eggs, but most of them are a bunch of wasters. Going along with every government policy just to keep the money rolling in whilst telling disabled people *what to do*. Then, when it comes to something that actually matters, they have no influence at all!"

"But what do you expect them to do? They don't have a choice, do they? It's just…politics!"

"No!" bellowed Clare. "Why do people keep saying that? If you put your name to an issue and never get anything done, it's not politics, is it—that's just grandstanding! Politics is about getting things done! The right thing. What the heck are they doing exactly? Sod all!"

"But you still use their website."

"Of course...*now that's what you call politics*. It's convenient... It's a public forum and we're not breaking the rules, are we? If they don't want us using it, they can shut the thing down." Amber was no longer feeling unsettled, but was still no closer to understanding how Clare ended up at an unauthorised demonstration.

"So what about yesterday? That wasn't too clever, was it? Just randomly pitching up like that?"

"How's that?" barked Veronica.

"Otherwise anyone can just roll up and cause mayhem."

"Bollocks! It's convenient for them to lump us in the same group as psychos and anarchists. It's the primary seat of Government. Any law abiding citizen should be able to turn up when they like. Do they think they're runnin' a hotel? Yea, more like a brothel. Blackwood and Co probably aren't even Security-cleared and they get three-course lunches. We can't offer them shit though, can we? We're a ruddy burden, aren't we?" At that point, a hiss could be heard. The three turned to see a patient gesturing to them to keep it down. This was followed by one of the nurses reminding them where they were.

They could argue all day long as to the correct protocol surrounding demonstrations. Now though, was the time to come up with a plan of action in order to make sure Clare's efforts weren't in vein.

"So what do you two want to do then? Organise another demo? Try and go to the press? Chain your wheelchairs to something? Veronica and I were talking earlier and we reckon it might be worth going to see Samantha Barratt and Sir Henry Jacob."

"Sir Henry won't do much, he's DI all the way, he's one of these people who talks a lot but doesn't really say much," said Clare disparagingly. "We'll ask for his help but we'll keep it to a minimum. Barratt might be useful though..."

"But what do you ACTUALLY want to do?"

"I don't know!" yelped Clare, who seemed to me maddening with every question. "Let's just see if we can talk to Barratt and go from there."

It dawned on Amber that after the *Political Engagement* gig, she had an ounce of leverage with Sir Henry Jacob. In spite of the odd disrespectful question he asked of her, at the end of the day

Amber judged him to be more malleable than most of the other political-types she had come across.

"Actually guys, if Sir Henry is a waste of time, let's just go see him first. Waste of time or not, I reckon I could arrange a quick ten minute chat over a cup of coffee. It'll have to be at his office though."

"Right, well, d'you know what his availability is like?" asked Clare.

"He's out and about quite a bit, but during the PE piece I realised that he is almost always in his office all day Thursday. I say we try and catch him just after lunch. He gets very jolly when he's on a full stomach. Very odd. In any case, if there is any chance of him doing squat, that'll be the best time to ask. Say two o'clock-ish. Are you gonna be cool with that Clare? It won't be too soon, will it?"

"No, that's fine, assuming I get the all clear."

Concurring over where and when to meet, Amber and Veronica gave Clare a cuddle and asked her to pass on their best wishes to her mother, who had very cordially gone for an extended tea break.

For Amber, visiting the hospital didn't seem as discomfiting as what she had predicted beforehand—but she was definitely feeling a bit queasy. She was already well-acclimatised to the Greg Waters Hospital, having dashed there on a number of occasions, often in the middle of the night, when her father was deeply unwell. They could put a swimming pool in the basement, a PlayStation game's console next to every bed and a sixty-inch LED television on every ward. Nothing could interfere with the mournful vibe that suffocated you even before you reached the front door. For Amber, the feeling would take hold as soon as the thought of the place entered her head—*somebody was probably being resuscitated around the corner*—she would think. Then you'd have the aprons, the twenty syllable scientific words that were some kind of anagram-esque black magic, the aroma of disinfectant. But the worst one for Amber, would be when she'd walk down a corridor of private rooms, with most of the doors closed. But she'd then come across a door that was wide open, and the will to know would stop her in her tracks and look inside. Surveying the room, she would see a nurse adding the finishing touches after laying out new beddin, and then maybe disposing off some flowers that appeared to be withering away. *Yep, somebody had just died.*

It was harmful to the mind to be alone after having spent time in a place like that, and after arriving home, Amber quickly thought about what she ought to do. Hitting the sack wasn't an option. She wasn't someone who could sleep for extended periods. Eight hours was her absolute max, and even then her actual sleeping cycle woke her in the middle of the night. Waking up once in the middle of the night, that was fair enough, but twice? No, she wasn't a pensioner or suffering from psychiatric problems, she thought. *So what now then?* Sitting down and finding the right words to put to Sir Henry seemed like a good thing to do. Every mumble would push him to even higher levels of disinterest and insouciance than what he usually possessed when interacting with the common folk. This caused Amber to remember that Isabelle had done the note-taking the previous day for Sir Henry's meeting with Guy Freedman. The meeting she had wormed herself out of. She tried to convince herself it was a warped case of serendipity. She was in a position to help Clare as a result of abandoning a shit-awful Committee meeting. That though, left her feeling restive. Her mind was telling her that, had she not been at the demonstration, she wouldn't have felt anywhere near as screwed-up as she actually did. It was witnessing everything first hand that really made any difference. *Enough of the philosophising!* It was time to give Isabelle a ring. Amber didn't usually ring her outside of office hours, but Isabelle was well-aware of the goings-on of recent days and probably wouldn't mind. The desired topic of conversation arrived quickly, and Isabelle gave Amber good insights into how to approach Sir Henry. Isabelle then began to move on to more unnerving matters.

"They began to talk about you actually and the antics you got up to…once the bullshit was over obviously…"

"What?" Amber was feeling fretful. "How the hell did they find out? The demonstration was at the same time as your meeting, wasn't it?"

"Not quite. The demonstration wasn't entirely received as innocuously as you think. When that lot pulled up unannounced, the boys in blue temporarily closed Nightingale Road, so as a result we got to Sir Henry's place about forty-five minutes late. He had lost his patience the way he usually does and was already having his next meeting. Within five minutes of us sitting down, some guy comes in checking with Freedman if he knows who you are. Then he quickly told him what had happened and just left."

"But HOW did he…shit…when one of those slobs was on top of me I had to say I was from Guy's office to get him off me! What did he say?"

"Nothing immediately. He just mumbled and said he'd deal with you when he sees you."

"Great!"

"There's more…at the end he tells me thanks and then just tells me to go because he and Sir Henry want to talk about the demonstration. But, to be honest, I wouldn't worry about it too much. He didn't seem pissed or anything. It's not like it's made front page news or anything. You'll probably just get a dressing down and that will be that. They'll probably be more annoyed with me than you."

"Why do you say that?"

"Five minutes after I left I walked back in and interrupted them! You know how Guy is when it comes to interruptions!"

"Why did you go back for?"

"Oh, well, it was getting quite boring at one point and so I began to use my mobile as a Dictaphone just in case I forgot something. They told me to leave a bit randomly, and so I forgot my mobile and then had to go back and get it."

That night was a restless one for Amber. Had she unwittingly jeopardised her internship? Even if she had, did she actually care? Was loyalty to Clare now the priority? She'd surely have her answers in the morning, when she'd inevitably have to face Guy Freedman.

Breakfast wasn't on the agenda for Amber the following morning. Having reflected on her predicament, she'd found that she'd been infused with a new sense of momentum. Even if she lost her internship, the bottom line was that she wasn't really into the political happenings to the same extent Marcus, Isabelle and the others were. It wasn't lost on her, however, that given the situation she was in, political nous was something she was in need of. If she lost her internship, then she could cut her losses and move on to something that suited her better. If, however, she caught a break, then that would be the signal for her to pull her socks up and get to grips with the world she inhabited. Arriving in the office, she didn't have to wait long. She hadn't even taken her jacket off when Tom strode over and informed her that Freedman wanted to see her in his office straight away. *Here we go*, thought Amber. Amber hesitantly knocked on the door and was summoned to enter.

"Ah Amber. How are you? All recovered from your little escapade?" Freedman wasn't one for concealing his emotions, when he was pissed, *he was pissed*. His voice was actually reasonably chipper; a good sign as far as Amber was concerned.

"I just wanted to get to the bottom of this thing you've been involved in. Naturally, I appreciate the difficult situation you found yourself in. However, I'm sure you can gather that this wasn't something that had my blessing."

"Oh no Guy, absolutely. Just to clarify, I wasn't involved in the demonstration or anything. I was just looking on and saw someone get their head smashed in. So I went to try and help and ended up being floored by this big ape. I only said I was from your office just to get him off me. I didn't mean it in the sense that I was there and I had your backing." As she explained herself, Amber began to feel like her hair was on fire. The exchange had barely been going for thirty seconds, but Amber was already feeling unable to hold herself together.

"OK, well, that makes more sense." *Er, hang on!* That mollifying comment wasn't like Guy. Her alarm bells were ringing, but she was at least feeling more secure in a weird, contradictory way.

"Well, fine then. We'll leave it at that. I just wanted to make sure you weren't invoking my name in order to start social rebellions." Freedman smiled. But for Amber, there was something devious in the way he was coming across. She couldn't put her finger on it. This was a guy who practically has seizures when she arrives late in the office. Now here he was, being charitable and even making an attempt at humour even though on a technicality, he may have been right that his name shouldn't have been used in the circumstances. Freedman was the kind of guy who loved technicalities. He was astute as using them to his advantage. Amber was in the clear, but her new found appetite for realism gave her a feeling that this probably wasn't the end of the matter. Something was afoot, she just didn't know what.

The mood in the office for the morning wasn't a talkative one. The others had automatically assumed Guy Freedman was in a foul mood. For the time being, she didn't bother setting them straight. On the face of it, Guy hadn't terminated her involvement with Clare and Veronica. For now, she was in the clear and so was eager to follow-through with their plan to meet Sir Henry Jacob. Amber was taking a bit of a gamble. She wasn't bothering to phone in advance and book an appointment in case she was blown-off. Based on her previous dealings with Sir Henry, she felt that if they got to him just on time, it would strengthen their hand. Sir Henry was more prone to agreeing to do something when not having been fully briefed on a matter.

The offices of Political Engagement were in Media City. Media City consisted of a series of clusters, each cluster usually belonging to one conglomerate or other. There were though various independent outlets based there. Organisations from across the media spectrum had some form of presence, whether it was print, television, radio or web-based. The City was draped along the southern banks of the river, not too far from the Parliamentary Village. All this made for a rather glossy skyline. Most of the political magazines were based in the same complex, Carpenter's House. The comical set-up of having ideological opponents who probably vomited at the thought of having to breathe the same air as their enemies made for some tempestuous stories. People sneaking into a rival's office late at night and pissing into the water cooler. Right-wingers on the second floor emailing viruses to left-wingers on the fourth—or vice versa. People going out of their way to use one of the lavatories on a different floor, particularly when they'd had a big lunch. None of this behaviour was ever confirmed—or officially denied. So for outsiders it always provided a strange thrill to be there.

Amber, Clare and Veronica arrived shortly after quarter to two. Sitting by the fountains opposite the main entrance, they maintained the shortest reconnaissance mission in history, as within five minutes of their arrival, Sir Henry arrived back from lunch and approached the building.

"Amber, you've definitely cleared it with your buddy at reception?" asked Veronica.

"Yep. But I suggest we leave it a few minutes at most. He tends to get calls constantly."

They procrastinated for a minute longer before making for the main entrance. Amber looked across to her friend at reception and nodded, before receiving a confirmation nod in response. Approaching the lift doors, Bob O'Hara of all people was getting out as the lift doors opened. Veronica courteously reversed her wheelchair to give the obese O'Hara sufficient room to leave. It didn't stop him from tutting as he passed.

"What the...? Did you just tut at me? You can see my excuse, can't you? What's your excuse for being such a massive shitbag? Oh you haven't got one, have you? You just happen to be a massive shitbag!" O'Hara turned his head whilst rooted to the spot and stared a black hole through Veronica. Veronica wasn't remotely intimidated and stared a hole of oblivion through O'Hara. O'Hara gently walked forward a few paces and bent down so that he could be face-to-face with Veronica.

"I could break your neck with a simple flick of the wrists, but there wouldn't be any fun in that." He stood up, smiled and walked away. Amber and Clare shuffled into the lift as quick as they could, wanting to avoid any further scenes.

"Flippin' 'eck Roni, you'll get us thrown out!" said Clare, somehow roaring and whispering at the same time.

"Sorry, but he's a prat."

Getting off at the eighth floor, Amber sprung ahead, and as she set off, turned to the other two.

"Let me grab him first, don't want to make it out to be an ambush—even though it is! I'll just ask him for a few minutes of his time and say you're waiting outside." Sir Henry had asked for a traditional private office, which meant there was no need to walk through the entire Political Engagement work area and risk raised eyebrows. It was hard to miss the door to Sir Henry's office; his name was carved elegantly in large letters above the door. This was though a bit abnormal for someone who had an above average number of blind visitors—*how could they reach? It wasn't even proper brail,* Amber thought. She rattled the door with her knuckles.

"Come in," Sir Henry's deep, appealing voice rattled the door in riposte, and Amber stuck her head around the door.

"Hi Sir Henry." Amber was trying her best to sound warm and toasty.

"Amber Watts. What brings you here?"

Well at least he recognises me! Amber trundled into the room.

"Sorry to bother you so soon after lunch..."

"No bother." *Sir Henry seemed to be in an approachable mood,* thought Amber.

"A couple of friends and I wanted to get your advice on something. Just for a few minutes. Would it be OK if they came in?"

"Absolutely. But not too long though." Amber walked back a couple of steps to reach the door, before opening it and signalling for the others to come in.

"Ah! Some fellow four-wheelers. So, how can I help?" *What was what? A second unexpected attempt at humour in one day. OK, fine, whatever.* Veronica was on a rush and began to talk immediately, foregoing any introductions.

"So what it is, is that, on Tuesday, Clare here attended a demonstration at Parliament House. Now fair enough, it wasn't technically authorised...but still. She went to put out a banner and got dragged out of her wheelchair and got her head pounded."

"I've been notified of this incident already as you can probably imagine." Sir Henry sounded very unemotional.

"Can you suggest anything we can do? How about putting something in Political Engagement?" advocated Clare. Sir Henry put his hands behind his head and chewed over for a moment.

"It's not really 'that kind' of a magazine. When you publish the type of magazine we do, you need to play by the 'rules of the game' or else no one of note will ever contribute anything. I'm sure you can see that, can't you?" Veronica looked at Amber with a 'I told you so' sort of stare.

"Can you do ANYTHING?" queried Amber fervently, a bit riled by Veronica's look.

"To be honest they can just play the security card and that'll be that. I mean nobody saw anything, did they? So it's your words against theirs. But ok, I'll have a chat with Terrance Winchester who's on the Security Committee. He's the kind of guy who can have a few off-the-record conversations without ruffling any feathers. He may be able to pull an unofficial apology from someone. How does that sound?" That was a rhetorical question, but in any event Clare and Veronica seemed to be pacified. On the other hand, Amber was now increasingly disturbed. It clearly hadn't registered with the other two—*but how did Sir Henry know nobody saw anything? How could he be so sure?* On paper there were any number of potential witnesses—the demonstrators, the other guards, people at the window and stray members of the public that Amber failed to glimpse at the time. She kept her mouth shut. They thanked

Sir Henry for his time and left. The friends exited the building and stood outside the main entrance for a few minutes. They each had plans and went in different directions. As far as Amber was aware, Freedman wasn't due in the office that afternoon, so she decided to extend her lunch break. Her visit to the hospital was still playing on her mind. Since visiting Clare, she had begun to acknowledge her feelings and had begun to be more honest with herself about why she had really felt squeamish. It wasn't just about being reminded of her father's passing. It was more to do with the ubiquitous sense of vulnerability she'd been left with. There were people around her who were suffering far greater trials and tribulations than she was. But her mother and father had until recently acted as her canopy, shading her from the convulsions of the world outside. The canopy now had a gaping hole, but she kept telling herself she wasn't ready to build something to replace it. But she realised that's the mistake she was making. This wasn't about replacement; it was about moving on and learning how to cope. Recent events were beginning to push her in the right direction.

Sir Henry had spent the afternoon perusing documents in his office. He was shuffling some papers when his arms came to a halt. He yanked open his desk draw and glanced at some photographs. He then jangled his keys for a few seconds. Picking his mobile phone up, he began to dial. There were barely two seconds before it was answered. Whoever it was, they were expecting him.

"I'm sorry it's taken a while to get back to you—yes, you were absolutely right. She left a while ago with two of her friends... No, well, I said I'd have a quiet word with Terrance, that'll placate them for now. If it doesn't, we'll see what we can do...what were they thinking jeopardising things when we're this close...? That guy can't help himself...! And we're positive nobody has anything they can use as evidence...? You *are* aware that if people find out just ONE member of Longacre Green Waterside were there then we've got a bit of a problem on our hands... Yes, we'll keep a watching brief for now... Likewise, let me know immediately if you hear anything of interest... Oh, can we do more thing? Let's just get our friends to look over camera footage in the area so we can see anyone who's seen something they shouldn't have...great." Sir Henry's door was then flung open. "You'll need to excuse me; I have a visitor." He put the phone down and gestured to his guest to come in. "Are you all right with everything?"

"Yes, I'm fine. But I'd appreciate more of a helping hand every now and then."

"Everything is absolutely fine don't worry. Just stick to what I've told you and all will be well. Does anybody suspect anything?"

"No. Not a thing."

Chapter Four

Samantha Barratt was MP for Caledonian Park. Clare lived in her constituency, so she decided to do things the old fashioned way and make an appointment with her at one of her surgeries. Clare and Samantha Barratt had known each other for a long time. Barratt had often supported Clare when it came to her constant battles with the local council or social services. Barratt trusted Clare, which meant they could have as open a discussion as they liked. Barratt was noticeably more sociable than some of her colleagues, and this was reflected in the location of her surgery. Many MPs held their surgeries on the fourth floor in the middle of nowhere. Barratt held hers in the Community Centre, within minutes of the High Street and Caledonian Park Tube Station. She even held regular appointments on Saturday and Sunday afternoons, so that people who weren't in a position to take time off work could come and see her.

Clare, Veronica and Amber were thankful for her accommodating nature, regardless of whether the intrinsic nature of the job surely called for such supportive measures. A cursory glance at the antics of some of her colleagues suggested many had a poor understanding of what representation actually meant. Meeting on a Saturday afternoon meant Amber and Co could indulge in a more enjoyable lunch rather than having to scoff down a cheese sandwich. The timing was also exquisite because a couple of the morning papers had raised suspicions as to how genuine Giles Gibbs' resignation was. *The Tribune* had a front page with a picture of Gibbs with the accompanying headline, "Did he walk? Or was he pushed?" It was a great chance to find out how much Barratt knew, and so all three were feeling exuberant in their desire to get on with things. Barratt's door creaked open. Her office assistant appeared in the frame of the door and invited them to come in. Tea had been prepared, but only two cups.

"Oh, I didn't realise you weren't coming alone. Chris could you make two extra cuppas?"

"Oh, that's OK Sam," responded Veronica on behalf of everyone. "We've all just had a lovely lunch."

"I'll have mine though!" fired Clare, the avid tea drinker.

"Well, park yourselves around the table. How can I be of service?" Barratt noticed both Clare and Veronica holding copies of *The Tribune.* "What do you make of that then?" she asked, pointing at the papers and smiling. She was greeted with reciprocal smiles and brightened faces. Clearly she was happy to discuss it! Amber was the first to respond.

"Well, if it was true, I wouldn't be surprised. It was just SO random… Hayes and Freedman say it was on the cards, but I'm not so sure…"

Veronica nodded, before adding, "I still think it's a crazy mistake on the part of Hayes and that lot. Everyone agrees Gibbs was a safe pair of hands."

Barratt was flicking a pen around in her hand, obviously deliberating about something in her head.

"It's quite concerning. The public isn't all that informed and I think Guy and Alex have taken advantage. They're a couple of funny ones."

"In what way?" semi-gurgled Clare whilst sipping her tea.

"Well, you work with Guy, Amber, so you already know he's a bit of a narcissist—even for a politician. But Hayes though, you need to keep an eye on him—he's definitely a funny one. I certainly am. His father was a bit of a freak and he seems like one to me as well. I mean it's all out there. Just read some of the reports he authored when he was working at the Grove Chambers Institute. You'd think he was trying to finish what his father started. And here he is. He's sleep-walked his way to the leadership. How, I have no idea." Barratt seemed to be all too happy to provide a frank and brazen analysis of her party leaders.

"Did he work at Grove Chambers?" gasped Veronica.

"Very briefly. Even they found him an embarrassment."

"Can I ask, why do you think his dad was a freak?" questioned Amber.

"I assume you've heard of the Kershal Wood Affair?"
Amber nodded.

"That was mostly him."

All three had become diverted from what they had gone in there for, and Clare plugged away with more questions, sensing that an engrossing story was at hand. There were many versions of the Kershal Wood affair darting around; she gleamed at the chance to hear a version from someone who they all trusted to a degree.

"Forgive me Sam, but I'm not all that familiar with the Kershal Wood stuff. Could you enlighten me briefly?"

"Well, there are all sorts of versions of events flying about. There are a lot of apologists out there. But a lot of the smart ones at the time were able to see through the spin that came out. Anyway, it's pretty well-documented now so guys like Hayes can't run from it."

"So what went on then?" Clare asked, trying her best not to sound impatient.

"So you're all familiar with where it is, right? Out there in the middle of nowhere?"

They all nodded.

"So, in the late sixties, Alexander Hayes' dad was a senior patron for a firm called the National Improvement and Development Fund. They used to do all this research into tropical diseases—or so they said. Then it came out that it was all a front and, instead, they were running a covert sterilisation programme."

"Fu...!" squawked Clare. "Oh! Sorry Sam..." Barratt smiled. "So what happened?"

"Well it was a scandal as you can imagine. When more details emerged it was quite shocking actually. They were paying people off in exchange for getting sterilised. Almost anyone who wasn't white and didn't go to Cambridge. They were targeting disabled people and poor people, but would go after a lot of black people as well. But in general they were going after anyone who wouldn't fit with their idea of genetic Puritanism."

"How were they getting them?" Veronica was now fully absorbed into the conversation.

"Well as I was saying, they were using the tropical disease thing as a front. They would make up all sorts of bullshit like 'such and such is at risk of a specific illness because of their disability or because they're from this or that country'. Then they would advocate sterilisation as a preventative measure. A lot of the people that went there were actually referred there by shitty doctors. Others fell for their bogus scientific leaflets. I mean it's brilliant, science. It has the same power as politics. You can use pseudoscientific piffle to give respectability to almost any position, and back then, obviously, information wasn't as widespread as it is today."

"So who blew the whistle?"

"Some brave souls eventually went to the police—who didn't do anything at first—useless fools, do excuse my French. But more and more people started to come forward until one day the Development Fund's HQ in Kershal Wood was raided at dawn out of the blue. Then all this came out and started to hit the papers."

Amber was as pumped up as the others, but was still mildly guarded.

"I appreciate his dad might have been a bit of a dick, but can we be so sure that he himself is as bad as that?"

Barratt was instant in her response.

"Oh, absolutely. He's a complete apologist for his father. He uses the relationship thing as cover in order to not condemn him. Just have a look at the Grove Chambers stuff. He believes in the politics of data…if you know what I mean. I mean just to state the obvious, you won't ever catch him making those sort of public comments—these are only things you'll pick up if you're around him for a long enough time—in a private sense."

"Sorry hang on," intruded Veronica. "So why did they push Giles Gibbs? If they did actually push him that is…"

"Simple. He'd done what was expected of him. Put the Party in a respectable, electable position. This government won't win another term after the debacle they've presided over. So as long as Hayes and Co don't put their foot in it, then they're away home and dry. Giles lacked the killer instinct to go far in the job… But there is something else I think, something I would never say in public anyway…"

"What's that? We're not wearing a wire!" joked Veronica.

"You're probably aware Giles has a severely disabled daughter. I think Hayes and Freedman manipulated that angle very intelligently. I mean, nobody is going to publicly accuse them of having heartless anti-disabled people policies, are they?" The girls remained silent, taking on board this new level of moral despotism Samantha Barratt had illustrated.

"But anyway, enough chat. Let's get down to business. How can I help?"

They had more questions, but were wise enough to move on. With that, Clare started to explain.

"Well it's just to reiterate what I said on the phone really. That demonstration earlier in the week. To cut a long story short the bottom line is I was essentially assaulted and we were wondering if you had any suggestions as to what I could do about it?" Amber then appeared to impetuously butt in.

"I'm really sorry Sam but can I just ask you quickly. I was in that committee room when the demonstration was taking place and you seemed to be, well, for want of a better word, dismissive of it…"

"No, not dismissive. There is a way of handling those situations. We've been pushing to grill Blackwood for a while and it would have been foolish to throw away the opportunity. For the record, I have absolutely no objections to the demonstration, and so I'll try and advise as best as I can… Getting back to this, you told me that nobody saw what happened—are you sure? It's a bit strange."

Amber was the only one of them who could provide testimony as to the lack of witnesses, so she carried on talking, turning impertinence to insightfulness.

"There were the demonstrators there obviously, but in terms of members of the public, no, not really. The area they were demonstrating in was sort of out of the way—you had to go out of your way to get there. Even then, you would have thought noise would have alerted someone, but no. I'd say the only real hope would be the guys at the windows. I mean, one second, people were there, and the next second, they weren't. Where the heck did they all go?"

"When events happen really close to the perimeter they normally do a PA message asking people to stay away from the windows. But, I think, your instincts are right. It's worth doing a bit of discreet sleuthing and seeing if anyone saw anything or whatever."

Veronica sliced in.

"We figured we'd try and get a prosecution or something. Assault. Might not sound a lot but you know, it would be symbolic."

"Well Clare was put in hospital with concussion so it's more than reasonable—reasonable being the operative word. Without finding someone other than Amber and the other demonstrators, it's essentially your word against theirs. It'll be a waste of time pursuing anything in that case. You know how the security establishment like to close ranks, and if this drags on and becomes high profile, then that's what they'll do. You told me they took everyone's phone, right? It might shock you but they can do that. So my advice is, try and see if you can find anyone else who saw something. That part of the building houses the committees so there's no need going half way around the world. But if you can't find anyone, I'd take it on the chin and move on to be honest."

Clare was disheartened, knowing that the possibility of finding an independent witness was slim.

"If we can't find anyone, do you have any ideas for a Plan B?"

"Keep on doing what you're doing. Organise, inform and demonstrate—LEGALLY. I'll put down a few questions in the House, piss a few people off."

"This is ridiculous!" spouted an incensed Veronica. "Someone has been assaulted on the Parliamentary Estate! How could nobody have seen? How come nobody seems to care?"

"Sadly, that's the way of the world. I mean, any scandal that's remotely close to the heart of government seems to have a habit of being brushed under the carpet. I mean take that whole paedophile ring thing. I mean on paper you would think anyone and everyone would be all over it. But at best it got treated as a third rate story. Which does make me slightly nervous about this particular incident. So keep your eyes open and your ears tuned ladies."

Preparing to leave the office, Amber's sense of agitation about what Sir Henry had said was unremitting. She stood up and promptly sat back down again.

"Everything OK Amber?" Barratt was spooked by the way Amber re-seated herself with purpose.

"Something is really bugging me, and I just wanted your view on it"

"Go on."

"The other day we went to see Sir Henry…"

"You went to see Sir Henry?"

"Yea, and when we were talking, he said there were no witnesses, but the way he said it, in such a matter-of-fact way, with such confidence, it freaked me out. How could he be so sure?"

Veronica looked at Amber.

"You didn't mention this before... Oh, actually Sam, Sir Henry also said he'd speak to Terrance Winchester."

"*Did he really?*" Barratt's playful voice suggested she didn't think much of Sir Henry's offer. "I'm afraid he's thrown you a banana skin there. You're likely to get more sense out of a lobotomised pineapple. He's done that to shut you up."

"But why would he do that?" Clare was irked.

"That's how he is. But let me talk to Terrance as well. Let Sir Henry know I'm taking an interest. I'll also put down a few questions in the House. It'll look bad if they interfered with opposition backbenchers putting down questions. As for your first point Amber, I'm not sure what to make of that. But I'll keep an ear out for anything untoward. In the meantime, do as I've already advised."

Leaving Samantha Barratt's office, the buoyancy they had come with remained partially intact, but there was no denying that the options available to them had stifled their impetus. The priority was indeed to try and find someone who may have seen the events, but all three had that nagging feeling. *This whole thing stinks, and something needed to be done.* As they were leaving, Veronica attempted to reassure Amber about her strange feeling.

"Don't worry Amber. Sir Henry is harmless."

Samantha Barratt hadn't revealed the full history of the Hayes family's involvement in dubious sciences. Although his father was closely associated with the National Improvement and Development Fund, it was Hayes' grandfather who had originally established himself as a foremost psychiatrist and supposed medical expert in the early twentieth century. He trained as a surgeon, but eventually traded the knife for an enormous chair, having been influenced by a number of writers that wrote about the supposed links between mental degradation and genetic integrity. It was a time of immense scientific intrigue—often for the wrong reasons. Colonial endeavours and rivalry between the leading nations of the day caused many intellectuals to investigate how the health of the masses could be improved in order to advance the interests of the nation. It was the poor and the downtrodden who suffered at the hands of the new intellectual curiosity. Hayes' grandfather had established an asylum in 1911. He was obsessed with proving the hereditary nature of those he considered feebleminded and was one of a number of public intellectuals that promoted methods, such as forced sterilisation, in order to maintain the safety of the public. Though never technically legal at the time, those targeted weren't in a position to question what was being done to them in the name of science. A number of high-profile institutions—from universities to research laboratories—made generous donations to Hayes' grandfather. He also had the ear of a number of powerful politicians. With war and conquest the habitual topics for discussion among power-brokers, Hayes' grandfather did an excellent job transferring the dexterity in his medically trained hands to his tongue. His speeches on social organisation were always well-received by the kingpins of his time. He wasn't looking for wealth or prestige, but it soon began to be poured on him as he started to acquire a small and well-connected following. The movement appeared to be on the cusp of making a wider mainstream breakthrough until the war intervened. Funding for Hayes' institution began to dry up as his financiers turned their attention to the war effort. Hayes' grandfather continued to contribute to the leading publications of his day. He had been wise with his investments, and upon anticipating the forthcoming financial squeeze, he began to consolidate his earnings. Though in good health, Hayes' grandfather was somehow able to escape conscription into the army, taking full advantage of the powerful friends and acquaintances he had made. As the war came to an end, he established a national newspaper. Trying to take advantage of the ever increasing literacy levels of the country, *The National* quickly ensconced itself into the psyche of the masses. Within ten years, it had established itself as the standard bearer for 'working people'. As time passed, the craze for genetic purity was losing its edge, largely thanks to the horrors that revealed themselves during the various battles taking place across the world. The targets of ridicule and humiliation remained the same, however. Changing times simply called for new methods to be developed and new intellectuals to propagate them.

Chapter Five

For Amber, weekends were a kind of exorcism for the five days that had just passed. The upheaval of recent days made this specific weekend a good candidate for mental hedonism. There were any number of activities she could indulge in: the movies, cycling, eating…sleeping. *Ah sleep*, precious little of that she'd done in the last week, she thought to herself, as she sat on her sofa, checking out how extensive the weekend's engineering works were in the event she and Clare planned to do something together that evening or the following day. Location-wise, some of their favourite places were in annoyingly distant areas. If Clare was going to attend, available transport would be key. Amber wanted to take Clare to her favourite restaurant, a delightful Turkish outfit south of the river. It turned out that the majority of the underground line they needed was suspended for that weekend. Amber sent a text message to Clare.

"No underground this weekend. Want to do anything regardless?"

There was no guarantee she'd respond immediately, so Amber left her phone on the table and went to her room. She was just about to have a nap when something Samantha Barratt said popped into her head: the Grove Chambers Institute. She had heard and seen the name come up several times through her studies and when working in Guy Freedman's office, but as far as she was aware, it was just one of several dozen think-tanks, just going around churning out an endless array of policy initiatives and putting them in front of any MP devoid of principle or sophistication of thought—and there were plenty who had those characteristics. Amber's feelings towards think-tanks were of general apathy; they were just part of the political circle of life. Barratt's depiction of Grove Chamber was causing Amber to question her stance. Was the sense of inevitability justifiable? *Think-tanks and policy institutes were a sign of a healthy democracy*, said one of her revision notes that she'd just pulled out from her university folders. The associated notes gave a long-list of why. It was the usual Spin Doctor's long-list—participation, generating ideas, freedom of thought. Her notes didn't say much about accountability or corruption or the skewing of representation, though this might have been because she was never the best at note-taking during lectures. Exposure to the cycle of policy-making meant that Amber was privy to the real interactions between the policy wonks and MPs, masked by all the verbal diarrhoea spouted at key note speeches or in newspaper interviews. Marcus once told her about his first internship stint, for the then Health Secretary, Marshall Mears. When it came to drafting the Home Assistance Act, rather than using the qualified people in the Parliamentary Drafting Unit, he would cut them out of the loop as often as he could and instead send key clauses over to the Thomas Foundation. Marcus told her how on one occasion the Drafting Unit spent three weeks on coming up with suitable wording for a contentious section of the Bill, but the Thomas Foundation wanted it re-written because they thought it ought to be *more* ambiguous. They sent it back within two hours. On that occasion, Mears was one of the very few politicians who actually got the blame when it became obvious that the legislation was so bad that it couldn't be delivered due to all the contradictions in the text. He tried his level best to point the finger at the Drafting Unit. He didn't have the backing of the PM and was eventually told to piss off. It turned out that he wasn't to be in the dole queue for a long time. Within a couple of months, he was appointed Policy Director at the Thomas Foundation. The Home Assistance Act was meant to have been a barnstorming new development in universal health care. A report, published a couple of years before the Bill was finalised, eviscerated a number of care homes that were being run for profit rather than the well-being of the patients. Following the report's publication, there was a clamour for a comprehensive set of regulations for those running the firms. More tellingly, the original aim of the Bill was to restrict the amount that the various private-equity firms and property developers could invest in such places. This didn't go down well with the Thomas Foundation, an unashamed cheerleader for private health care at any cost. For the entire duration of the Bill's passing, they used every point of access at their disposal to massage Mears' ego and kibosh the Bill if they could help it. In the end, they invariably succeeded, and two years of public engagement, consultation and heavy debate had gone down the drain. It was the last time Amber could remember an example of wholehearted public opinion being behind something. Things had gone downhill since then.

Amber would look into the Thomas Foundation in more detail a little later on. For now, she decided to delay her nap and see what she could find out about the Grove Chambers Institute. It made sense to make their website her first port of call. The Grove Chambers' name did come up on a relatively regular occurrence when there was a consultation going on as part of a new piece of legislation or when Guy Freedman would receive an invitation to attend a function of some sort. But it didn't come up to the extent where Amber had to work alongside actual Researchers and Policy Analysts for long stints or digest a report. Consequently, Amber didn't quite know what they were *really* all about. Scouring the homepage, it wasn't immediately clear what their raison d'être was. There was something called the 'Carl Kelly's Immigration Blog', an area of the website dedicated to Urban Regeneration, another area apparently dedicated to 'The Urbanisation of Medicine'—whatever that meant, and a vast area of the website dedicated to statistical analysis. Not really getting anywhere, Amber decided to take the shortcut route to what she was looking for and just go straight to the 'About Us' and 'What We Do' sections. There wasn't actually much there, but there was enough for Amber to understand what Samantha Barratt was getting at when she mentioned the 'politics of data'.

"The Grove Chambers Institute is a non-aligned Policy and Research Organisation, as defined under the Public Research Regulations 2009. Grove Chambers has two inter-dependent aims. The first is to seek a step-change in the way research and statistics are used in this country. Hundreds of public and private institutions are producing surveys and reports aimed at determining the opinions and habits of the general public in order to inform a new policy or a new product for the market. Grove Chambers believes that the mountain of data that these activities produce can be put to use in a more strategic manner. Grove Chambers is calling for all such data to be made available by way of a national information database. Having such a wealth of information can then be used to inform national policy-making that is genuinely in the national interest. For Grove Chambers, such data would allow it to fully embrace its second aim. Recent research by Grove Chambers has found that the integration of Medical Anthropology and Urbanisation and Development can lead to ground-breaking changes in social policy. However, these changes can only be realised if there is a step change in the way these fields are allowed to gather, analyse and interpret data."

That is some fully loaded stuff. Amber sat back in her chair. Every government policy is based on some combination of either making money or reducing spending, partially fulfilling an election manifesto to maintain credibility or creating a headache for the incoming government if defeat was almost certain, reacting to a negative opinion poll or story in a newspaper that had been blown out of all proportion. Well-meaning civil servants and ill-meaning policy gurus and special advisors would be behind the scenes doing the dishes. And yet, there was always an unspoken acknowledgement that really, the primary aim for any government was maintaining the status quo. Everyone of relevance thought this to be the case. A significant chunk of the public appeared to have moved on from the intoxication of apathy and had seemed to actively embrace this way of thinking. Nothing ever *really* got done because doing much more would lead to riots or World War Three. For this cohort, muddling through was the best way forward. It was politics' own warped version of Stockholm syndrome.

Why aren't these bastards doing anything to make our lives better?—We need to do something about these bastard politicians quick!—Actually if we do anything of relevance we'll all be killed!— Leave the politicians alone! Poor bastards, it's not their fault! There isn't much they can do really, is there? Just be thankful you're not lying in a ditch somewhere.

For the time being, although a large minority, it was just only a minority of the public that had been duped into silence—but Amber was always nervous that the numbers were growing. There were plenty of people out there who knew exactly what it meant to live in a society of rights and responsibilities, people who knew exactly what a reasonable balance was. It was for this reason the ramblings of an organisation like Grove Chambers hadn't seeped into the mainstream—yet. On a personal note, Amber was trying her resolute best not to trip over her own gullibility. In the past, she would be easily taken in by the sort of thing she had just read on the

Grove Chambers website. She assumed such oratorical nonsense was a hallmark of most think-tanks and policy institutes. Recent events, however, were making her appraise such grand statements more heedfully. *The politics of data*—this phrase seemed to sum up what Grove Chambers was all about, but at the same time it was hard to pick it apart. It was now time to do the really rubbish stuff and read a couple of articles on the website, just to try and add a bit more meat to the bones of what Samantha Barratt was getting at. Jumping from page to page, Amber was slowly getting a better idea of what Grove Chambers wanted to promote. Her grasp of political language had vanished since leaving university and so she had to re-read things until they had almost hypnotised her. Most of the apposite information was in the immigration blog and the medicine section. The statistics and data area of the website appeared to be filled with donkey twaddle. Amber may not have had a mathematician's mind, but she recognised bullshit when she saw it. None of it seemed to be of relevance. That was probably why they put it all on a public-facing website. Algorithms and statistics tend to generate an aura of respectability. As for the information written in plain English, it was quite clear what these guys were all about. They seemed to want to completely remove the human element from the policy-making process. It wasn't about what people wanted or needed, it was about what the state thought was in the state's interest. Everything could be codified. Everything could be stratified. It was all symbolised in two specific articles. An article on the immigration blog seemed to be making some of sort veiled racialist point about the need for different 'management strategies' for different 'social' groups. There seemed to be an intentional desultory running through the article. Screaming about immigration gained the reader's attention, but this article was more than just about immigration. The article seemed to be making a dogged attempt to use the anti-immigration buzzwords of recent times and expand them to other areas of society. The rationale was quite clear: if people tolerated the divide and conquer rhetoric of immigration policy, they might accept it in other areas as well. The article was dripping with mendaciousness. Some quick digging showed that the statistics used to support the assertions in the article were obtained after some sort of emotive event had occurred—in most cases an event not even in the country. A section of the article talked about how the recently initiated immigration points system could be taken as a standard and applied to people who were applying for benefits. This was one area of policy Amber knew all too well. In the first instance, the points system was clearly racialist in nature, giving preferential treatment to those with qualifications from European nations even though every academic on Earth thought the education systems of the Far East were superior to what most European countries had to offer. But the system also enforced a quota from certain parts of the world. An interrogation of the quota figures showed a correlation between a decline in the maximum number of people allowed from certain countries and darkness of skin colour. Amber came across that hideous statistic from a refugee rights' agency. There were other more well-known morally questionable elements of the point's scheme. The most obvious was the relationship between who wasn't allowed into the country and involvement in their countries of origin, usually in the role of a reliable arms exporter during a civil war. Despite having no real narrative, support for the scheme was asserted on the back of opinion polls that always seemed to be taken at very specific times, usually the day after SJTV had finished broadcasting back-to-pack pseudo-documentaries declaring the pending collapse of the British state as a result of the imminent arrival of the 'herds'.

That was the basis of the system. As for applying it to 'benefit claimants', the now standard euphemism for all disabled people, Amber shuddered at the senseless malignance of it all. A steady stream of stories concerning useless layabouts living lives of luxury whilst the rest of the country slaved away didn't really lead to a concerted moral attack on laziness. It did, however, lead to hardened attitudes towards disabled recipients of state benefits. As usual, Bob O'Hara was chief cheerleader within the tabloid press. SJTV would broadcast reality TV shows that seemed to have the aim of running concurrently with what the tabloids were saying. Nobody really understood why those featured on the shows were deemed disabled. Most had experienced some form of incapacity and had dropped out of work years ago. Admittedly, some had taken full advantage of the inability of successive governments to address the needs of those at the margins of society. Most though appeared to be…lost and, in many cases, terrified of life. The shows would purposely feature people with no visible frailties. Wheelchairs, canes, assistance dogs, adapted bathrooms; those were an inconvenience. Things had to be kept simple for the viewer—this fat ugly piece of shit needs to get off his backside, stop breeding and go and get a job. It was in this context that the article was written—it's not just immigrants who need keeping an eye on, it's the useless sods—disabled sods if you will—already here that need sorting out, and immigration policy can teach us a thing or two. The article went on to essentially argue that disabled people ought to have access to state benefits in accordance with how useful they were. Infuriatingly, the article was given an extra touchy edge by giving an example of the type of person who deserved higher levels of access to state benefits, in this case a former army soldier who had a limb amputated due to combat action. Amber's re-awakening political mind was sickened by the divisive play on patriotism. The higher moral worth attached to a soldier was acceptable because apparently when it comes to the national interest a solider has a clear role in defending that interest. It didn't matter what profession you were in, how educated you were, how much you participated in society or how much of a contribution to society you made. And to top everything, any idea that the state had a responsibility to protect the most vulnerable was dismissed as an unattainable pipe-dream.

Amber rubbed her eyes. Maybe in her newly acquired sense of political articulation she was over-analysing. It was time to take a step back and put things in to perspective. Apart from the immigration points system, nothing she had read was actually law, nor to her knowledge was it being proposed in any manifesto—not for the time-being at least. *But that wasn't the point!* How the heck could Alexander Hayes go from writing for this kind of organisation to become leader of the opposition? Amber knew all about the infamous 'climate of opinion'—and that's what this was all about. Bogus surveys and TV shows had softened a chunk of the public into thinking in a way that they wouldn't have done previously. Amber thought about it a bit more, and in a crazy kind of way, the sheer lunacy shown in a point of view that can only be described as a utilitarian form of fascism would give it more attention than it deserved. People would say, *most of it is utter nonsense but when he says such-and-such a thing I think he has a point; we should bin the rest of it and keep that bit.* And there it is; the research had done its job; it had entered the world of civilisation and respectability. The work done for *Political Engagement* was also beginning to trouble Amber. Guy Freedman and Alexander Hayes were parliamentary interlocutors. They, along with Giles Gibbs were the strategic brain of the Party. What Amber had just read didn't fit into any of the points made in the published article. Putting the two together was like having caviar and mashed potatoes; it just seemed weird. Amber fired off an email to Samantha Barratt in the midst of her mental bedlam to see what she thought of it all.

If there was any truism that Amber had taken on board from her studies and her short time as an intern, it was that money talks. Guy Freedman would go out of his way to try and make sure the financial links between his office and the various organisations he supported were suppressed to the maximum extent possible. Amber wanted to get a better idea of who some of the financial backers were behind Grove Chambers. A well-resourced office and comparatively well-remunerated staff didn't just pay for themselves. So who was paying for it? Amber had a look at the 'Our Supporters' section of the Grove Chambers Website. Most of the people on there were wealthy private individuals who were obscure to most of the general public but quite well-known to government insiders. One name, however, screamed out at Amber—Morgan & York. What the heck were they doing supporting this clap trap? When did Architecture and Urban Design develop a proclivity for immigration policy? Under the circumstances though that was a minor point. The real showstopper was the fact that James Jacob, son of Sir Henry, was a Senior Executive at the firm. What on earth did Sir Henry make of his son working for such an organisation? Morgan & York's website didn't really reveal anything of a malicious nature. And why would it? It was as interesting as one could expect the website of an architect's firm to be. Amber wasn't aware of any grief between James and Sir Henry. James Jacob was actually a close associate of Guy Freedman. Earlier that very week, James and Guy had met in The Sunflower to discuss some issue or other. It wasn't officially arranged by any of the team and didn't appear in any email calendar. You wouldn't have known it ever took place unless you had access to either of their inner circle—or were the landlord of The Sunflower. It was one of those personal get-togethers that doubled-up as a business meeting. Amber went over the times she had spoken with Sir Henry, to try to remember if James ever came up in a conversation, but nothing was coming to mind. It was cartoonishly stupid that James Jacob would be providing support to an organisation that apparently had a set of values totally at odds with those of his father. James' name wasn't explicitly on the website, just the name of Morgan & York. Was this just another case of everyday politics? The softening up of the *Political Engagement* article was understandable to a degree, but surely something like this couldn't be dismissed in the same context? Sir Henry Jacob was a wheelchair user and yet the organisation his son worked for was giving moral support to an institution that apparently despised anything that deviated from what an average Joe would consider to be normal. Reinforcing Amber's disquietude was Sir Henry's behaviour over the events that took place at the demonstration. Amber was in a state of chagrin; the situation seemed so implausible, and yet in reality, she couldn't join any dots to make greater sense of it all.

James Jacob had done well to keep himself out of the public limelight considering the amount of activities that could link him to those in senior political positions. Amber dug around at the back of her mind before realising there was something in James Jacob's past that, in hindsight, appeared to allude to a potential darker side. It wasn't something that was widely known—Amber only found out herself through Isabelle. He got a former secretary pregnant following a fling. At first, he seemed to be going along with the idea of having the child. He performed an about turn upon being informed that the child had a cleft lip. His former secretary failed to succumb to the pressure put on her by him to have an abortion. A simple operation sorted the issue a few months after the child was born, but James Jacob refused to have anything to do with mother or baby. *Goodness,* thought Amber. *If he's like that with something like a cleft lip, what on earth are his views like when it comes to more serious disabilities?*

Think-tanks and policy institutes were skilful at generating a mundane image of themselves to the general public. *This is all just boring, run-of-the-mill policy work, nothing to see here*. Amber had fallen for that line herself. As a result, the writings of Grove Chambers hadn't really received extensive exposure. This was something to be thankful for on the one hand, but still concerning on the other. The press, tabloid and quality alike, would hound people out of office for what would seem far less serious mutterings. If there was one person who could add some light to any of this, it was Henrietta Barnes from *The Tribune*. Barnes never wrote about the nitty-gritty of the think-tank/government axis in her actual weekly column because she most likely realised that, despite having a more

74

educated readership than compared to *The National*, a lot of people would never be able to appreciate the deceitfulness in the relationship that the nuances betrayed. When it came to the boredom of think-tanks and policy wonks, the tedium of it all meant that this was definitely a case where apathy *was* the correct mindset. As a result, Henrietta Barnes left her more recherché material for the magazine and website that was attached to the Jemima Centre. The Jemima Centre was originally set up as a charity and research centre for those with mental health problems. The Kershal Wood affair wasn't the only act of repugnance aimed in the direction of the most vulnerable that had come to light in the last forty years. More recently in fact, a number of whistle-blowers within the mental health establishment had blown the lid off a series of inhumane practices that were being inflicted upon patients at a clutch of psychiatric wards. These weren't the sort of dark arts promoted by the likes of Alexander Hayes' father in a bygone era. The activities were far less subtle—almost animalistic. People were being chained to their beds, being left to sleep on soiled mattresses and often being left untreated after suffering an episode. The government's response was lukewarm at best, with only a handful of perpetrators seeing the inside of a court room. The government had tied its own hands by way of the Mental Health and Readjustment Act, a terrifyingly paternalistic piece of law that watered down even the most basic of patient rights. Henrietta Barnes was one of the very few people who had actually lived in one of the effected wards but had come out with her sanity somehow intact. The experience drove her and a few like-minded individuals to establish the Jemima Centre. The original aim of the centre was to provide insight and analysis on debates around mental health. The mental well-being of the nation was a ticking time-bomb and the centre aimed to prize open a wider debate on the issue. Supporters of the centre soon realised, however, that the mental health issue was still too raw for many people to talk about. Of more relevance was the observation that they were spending too much time looking at the issue in a closed-off box, not taking into account the various social phenomena that underpinned the slaughter of the psyche. From then on, the centre began to pump out mountainous amounts of briefing material, flyers, posters and policy papers on every social ill-conceivable. A sense of purpose was often missing from a lot of it, but what it did provide was a genuine reservoir of knowledge and analysis on issues that the government of the day simply brushed under the carpet. The Jemima Centre had made itself indispensable in the world of those looking for a progressive step-change in government policy. It alone acted as a counterweight to the fifteen or so policy institutes that acted as what Henrietta Barnes called, "The Permanent Cabinet."

It appeared that Henrietta Barnes had been tracking the work of the Grove Chambers Institute for some time and had been publishing her thoughts within the Jemima Centre magazine. The magazine only had a circulation of around twenty thousand, but the shortfall in readership was cancelled out by the magazine's website, where a collection of blogs, extended essays and opinion pieces meant the paper-version would most likely come to an end sooner rather than later. Barnes' analysis of Grove Chambers was punctilious and brutal. Barnes had identified what she thought to be "the Machiavellian rise of an insular nexus of powerful individuals who appeared to adhere to a shared belief in neo-eugenics and who were beginning to discreetly make their power felt behind the closed doors of the Parliamentary Village." Barnes had written about a number of off-the-record meetings that had taken place between ministers, opposition MPs, representatives from Grove Chambers and some of its affiliates and like-minded organisations. Incidents of meetings began to serrate Amber's memory. Many were dismissive of Barnes' sensationalistic characterisations due to her lack of solid information. Much of her information was attributed to just 'sources', however, Amber was in a position to verify at least some of the meetings Barnes was referring to. Her most recent article on the subject was lambasted in the comments section due to her implying that Guy Freedman had met James Jacob informally to talk about 'policy matters' in a pub. Two men of that calibre wouldn't be so stupid, people said. Close associates were now guilty of having a drink together. Her wording made it sound unnatural. Amber knew, however, that the meeting between James and Guy definitely took place. More pressingly, having observed the two of them on several occasions, she knew that swapping holiday snaps was never on the agenda when they got together. Business and future government were the primary items for discussion. Then there were other meetings that surely only a handful of people would have known about? Amber recalled an occasion when Howard Blackwood and Guy Freedman had a private appointment in Guy's office. Neither she nor the others were asked to take notes or sit in at the meeting.

Making three cups of tea was as far as anybody had to extend themselves on that particular afternoon. So Amber could verify some of the meetings that were taking place. But how was Barnes getting wind of not only the meetings, but what was apparently being decided at those meetings? She appeared to be using her political intuition and some common sense. After each meeting, there would be an almost instant reaction by way of a new policy initiative on The Union Party website or a random television or radio interview that nobody had been briefed about up to that point, an initiative that appeared to be completely at odds with what the Party had been banging on about in public forums, magazine interviews and key note speeches. Furtively, these sorts of announcements were often made by junior ministers. Critics dismissed the announcements as purely an outcome of personality politics or short-termism. That's the way things got done sometimes. If somebody had a bright idea, it had to be expressed there and then. It was just the spin-doctors doing their thing. Keeping official announcements for official engagements and using other ad-hoc forums to toss out some idea if suitable for the climate—or, it would appear, if pressured by some corporation or organisation.

Personal examples of the latticework began to abound in Amber's head. Most symbolic was the Union Party's Summertime Ball. Such events in poorer countries were dismissed as cronyism and a sign of under-development, but here it was apparently all part of the democratic process. The event was under the patronage of the Union Party but was actually paid for by Mortimer Brothers. People normally associate debauchery when such a large number of men and their guests decide to frolic in the summer sunshine. Amber didn't recall anything like that. The sort of things that did happen, however, was far worse in some ways. Future amendments to the Public Research Regulations were actually agreed at the ball. A number of academic institutions had successfully called for a neutrality principle to be enshrined into the regulations. Practically all think-tanks and research firms were private institutions. But an exponential increase in the amount of papers being published caused leading academics to argue that firms could publish what they like, but that they had to have a publicly available register of interests so that they couldn't hang onto the coattails of prestigious universities and use them as cover. Naturally the backers of the Permanent

Cabinet were aghast at the inclusion of the clause. So, at the Summertime Ball, while the majority of the audience were enjoying an auction with the aim of hoping to secure a private dinner with someone from the corridors of power, leading figures in the Union Party were locked away with policy gurus agreeing to make the necessary changes if there was to be a future Union government.

Amber had taken in a lot and decided not to look further into the Thomas Foundation for the time being. Her vibrating phone almost knocked a glass of water off the table. Clare had replied back to say that she was tied up with family that weekend and couldn't make it.

Right! Now it really is time for a nap! But as Amber hopped into bed she received a response from Samantha Barratt.

"If you take a look at the speeches I've made, this is an issue I've highlighted in the House on many occasions. But to be honest Amber, this sort of stuff falls on death ears. You have to ask yourself, how many members of the public have the time to read and process stuff published by the likes of Grove Chambers? It's the ultimate paradox—you only appreciate the power of the spider's web once you've been caught in it. Anyway have a good evening, Samantha."

Chapter Six

Barely a week had passed since Giles Gibbs had stepped down as leader of the Union Party, but the team was doing a steady job of managing the readjustment process. Although in reality, there was a sense of inevitability throughout the early days under the new leadership. For someone who relied on a team of interns and special advisers to hold things together, Guy Freedman's instructions since Gibbs' departure were conspicuously clear and to the point. One of the less-talked about outcomes of the change in leadership was a change in portfolio management for Guy Freedman. Homeland Affairs wasn't the most alluring area a minister or shadow minister could work in, but in recent years, it had come to be a badge of honour for any minister with leadership aspirations. The economy had been joined by law and order as the benchmark that made or broke ministerial careers. Freedman didn't have the intellectual vigour to deal with immigration or race relations, but if you were to give him five minutes, he was enough of a wordsmith to turn the Orange Tiger Butterfly into an axe-wielding maniac. He had a pinpricked look on his face immediately after the weekend, clearly unimpressed with what had been written in some of the newspapers. On the whole though, he was relatively relaxed. He had his allies in the press, and the events of the past week had instilled momentum in everything he did. One of the very few changes pushed through by the current administration was the increasing of Prime Minister's Questions from once a week to twice a week—every Tuesday and Thursday, midday to half past twelve. The bulk of Monday was taken up with the team doing background research and networking as part of attempts to get to grips with their new area. They never really had to get involved in the heavy-duty side of things, that's what the special advisers were there for. But Freedman expected everyone to possess the basics in terms of policy positions and important numbers on speed-dial if needed. A portion of the day was also dedicated to doing background research for Union MPs who were planning to put questions to the Prime Minister. Under different circumstances, this would have been an ideal opportunity to throw some light on what happened to Clare. But Amber's involvement caused Guy Freedman to tell her that in no uncertain terms should she discuss the matter with Union MPs who were looking to pester the Prime Minister.

"How are we all on this fine Monday afternoon then?" Tom was surprisingly chirpy for the first day of the week, probably because Arsenal had won at the weekend. There was no immediate answer from his colleagues, who were all engrossed in their computer monitors. Marcus had been asked to do some quotidian background research into a speech the government was delivering later on the topic of prison reform so that Freedman had some material to offer an immediate public rebuttal. The special advisers naturally did the bulk of the hardcore preparation such as key messages and applying the right tone. But Freedman did use material provided by his interns when he thought the stakes weren't too high. Freedman recognised that his team of interns may not be PR experts, but having left university recently, were quite fastidious when it came to researching facts and figures. With the amount of material they consumed through reading and research, Amber & Co should have been semi-experts in the areas they had worked in so far. Far more seemed to leave their heads than stay in though.

Prison reform wasn't normally a core part of the law and order patchwork that all politicians needed to be knowledgeable about if they wanted to be perceived as electable. It was high on the agenda for the forthcoming election, partly because of the disturbances at a number of immigration detention centres and partly because of a riot that had taken place at Taunton Bridge young offender's institute. Reports in some sections of the media alleged misdemeanours on a grand scale by the security firm involved, Longacre Green Waterside (LGW). No official report was published, but sufficient public pressure meant LGW had all their government contracts taken away and were barred from tendering for any future central government contract for five years. The decision caused consternation in some circles, LGW being owned by Herron Tate, a private equity firm that was a donor for a number of high-ranking politicians from both sides of the political spectrum. Despite the shocking nature of some of the confirmed events that took place at

Taunton Bridge, the decision to withdraw the contracts caused a decline in the relationship between the business lobby and the government, which in turn contributed to a perception that the government was losing a grip on things, even though in this case the government did that rare thing of taking the principled line for once. But it seemed that competence and morality were too distinct things for a lot of people. Once you were judged as incompetent, all examples of good-conduct were dismissed as gesture politics.

"Do any of you guys know if there is a ready-made document I can use on the shared drive that covers our positions on justice and stuff?" Marcus was tiring of the excessive reading.

"I remember coming across something produced by one of the old interns when I was doing the *Political Engagement* stuff." Amber walked across and showed Marcus where it was.

"What the heck is all this?"

"Oh—I don't know—there are one or two things on here that are password protected like that. That one there, that's the one you need." Amber pressed her index finger into the glass as if to convey a sense of definiteness and went back to her chair. Marcus began to summate the information, but there wasn't anything suave about the content of Union policies.

"So basically lock them up and throw away the key." Marcus seemed accepting of most of what he was reading or just feeling spectacularly pococurante. Isabelle on the other hand told it like it was.

"Come off it Marcus. How nobody got done for Taunton Bridge, we'll never know. You should go read the Jemima Centre report on it. It's shameful. But do you know when it stopped making front page news, they actually did all-night Youth Offender Tribunals to punish the people that took part. They can mobilise the full force of the law to bury a bunch of nobodies, but they do sod all when some rat legally embezzles millions. *'No actual crime has been committed'* they scream—well, then make it a crime then." Marcus knew better than to argue with Isabelle, and so didn't make any counter-remark.

With the weekend being a total blowout, Amber and Clare decided to compensate by going to a local restaurant for dinner, in their minds it was still the weekend, and that was good enough for them. Parliament House Italia was usefully located close to Parliament House and the Private Offices. Central Chapel Tube

Station was thankfully accessible, and so Amber and Clare arrived for their 7pm reservation with time to spare. Amber was relived as she took her seat at the table.

"Finally—it's freezing outside!"

"I hear you! Even with thick gloves my hands feel like they're gonna fall off from all the pushing!"

The restaurant was relatively busy. Although there were a couple of empty tables, they had reservation cards placed on them. Amber flicked her eyes around the tables. Being so close to the Private Offices and Parliament House, it wasn't uncommon to be able to spot the odd politician or a tabloid chancer looking for their next story. Amber couldn't spot any chances, but on the far side, away from the immodestly sized windows, Amber was certain she had spotted Giles Gibbs sitting down with his wife for some dinner. She merrily popped out of her chair and went over to say hello.

"Hi Giles. It's Amber from Guy Freedman's office. You might not remember me; we spoke a few times when I was working with Sir Henry."

"Yes, I remember. Good evening Amber. How are you?" Giles Gibbs tended to be more amiable than some of his ex-Parliamentary colleagues.

"Oh, you know the life of an intern—useless one second, industrious the next. How have the first few days been?"

"Oh, lovely…spending a lot of time gardening and annoying the wife and kids." He smiled at his wife Lisa, who lovingly smiled back.

"Sounds awesome, well, I won't ruin your evening any further. It was nice to see you again."

"And you Amber." Amber aimed a gentle waive and smile in both their directions and returned to her seat.

"How is he?"

"Yea, he's all right I think. I always preferred him to most of the others. I think he had a sanitising effect on Guy. It was probably one of the reasons why they got rid of him. But anyway, didn't come here to talk about politics—how goes your flat search?"

"Non-existent, I'm afraid. Can't find a thing, and even the stuff I do find is either too expensive or on the twentieth floor with no lift. I'm telling you, history is gonna remember us as the shoebox generation."

"How does your mum feel?"

"Oh, she's all right. She's happy for me to stay as long as I want. But I've always thought it would be nice to have a place of my own or at least start looking for one at the minimum."

"I hear what you're saying. But, I think, independence is more desirable in some areas than others. I think your mum would be really pleased if you hung around. And I think you're right, we are the shoebox generation, largely because of the government, but a small part is down to us as well…"

"How d'you mean?"

"For example if things really are that expensive, then people should take it on board rather than just carry on as normal. I mean there's nothing wrong with living with your parents. I mean, all these pricks on chat shows and comedy shows passing judgment on people, there isn't any shame in it. It's all right for most of them—half of these people get a place of their own and their mummies and daddies are subsidising everything for them anyway!"

In the time that passed between them entering the restaurant and sitting down at their table, Amber had apparently become an economist and a social commentator. She was worried that she had inflamed Clare's senses, but Clare took the advice in the right spirit.

"No, I see what you mean. I'm definitely not ashamed. I'd gladly stay at home forever. But I just always get this feeling I'm a burden for her."

"Nonsense—you only feel like that now because you ain't got a job. Once that changes, your mood would change as well. Anyways, I'm pretty sure as with most people who move out, you'd be more of a burden on your own. She'd constantly be phoning, going over, asking you to come on over. If you didn't get along with each other, that might have changed things but you do, so it makes more sense if you're under the same roof."

Clare admired the patterns carved into the lamp shade in front of her whilst excogitating over Amber's advice for a few moments. A few moments soon turned into over twenty minutes as their order appeared to be increasingly delayed. Then, bizarrely, a small piece of meat landed next to Clare, and within seconds another piece seemed to flick the back of her wheelchair. She turned, Amber swayed her head to the right, and there appeared to be a mischievous little boy smiling at them, with some fish in his hands, and his parents looking on, with no sense of alarm. Amber gestured to them, pointing at the meat that had been thrown and then pointing to the boy. The parents remained straight-faced.

"I'll sort this out." Amber got out of her chair and walked over to the boy.

"Are you gonna come over and clean that up?"

"Shut up." The boy's father then finally said something.

"Can't you just get the waiter to sort it out?"

Amber walloped her hand on the table, bent down to make eye contact with him and in a quiet, poisonous voice said, "If that little shit doesn't go over there right now and clean that stuff up, I'm gonna drag him over there and use his but-ugly face to do it myself."

A waiter appeared and asked if there was a problem.

"Yes, this young lady is sitting over there with her friend and this little brat here has been throwing things at their table." Amber had been staring at the boy's father the entire time but she then jumped up and turned around. There was Giles Gibbs, who had seen what happened and had come over to intervene. The waiter knew exactly who he was and didn't even bother to check the other version of events.

"Excuse me Sir please control your child or else I shall have to ask you to leave. My apologies Miss, we will move you to one of our premium tables immediately complements of the house."

"We can't sit in your premium area; it's up the stairs and my friend is in a wheelchair. Can you just seat us at a clean table? And can you also serve us our food please. We've been here for almost half an hour."

"Yes, of course Miss. Immediately."

Amber whispered, "Cheers" as she walked passed Giles and over to her new table that was being set up.

Later that evening, Amber was looking forward to seeing Giles in more familiar surroundings. *Review of the Day* was due to broadcast an interview with him. Amber wasn't expecting it to be anything explosive, but it was at least a chance to hear what he thought how the change in leadership had gone. Everything Amber had come across so far was comment pieces. It was a pre-recorded piece, which meant there wouldn't be a chance for Sir Richard Willis to turn it into a pointless self-righteous exhibition of his interviewing skills.

"Giles Gibbs, would you say that the Union Party is in a better place now that you've let go of the rains?"

"I think the Party is heading in the direction its leadership and supporters would expect it to." That was a somewhat cryptic answer under the circumstances. Sir Richard was almost certainly expecting a ringing endorsement of both Giles and the new leadership.

"And is that a direction you endorse? Having been leader for close to three years you are of course largely responsible for what is slowly turning into an unassailable lead in opinion polls?"

"I think what I did was put the Party on a clear footing. I'm obviously very pleased with my achievements as leader but I don't think now is the time to talk about that. There is an election that needs winning and we need to concentrate on that."

"May I say that you're probably the most magnanimous politician in British history?" Sir Richard was obviously taking the piss but he had a point. Giles Gibbs sounded like he was neutering himself.

"No, I don't think I'm at all magnanimous. As I've just said, I think under my leadership, we've managed to articulate a far more robust policy stance than we have done in previous years."

"So what are some of these policies?"

"Well I think we're now shaping the thinking of others on a number of key areas—engagement with small business…new perspectives on immigration…substantive changes to environmental laws. These are all areas where we've had a major impact…where I think the electorate sees many benefits of having the Union Party in government—areas where quite frankly the government has attempted to steal our ideas."

"Is that it?"

"What do you mean?"

"For someone who has been Party leader for nearly three years you don't have much more to show for than a few business and environmental policy initiatives?"

"I suppose I am magnanimous," chuckled Gibbs. It was a good thing this was pre-recorded. If Gibbs had come out with these sorts of answers in a live interview, Sir Richard would have torn him apart. As it was, it was recorded in Gibbs' study, just a couple of days after he had stepped down. Sir Richard obviously thought this wasn't the place for journalistic bravado. Amber wasn't having any of it though. Gibbs' answers were so innocuous they were actually meretricious.

"So tell me about the lover's tiff your Party had over the Public Advertising Bill…"

"I don't think there's much to say about that to be honest. We supported a government initiative. It's as simple as that."

"An initiative that wouldn't have passed without your backing…tell me…is it common practice for deals to be done with some backbenchers at the expense of others?"

"Well as you know the Public Advertising Bill has supporters and opponents in both the main parties. The strategic decision of the leadership as a whole was to support the Bill, which I'm totally comfortable with." Giles may have been comfortable with the vote, but this was a distinctly uncomfortable interview. For someone who was looking forward to spending more time with his family, he came across as being troubled.

"So there is no relationship between the vote in the house and your departure?"

"Absolutely not."

"So what message do you think Alexander Hayes would want to hear coming from you? You're no longer a politician, is there any specific advice that you would give the leadership now that you're at a safe distance as it were?"

"I think the message for the Party is that it's business as usual. As I've said previously, senior colleagues knew of my decision to stand down in advance so there has been sufficient planning in terms of a transition period."

"And how about advice—is there anything you're happy to say now that you may not have said previously?"

"No, I don't think so. I think they know what they're doing." Giles was trying to come across as light-hearted as possible, but clearly something was bugging him.

"Not the most ringing endorsement…"

"Look…well…party leaders don't like to be talked about publicly by their predecessors—nor do they like to be told they should do this or they should do that. They've got a plan and I'm sure they'll get on with it. It's not for me to say either way…" Giles was clearly intonating some sort of disharmony about this 'plan'— Sir Richard tried to prod away in his usual crafty way, but during the interview Giles must have realised how evasive he was being.

He changed his approach from, 'It's got nothing to do with me' to the 'I'm retired and I don't care anymore'.

"Look Sir Richard, I know you do these interviews looking to see who slips on the banana skin, but really, I'm trying to move on quickly so that I can get used to the life of not being in the public eye. Some politicians leave Parliament with dreams of world domination, but I've had enough of that life."

Sir Richard, Guy Freedman and Alexander Hayes would have been relatively happy with that public confirmation of disengagement, but again, Amber knew better. Giles Gibbs had political antenna sticking out of every orifice of his body, despite lacking a politician's killer instinct. He may have lacked the willpower to act when it mattered, but he knew exactly what was going on and when, and Amber suspected that his peaceable remarks weren't reflective of his long-term outlook.

Working as an intern for a frontline MP had a particular attraction on Tuesdays and Thursdays. The standard half hour lunchtime break could be stretched to one-and-a-half or even two hours as people were allowed to absorb the pantomime of Prime Minister's Questions. MPs, special advisers and political hacks would congregate around the private canteens dotted around Parliament House in a fashion akin to holidaymakers in the Mediterranean summer. Amber was always amused how stories of powerful cliques, plots and rebellions would more often than not spring from an insipid, steeply-priced tea room. There were always more comical stories, the veracity of which nobody could ratify apart from those on the inside. One such story that Amber would happily confirm were she to be asked was when Bob O'Hara got drunk one night and proceeded to get stuck in the ladies toilets, which he then proceeded to block—with the full force of his bowel muscles by most accounts. A number of women had complained of a fouls stench coming from one of the cubicles. When the door was opened, there was O'Hara, head leaning against the wall, fast asleep.

Amber knew that Samantha Barratt was due to ask a question, so she made sure she got to the Chamber early in order to get a seat in the public gallery. It provided a stunning birds-eye view of the entire chamber, with the exception of the standing areas near the two exits. Tom was always up for a lunch break in the public gallery and so had accompanied Amber.

"Why did you wanna come so early?"

"Because there isn't a safety net underneath the gallery in the event it gets overcrowded and someone starts shoving me in the back and I throw them overboard."

"Fair enough…any interesting characters today?"

"No, not that I can see from the list. I think most people want to see how the PM handles Alexander. It didn't go all that well first time, did it? Alexander got a free ride. Let's see what happens this time." Amber didn't want to tell Tom about the business with Samantha Barratt—not just yet anyway. There was no point in getting him involved—it was just one extra person who she'd have to make sure didn't say the wrong thing.

"Questions for the Prime Minister!" barked the Speaker of the House, Chandler Perryman. "Alex Wilshaw!"

"Thank you Mr Speaker. Mr Speaker, in my constituency East Porters, at the time when this government came to power, youth unemployment was at record levels. Since then, the apprenticeship scheme and other policies instituted by this government have contributed to a dramatic reduction in the numbers of those not in education, employment or training. Would the Prime Minister join me in congratulating those who have seized their opportunities, as well as joining me in condemning those on the opposition benches who are licking their lips at the mere thought of taking it all away again?"

That was a fairly straightforward beginning to the session for the Prime Minister.

"I know my Right Honourable friend has been doing some outstanding work with young people in East Porters, I say long may it continue, and it CAN only continue with the future-proof policies of an Alliance administration, not with the shambles on offer from those on the opposition benches!" The Saturday night, bar-fight-esque howling had begun.

"Julia Morris!"

"Thank you Mr Speaker. Mr Speaker, as we draw deeper into the winter, many of my constituents are naturally concerned about the energy bills they face coughing up. Could the Prime Minister explain why such little has been done to neutralise the corrosive effect of what can only be described as the mafia masquerading as energy companies?"

Members on the government benches mockingly aimed gun gestures at the opposition front bench; Hayes, Freedman and the others just shook their heads.

"This government has done more than any in recent years to address the issue of winter energy bills. We've introduced the Fuel Allowance for over 70s, as well as promoting a raft of subsidised sustainable energy solutions. In comparison, he and his colleagues are taking it in turns to suggest how much more they can de-regulate the market—a market they de-regulated so much the last time they were in government, stories of people finding their relatives frozen at the bottom of the stairs almost reaching a weekly occurrence."

That piece of theatre didn't go down well with opposition MPs. Screams of 'bullshit' and 'liar' could be heard as the Chamber continued its descent into routine petulance and megalomania. The Prime Minister's remark was more an extreme exaggeration rather than outright dishonesty. The last time the Union Party was in power, the situation with the big energy firms got to preposterous levels. For a short period of time, the Party allowed one of the major firms—and later to be revealed major donors to the Party, Bloom Energy, to undertake what many observers regarded as a suspect remote energy measurement project. They portrayed it as just using technology to get more accurate fuel use measurements. Instruments were installed in what the Union Party described as the most vulnerable group—old ages pensioners. They were supposed to allow the firm far greater energy use levels—by allowing the firm to remotely connect to the instruments. But only the well-informed knew that the devices were more than what they appeared to be. It turned out that Bloom were recording usage habits and then bombarding customers with random letters suggesting how to improve energy use based on cutting edge research—*do you need to have that cup of tea so hot? That piece of meat doesn't need to be heated that long. Have fewer pieces of toast.* But in a few admittedly rare cases, some Bloom workers were actually remotely switching off energy supplies. Those who lost their jobs always said they were only following orders that had come from senior management, but naturally no proof was found and nobody at a senior level was hung out to dry.

Amber leaned forward as if she was about to see her son or daughter perform their first piano recital; she wasn't of course.

Samantha Barratt was up next, and this was what she had come to see.

"Samantha Barratt!"

"Thank you Mr Speaker. Mr Speaker, I'm sure the Prime Minister would agree that in this country we strive to make the lives of disabled people as comfortable as possible. That being the case, could the Prime Minister explain why an innocent yet admittedly unauthorised demonstration recently held on the grounds of Parliament House led to a shameful, unprovoked assault on a young wheelchair user?" There was an atypical silence, the sort when someone makes a joke about a dead person in the presence of a relative, not realising they were there.

"As my Right Honourable friend highlights, that particular demonstration was unauthorised. However, in any case, I am happy to defend the conduct of those who work to protect the parliamentary buildings. A proper review will take place to make sure security guidelines are clear for all. I won't comment on that particular case as I don't think that is appropriate, however, as I said we will review procedures to make sure things are fit for purpose."

Amber wasn't sure who would be more pleased with that response—The Prime Minister or Guy Freedman. As Barratt was speaking, Amber studied Guy's face. For a moment it looked like it was about to rupture. He had the look of a man who'd just woken up, looked out his window and discovered his favourite y-fronts missing from his washing line. It was very outré for a Prime Minister's response to a question to relax a leading member of the opposition, but that it did. Freedman wasn't totally at ease though. He was heatedly whispering things into Hayes' ear. Amber was at an excellent vantage point to try and lip read what was being said, but it was no use though. Hayes, along with most of his frontbench colleagues, had become extremely adept in the art of minimal lip movement when talking in the chamber.

Amber was also monitoring live analysis of Prime Minister's Questions on her smartphone. She was switching between the First Broadcasting Service (FBS), *The Tribune*, and *The National*. Harry Sullivan, the FBS's Chief Political Editor was largely implying that this week was going far more smoothly for the PM than in recent outings, but he made the point that being so far behind in the opinion polls, was it too little too late? But he did caution that a lot can happen in eighteen months. Over at *The National*, Bob O'Hara was doing his best impression of a Rottweiler that hadn't eaten in three days—psychotic and deranged whenever an issue of social conscious was raised—something that was an increasingly rare occurrence in the Chamber anyway—but that wasn't good enough for O'Hara; "Effing Barratt—that woman is always making a mountain out of a molehill."

A hop over to the *Disability Institute* Website revealed that the various chat rooms used by Veronica & Co had been taken down. DI clearly didn't appreciate their site being used as a venue for self-criticism. Amber switched over to Henrietta Barnes' live blog on *The Tribune* Website, but for some reason she wasn't making a bigger deal out of Samantha Barratt's question. Barnes would normally be very astute in picking up on the potential banana skins. On this occasion she wasn't going beyond the 'incompetent security' line, rather than blithering and blustering and demanding a full inquiry. Amber was displeased and resolved to try and catch-up with Henrietta at some point. A charity shindig was coming up in the next few days; Amber would see her then.

A soul-destroying dark night sky and an urban fox dragging what appeared to be a kitten across the street compounded what Amber predicted would be an upsetting evening. Clare's nerve disorder had flared up again, and Amber was paying a visit to see how she was going. It was also a chance for them to gather their thoughts concerning everything that was going on. Amber rang the doorbell, and Clare's mum arrived shortly to greet her.

"Hey Mrs T!"

"Ah Amber. Come on in. I hope you didn't get too much of a soaking."

"Nah I'm all right, it only started to properly come down just as I turned on to your street."

"Here, let me take your coat. You can let it dry down here whilst you're chatting to Clare."

Amber handed her jacket to Clare's mum.

"How is she doing?"

"Better than this morning thankfully. She can sit up more comfortably now."

Amber nodded and walked down the passage way to Clare's room.

"I'm cooking a meal so no ordering takeaway!"

"Wouldn't dream of it Mrs T! It smells fantastic!"

Entering Clare's room, Amber saw her friend sitting up in bed, using her smartphone. Clare looked up with a smile.

"Hey Amber. How goes you? There is some popcorn over there…" Clare began to stretch to pass the popcorn to Amber.

"It's cool it's cool, I'll get it… Your mum tells me you're feeling a bit better today?" Amber perched herself at the end of the bed, opposite some of Clare's vibrant watercolours that were displayed on the wall.

"I suppose so. I had a nightmare going to the loo and stuff last night and this morning as you can probably guess. But yea, I think I'm over the worst of it now."

"How's your mum doing?"

"Oh you know, she never lets it get to her, which is worrying in itself I suppose. At times, I think it might be better if she just screamed at the top of her voice just to let it all out. In any case, all this has put an end to me getting a place of my own for the time being." Amber and Clare paused for a moment to gulp down some popcorn.

"These episodes never used to be so close together. Before it happened a few times a year, now it's twice in two months. Is your medication all right?"

"No, that's the thing. The doctor always said as the years go by the more chance the drugs would be less effective…"

"So what are they gonna do?" Amber had the shivers at the thought of Clare's condition deteriorating.

"There are a couple of new things that have come out recently. Gonna go in next week and discuss it with the doc. But let's not depress ourselves. Did you watch PMQs? Samantha asked about the demo. What's the reaction been like?"

"Practically nothing. She got fobbed off in the chamber and it's been almost dismissed out of hand in the bullshit afterwards."

"This is weird!"

"I know right?"

"I've said it before and I'll say it again! Someone has been assaulted on the Parliamentary estate and nobody gives a shit? Round the corner from an election? Nah sorry, something else is going on here." Clare seemed to be pinning all her hopes on this being more than just the political machine doing what the political machine does best.

"Let me catch up with Samantha Barratt in the next day or so. I'm going to a charity thing as well this week. I'm pretty sure Henrietta Barnes will be there—as well as Samantha. Henrietta is the only one who might push things I think." Amber concealed her displeasure at Barnes not making more of PMQs.

"Did you reach the comments by that dickhead O'Hara? That guy is suffering from serious psychological problems; I think everyone at the National is to be honest with you."

"Yea you know I've never got the inside low-down on him actually. You know, was he raised a dickhead or did his friends convince him to become one? I think I'll add him to my list."

"What list is this?" Clare was thoroughly enjoying her popcorn as the two talked away.

"Ha! Not that kind of list. I've been trying to get a better idea about some of these organisations that Sam told us about, principally Grove Chambers. It's quite shocking actually. If anybody outside the Parliamentary axis produced some of that stuff, I'm sure they'd be arrested for breaking some law or other."

"Well, let me know if anything interesting turns up. I've been trying to be constructive as well actually...well as much as is practically possible from a flippin' bed."

"Go on..."

"Did you see our forums on the Disability Institute website got shut down?"

"Yea I saw that..."

"No bother, we knew we couldn't go on using that forever. Anyhoo, we've nobbled some of their members, and I've managed to create a new website we can all use. Well, actually Veronica is more of the techie—I'm more of the creative person."

"Ace—what are you calling yourselves? Sticking with Gold Front?"

"What are WE calling ourselves—you're with us, aren't you?" Clare had an enormous smirk on her face.

"Defo—so what are we calling ourselves?"

"Well, it might change again, but for now, we're calling ourselves Blind Spot."

"Why d'you settle on that?"

"Sums up our predicament don't you think?"

"I suppose so. Wasn't Veronica meant to be coming over tonight as well?"

"She was, yea. But she sent me a text to say she couldn't make it. She'd double booked herself apparently. Silly girl!"

Chapter Seven

The incumbent Alliance government was suffering a barrage of indignities at the hands of the press—both from the left and right. Having been in power for close to ten years, any sense of a coherent policy framework had been jettisoned in the belief that, as defeat in the forthcoming elections seemed inevitable, individual prerogatives were now the driving force of the administration. The party had come to power on a wave of discontent surrounding the outgoing Unity government. A glut of sleaze scandals had caused the Unity government to fall apart at the seams, with Alliance positioning itself to take advantage at every opportunity, absolving them of the need to win the public over with the standard avalanche of un-costed policy initiatives. The administration started smoothly enough by making all the relevant overtures to key parts of the press and the business lobby. There was no ostensible difference between Union and Alliance when it came to prioritising friends and enemies. Alliance was generally perceived as a softer version of their Unity foes. Naturally, this was never observable in newspaper articles or television interviews, with members of the frontbench taking it in turns to aim broadsides at each other. The Alliance government set about a corrective course of government when it entered office, tweaking the policies of its predecessor as opposed to committing to any mass changes. The approach was partly dictated by the slender majority in Parliament—just twenty-five at the changeover of government. This in itself was a prickly matter for the leaders of the party. Schisms inside the Alliance were more pronounced than in the Unity Party, and the government was thus repeatedly susceptible to rebellions. The Whips' Office would work overtime just to keep an eye on any seedy interactions with opposition members. It was this fractious atmosphere within the government that had Hayes and Freedman licking their lips for several years. During the early years of the Alliance administration, both were still part of the backbenches, with no real indication that they were set to make a break for glory any time soon. Hayes and Freedman saw opportunities to insert themselves into the affairs of the Alliance administration while working from the shadows. Their early overtures to Alliance MPs were dismissed as being part and parcel of the state the Party found itself in. They weren't the first, nor would they be the last, to take advantage of government infighting. But for Hayes and Freedman, it wasn't about sowing dissention among the ranks. They were smart enough to understand the importance of maintaining a sense of equilibrium between various power brokers. Hayes and Freedman took the path of anonymous suffocation—never contributing to major discontent—but flicking small doses of itching powder on an open wound and then standing back and seeing what happened. At the end of Alliance's first term in office, the chicanery of Hayes, Freedman and their allies turned out not to be enough to win the public over, the national psyche showing its unique ability to organise its thoughts collectively despite the cleavages that lay beneath. On this rare occasion, the public was willing to overlook party disunity in favour of a modicum of continuity. Hayes and Freedman weren't too fussed; however, they'd got their elbows through the door, and at that moment in time, that was all that was required.

Unbeknown to observers and analysts, Hayes and Freedman had set the balls in motion for a future Unity government. In Alliance's first term, the interference was calculated and almost untraceable. As the second term progressed, Hayes, Freedman and their allies were on the move to seal the deal on a number of key pieces of legislation as well as cementing links with prominent but disgruntled members of Alliance. Shortly after the start of Alliance's second term, senior party figures began to commit the cardinal sin in politics of feeling a sense of security following the election victory—even though the majority had been reduced to ten. Hayes and Freedman began to identify allies that shared similar 'interests' to their own, allies who could be trusted to support their future cause. With senior figures in the Alliance government seemingly taking a totalitarian turn, finding recruits wasn't as difficult as one would suspect. Alliance and Unity were both firmly part of the establishment, and any attempt to usher in a new political paradigm needed the consent of both parties. What required more work was neutralising the consciences of those who purported to play by some kind of gentleman's rule book. Hayes and Freedman wanted to mould a political landscape that embraced the incentives that came with the recent breakthroughs in areas like medicine and technology—namely power and money—while divorcing themselves from any discussions surrounding ethics or probity. It's always difficult to spot when the sands begin to shift within a nation's political culture. For most countries the political mood takes a decisive turn following some kind of calamity—either a civil war or an assassination. The deadliest political turns, however, seemed to be the ones that seemed to creep up on a nation without warning, with nobody being able to spot the signs apart from a few diehard mavericks that seemed to be shunned by society for being too smart for their own good. Hayes and Freedman knew the importance of not allowing the pendulum to swing out of rhythm. For Hayes and Freedman, pinning down the moment of transformation was no easier for them than it was for anyone else. They might have been increasingly successful in winning future backers, but they were two people not willing to dilute any future settlement. What they were skilled at was successfully concluding that a mood change had taken place and knowing how to take full advantage. Shortly after Giles Gibbs' election as party leader, there came a time where the sheer weight of regressive Government policies would win their battle with public resistance. Over the years the public had somehow managed to sacrifice its stake in itself. Changes in the law seemed to be debated in some kind of virtual pit. Everyone could hear what was being debated in their name. Everyone could see what was being debated in their name. But nobody could add their voice. But in due course, everyone was able to feel the full effects of what was being discussed in their name. The election of Giles Gibbs was a pivotal moment in the plans of Hayes, Freedman and their allies. Here was a man that could act as an antidote to the public's misgivings. Gibbs' public persona was warm, appealing and more human than any of the other contenders running for the position. While Gibbs swept the public off its feet, Hayes and Freedman were working overtime behind the scenes with their collaborators in order to get various policy deals in place. Nobody questioned the increasingly close relationship between leading figures on the two frontbenches—because in truth nobody could detect them. Any attempts to conflate them were either half-hearted or dismissed as wild exaggerations. It was almost impossible to prove as the network only extended to a few people. Alliance Party figureheads hadn't lost all sense of perspective and only collaborated on what were judged to be low profile pieces of legislation. But what were low profile to Alliance were essential bits of ingredients for the likes of Hayes—changes to medical research practices, advertising regulations and amendments to social care procedures. Hayes and Freedman weren't stupid enough to touch more populist causes like taxes. And as for the ones they did touch—immigration or welfare for instance—it didn't really matter. The climate of opinion was already changing in their favour.

As time went on, general incompetence and misdemeanours began to erode what remained of Alliance's reputation. It was the passing of changes to the Freedom of Information Act that should have caused more people to detect the all-too-comfortable relationship between senior members of the parties. The Act had originally been introduced by the previous Unity administration as one of its symbolic attempts to maintain the illusion of transparency in the political system. Freedom of information was always a useful stick to beat any government with, but up to that point no administration had bothered to implement any legislation upon entering office. In truth, it was thrown into the mix by way of a gamble to keep Unity in power for as long as possible. Fast forward to the twilight of the Alliance Party's days in office, and Hayes, Freedman and their allies were working with their backbenchers to make sure that the restrictions being placed on the Act that they themselves had introduced would make it through the House. It was a poor political gamble on the part of the Alliance Party. They had believed that as it was a piece of legislation that had the 'genuine' backing of both parties, blame would be diluted. It was a particularly rookie error for a party that had now been in power for several years. Incumbent administrations always took the fall for a piece of legislation that had the backing of both sides of the house but not the backing of any substantive portion of the public. The very same outcome occurred when there was cross party agreement on the establishment of a new independent authority to set pay and expenses for Parliamentarians following a series of scandals. When the authority published a report recommending that the starting pay be raised substantially in exchange for the reigning in of expenses, there was an understandable outcry, but it was Alliance that took the battering in the polls.

Chapter Eight

Bob O'Hara's rise to being the darling tabloid journalist of the establishment was full of incident and controversy. Some people thought it all started for O'Hara when he left *The British Tribune* for *The National*. O'Hara had apparently finally broken free from the moralising chains of Barnes and the others and could now do his 'duty' with no inhibitions. Those inhibitions, however, weren't released after his departure from *The Tribune*. The ingredients that helped form O'Hara's often barbaric state of mind were supplied to him much earlier in his life.

Breyerton School, located in the suburbs of West London, had a long established reputation for being the starting point for a number of high-profile journalists. It was popular for being one of a handful of institutions that could challenge the academic pedigree of Cambridge and Oxford Universities. Surprisingly, those journalists associated with it didn't fit a particular political or social tradition. In fact, Henrietta Barnes had spent her final two years of school there on a scholarship and had the displeasure of being in attendance at the same time as O'Hara. From time to time, Barnes would write about her encounters with O'Hara, knowing full well it would whip him up into a frenzy. One of her earliest revelations concerning O'Hara was always regarded as one of the most infamous. Barnes alleged that on one occasion, O'Hara hit on her, but that she rejected his advances. When the incident was revealed, it was done in a tongue-in-cheek, nostalgic tone. Barnes was merely writing about the changing experiences of second-generation immigrants, and it was two lines in a three-page extended essay. O'Hara, however, was apoplectic. Going out of his way to deny the story, he used his column in the *Tribune* to tear into Barnes. It was quite the spectacle, a columnist calling into question the integrity of one of his own colleagues. *The Tribune's* editor, Hayley Wainwright, naturally thought the spice of the situation would sell extra copies, and that it did. As for the story itself, as it was a question of one word against the other, it really came down to whom out of Barnes and O'Hara had the most credibility, and on that front, there was only one winner. That one incident probably did the most in accelerating O'Hara's move to *The National*.

One slap down from the opposite sex doesn't always break the man. O'Hara's primary source of ignition came in his later years at Breyerton when, upon joining the Breyerton Speakers Convention, he fell into the company of one James Jacob. Jacob was probably closer to the archetype Breyerton student that the headmasters had in mind. His mother was one of a handful of female MPs in the House of Commons and his father, Henry, was a well-known business entrepreneur. O'Hara had no such luxurious family tapestry to invoke and, to his credit, had also attended Breyerton on a scholarship, just like Henrietta Barnes. To his discredit though, he was in awe of some of his wealthier peers. An important lesson of life that most parents try to endow their children with, is being grateful for what one has while having the aspiration for wanting something more, should the opportunity show itself. Such life lessons were lost on O'Hara, however, and James Jacob instantly realised that here was someone he could bounce around.

The Breyerton Speakers Convention was the chief venue through which students earned their reputations and budding future journalists were born. The set-up itself was straight-forward. The Head of the Convention would publish a motion six weeks in advance, and then either individuals or groups of no more than three would submit themselves to take part in the debate, and for organisational purposes, they would need to declare at least two weeks in advance whether they would be arguing for or against the motion. Jacob and O'Hara made their names at the exact same Convention, but for very different reasons. Jacob was arguing for the motion, "Fee-levying schools, contrary to established belief, play a positive role in the furthering of educational attainment for ALL students." O'Hara was opposing the motion—or that was how it was supposed to be. Just after the half-way point of the debate, O'Hara did a spectacular volte-face, declaring to the audience that he was engrossed by Jacob's arguments and had been convinced to change his stance on the position. The incident generated a lot of positive commentary for Jacob. Beneath Jacob's apparent success story, however, was actually a quid-pro-quo agreed between O'Hara and Jacob. Jacob promised O'Hara he could get him into an internship at his father's firm, and in exchange, O'Hara would perform a princely public climb down in their debate. To some, it may have been an easy decision, but it was difficult to underestimate Jacob's longing for limelight.

From then on, a friendship based on the fulfilling of promises and very little else began to transpire. O'Hara would be James Jacob's working-class poster boy chum and Jacob would be O'Hara's source of patronage. It didn't take long for O'Hara to dispense with the little moral conscious he had invested within himself. The pinnacle of their relationship came in their final year together at Breyerton. Jacob had become enamoured with the prospect of his father's inheritance. Henry Jacob had successfully steered a number of flagging firms back to economic health. That, combined with his philanthropic activities meant that he had been told of the Queen's intention to grant him a knighthood as part of her Birthday Honours List. Jacob had absolutely no respect for his father, in spite of the lush upbringing he had afforded him. From the second he discovered the nature of his inheritance, he wanted it at whatever cost. The only real solution for James Jacob was the elimination of his father, but being the wretched human being he was, he delegated the task to O'Hara. He didn't actually order O'Hara to take him out per se—but rather he asked him to make sure he was at least permanently neutralised. O'Hara did as instructed, with a twenty-thousand pound thank you cheque to help persuade him. It was arranged for Henry Jacob to be struck down by car one night upon leaving his office. O'Hara did some serious damage. Henry Jacob was left paralysed from the waist down. The outcome did nothing to further James Jacob's position. A man with a conscience may well have suffocated from conducting such depraved activities, but James Jacob was ice cold before the accident, and he continued to be so afterward. Bob O'Hara increasingly became the personal tool of James Jacob, a situation James Jacob pushed for more and more, sensing that O'Hara had the same immoral backbone as he did.

It was generally quite unusual for Breyerton Leavers to be offered an immediate opportunity at one of the national papers. Most of the more prestigious papers preferred their new recruits to come with exposure to the policy making environment or at least some exposure to regional or local newspapers. James Jacob took up a position with one of his father's firms, Morgan & York. O'Hara struggled to pin down anything as remotely glamorous as Morgan & York. It took an intervention from Jacob to settle O'Hara into somewhere that that would be of benefit to both of them. During a social gathering, James' father had introduced him to a colleague whom he met during his business travels—Alexander Hayes. According to Henry, Alexander Hayes was on the fast-track route to becoming a future British statesman. Having studied Philosophy and Economics at Cambridge, Hayes had quickly entered the world of political PR. He had also carried on some of his intellectual pursuits by working for the Grove Chambers Institute. Henry Jacob would often recall how Hayes had to shrug off the toxic baggage left by his father's misdemeanours in order to be taken seriously in the policy world. Back then Grove Chambers was a rookie institution eagerly recruiting analysts and researchers. Through developing its links with the likes of James Jacob and others of a similar ilk, it was soon among the more established policy institutes from the establishment. O'Hara didn't even have to apply for his role. James Jacob took care of the paperwork for him, guaranteeing the continuation of their slimy relationship.

Henry Jacob's accident hastened three things. His knighthood was rubberstamped during a stylish ceremony at the Palace. The accident also helped win Sir Henry favour with a number of high-profile disability charities, organisations that were always looking for public faces to help promote their causes. By extension, this new found chemistry between Sir Henry and the disability sector helped to further antagonise James' feelings towards his father. His attempts to eliminate him had only succeeded in presenting Sir Henry in a more favourable light to the wider world. Sir Henry was totally oblivious to his son's malicious intent and continued to support him financially through his business adventures. From James' perspective, if supporting the causes of disabled people was his father's new goal in life, then it was his goal to thwart any positive developments that may arise. Neither he nor O'Hara had any qualms about acting as a force for de-stabilisation. At their time together at Breyerton, they came dangerously close to being expelled after stealing a student's cane as part of a dare. They would have been expelled had it not been for Jacob bunging one of his senior tutors a large stash of money in order to make the disciplinary action go away. Jacob wasn't so dumb as to ask colleagues at Grove

Chambers to give their work an explicitly anti-disability bent. He always couched his words in policy or economic jargon—constantly warning about threats to employment, economic sustainability and the like.

James Jacob wasn't the primary driver of the agenda, however. That came from Alexander Hayes. He would never admit it, but Alexander Hayes came with a massive chip on his shoulder in the form of the work undertaken by his father at the National Improvement and Development Fund. Hayes always maintained that his father took the majority of the blame for the things that went on there, when in fact the culprits were numerous. Hayes' rage though was a front to conceal his true motives. Hayes was no scientist like his father, but he depicted himself as a heavy thinker. Heavily influenced by Darwinian and Eugenicist polemics of the late nineteenth and early twentieth century, he had convinced himself that large swathes of this thinking could be applied to numerous modern social problems in a benign and productive manner. Inevitably, things quickly got out of hand, and Hayes merely succeeded in bringing together a band of shady and powerful individuals committed to re-drawing the norms of a modern society. Think-tanks, such as Grove Chambers and the Thomas Foundation, had taken their cue from Hayes and James Jacob with great thirst, and gradually, the likes of O'Hara had positioned themselves to filter the message further through their journalistic connections.

After leaving Grove Chambers, O'Hara achieved his first newspaper gig working for a local outlet in Gloucestershire. He rightly achieved acclaim for his stories that exposed the homelessness scandal that had engulfed the local authority. It was by that time a rare foray into what O'Hara would describe in later years as 'the lesser issues'. His efforts were enough, however, to attract the attention of LUK Talk, one of the country's foremost talk radio stations. The editors at the station wanted O'Hara to take on the persona of the so-called 'Shock Jock'. No 'taking on' was necessary in O'Hara's case. He already came with the requisite mentality. Two revealing encounters during his phone-in sessions helped to cement his status as a thuggish, non-compromising commentator. The first was during a debate about sexual violence. A caller had rightly taken issue with his stance of making excuses for some men in some cases of rape, going so far as to assign some responsibility to the victim. He kept making distinctions between different 'types' of rape. On one level it wasn't surprising that O'Hara had such a warped and misogynistic attitude. His myopic view of society extended to his assessment of women being second class citizens. The second incident involved Veronica phoning in via a pseudonym to take issue with his assertions that some disabled people ought to be paid less than those doing the same job in order to 'prove themselves' to their employers that they were reliable workers. Veronica ran rings around O'Hara to the extent that he got so flustered he swore live on air. The exchange went viral on all the social media sites, and O'Hara was forced to make a grovelling apology.

Nobody was ever quite sure of how Bob O'Hara came to be given a column at *The British Tribune*. Those at *The National* thought it was a naïve attempt to tone down one of the establishment's most prized assets. Senior columnists at the *Tribune* were unimpressed for different reasons. They read it as a naked attempt to sell more copies, rather than being an opportunity to enhance the paper's reputation for high quality journalism; it would almost certainly do the opposite. The paper's editor, Hayley Wainwright, certainly saw an opportunity to pitch the newspaper to a different demographic. But her primary motivation was actually to counter some of the progressive voices that had begun to write columns for *The National* and similarly-minded publications. As far as Wainwright was concerned, the progressive voice had become diluted. Papers such as *The National* had done an outstanding job of drowning out the voices of the more socially aware at a time when their voices needed to be heard the most. Some journalists who said they would never work for a paper like *The National* soon found themselves changing their minds, justifying their position on the basis of promoting a more non-partisan approach to journalism. Their change of heart was also assisted by the higher salaries afforded to the paper's staff by its tax-dodging owners. Bob O'Hara had conflicted reasons for wanting to join the *Tribune*. O'Hara was a man who was heavily influenced by his own ego, and his ego told him he was an outstanding journalist that hadn't received the recognition he deserved. Before joining, O'Hara hated the *Tribune* with a passion, but he was also profoundly aware that in the world of print journalism, *The British Tribune* was—among most journalists at least—the newspaper of record for quality of journalism. A move to the paper would represent a confirmation of his ego and would probably accentuate it further.

Moving to *The British Tribune* brought about the inevitable reunion with Henrietta Barnes. Barnes and O'Hara's intra-paper warfare did lead to an increase in the Paper's circulation, as well as cementing each other's reputation. The acme of their internal sparring came a little over a year earlier, when a group of living wage campaigners scaled Parliament House in the middle of the night and occupied the roof for nearly 48-hours. It would have lasted longer, but the perpetrators were shot dead my marksman from a near-by rooftop. It was one of the main incidents that had caused the government's approval ratings to plummet, particularly when Barnes published an exclusive for the *Tribune* claiming that a feeble attempt was made behind the scenes to tarnish the names of the protesters in order to justify the extreme nature of the solution. The city had only just approved water cannon. The sight of armed police may well have been something the public was getting used to, but the Parliament House incident was an enthusiastic and spectacular misreading of public opinion at the time. But where Barnes was exposing the scheming of insiders, O'Hara was producing incessant and inflammatory articles about law and order and making sure people knew where their place in society was. He would often combine it with his favourite theme, the politics of envy. Everyone was envious of rich, powerful upper-class men, and people should just make their peace with what society had approved of. At times of utter convenience, O'Hara's bandwagoning antenna would assert itself in the most underhand ways. Simultaneously running ad-hoc fundraisers for some group or individual that had managed to garner publicity by by-passing the traditional press, while going bonkers the rest of the year. On one occasion, it ran a campaign to raise money for a group of families that were being evicted from their housing estate to make way for a new development. The rest of the year O'Hara would run articles moaning how single mothers and housing estates were an affront to the landscape. This particular campaign was even more crazy considering that the firm wanting to knock the estate down was part owned by the owner of *The National*, Reginald Parry, king of tax avoidance. That was another of O'Hara's favourite games—giving himself a haemorrhage over phony benefit claimants while not writing a single article on the grand levels of financial brinkmanship that had engulfed his more senior associates. O'Hara was selling pure nihilism dressed up as moral arrogance. The final straw for O'Hara was when Barnes published an article entitled "Meet the apologists of establishment brutality". O'Hara made Hayley Wainwright's job an easy one by simply resigning from the paper. Within days, he was writing for *The National*, his first few pieces dedicated to defaming the progressive low-lifers at the *Tribune*. O'Hara's depiction of the Taunton Bridge incident proved to be the one piece of journalism that encapsulated his credentials as a hot-headed Neanderthal of a columnist. His article came with the caption 'Animals', below a picture of some young offenders who were allegedly ringleaders in the rioting that took place—all the pictures were of boys from an ethnic minority background—even though the prison population was predominantly white. O'Hara skimmed over the various reports of guards organising fights between prisoners and people being tied to their beds. There was, however, an interview with the then Chief Executive of Longacre Green Waterside. There was extensive talk of discipline and tough love, but all done in an above board manner.

Chapter Nine

Terrance Winchester's office was more suave than that belonging to Guy Freedman on account of the paintings hung up on the walls. Winchester saw himself, and was seen by most of his colleagues, as an old Parliamentary grandee. Most MPs with his length of tenure had already acquired knighthoods or some other honorary title. Winchester was bound to get one that year as he was due to retire at the election. He had already accepted a non-executive directorship at the Old Market Art Gallery.

"Can I pour you a drink Samantha?"

"A bit early for the red stuff for me. Besides, I'm going to a charity function this evening so I'm sure I'll have a chance to indulge at some point. A cup of tea would be ideal though."

"Samuel, could you pour us both a cup of tea please? How do you like your tea, Sam?"

"Milk and two sugars please Samuel. Have you moved over to Terrance's office now Samuel? Alexander Hayes finally driven you to insanity? I don't blame you man!"

"Ha! No, nothing like that Sam. Terrance had reduced his hours in the office. Because Alexander obviously has a lot of people so Rein and I have had some time to pick up other things...so I asked Terrance and Alexander and they were both fine with it."

"Fair enough."

"So then tell me—what's on your mind?" Winchester was far more cordial than the likes of Hayes and Freedman, but he did come across slightly snooty, particularly when talking to his female Parliamentary colleagues. Samantha Barratt saw him as the best of a bad bunch, and so didn't take his poor interpersonal skills to heart.

"I just wanted to run something by you. This thing that happened the other day. The unauthorised demonstration. I've had some constituents ask about it and I just wanted to get the lowdown from you in terms of, well, really...what's it all about and from a

Parliamentary view—what have we done or are doing about it?" Barratt was trying her best to play the role of the loyal local MP that was dedicated to protecting the image of Parliament.

"Sorry, how do you mean Sam? In terms of investigations?"

"Yes, I suppose so. Has anything happened internally? I mean was the entire thing much ado about nothing?" Sounding dismissive, Barratt was hoping to neuter any red flags that may have been appearing in Winchester's head so that she could set him up for a fall.

"No need for a full investigation…nothing like that my dear. As you say just a bit of commotion… I think our chaps handled it perfectly fine."

"Excellent," Barratt smiled. "I was going to ask the head of security if he could write me one of those 'all is well' letters for me to give to my constituents…you know how it is…"

"Sounds super!"

"And I was also going to ask some of the boys from security if they'd be happy to meet some of my constituents if I brought them to Parliament…you know…good PR and all that." Barratt was toying with him to see what kind of response she would get.

"Well I don't know about that Sam, it seems a bit overkill to me." Winchester's body language didn't change completely, but he became decidedly more stony upon hearing Barratt's suggestion.

"Oh…come now Terrance. There aren't any security implications are there? I mean they are dotted all over the place in full public view. I think the Outreach team would definitely be fine with it."

"It seems a bit much, don't you think? I mean are you going to get them to meet HR and Finance next?" That semi-doltish response told Barratt that Winchester was definitely ill at ease with the subject matter.

"Don't be daft!" chuckled Barratt. "It's good for people to see the core workings of the place. And I think the best thing with having so much security is that there won't be any harm in people coming in and seeing how things are done. I mean we don't need to show them anything sensitive. Actually I was hoping that my constituents could meet the head officer that was in charge during the demonstration…no ill feeling, nothing to hide, you know…"

"Sorry, that's out of the question."

"Why on earth for? As you've already said, nothing went on, it was all done in accordance within guidelines I assume…"

"Yes, of course…" That 'Yes, of course' was enough for Barratt to realise there was an altogether different game at play. Winchester had essentially gone from saying that the aftermath of the demonstration was a non-event, to saying that the incident was dealt with in accordance with the proper guidelines. Non-events don't require guidelines. Pressingly, if it was a non-event, the meet and greet with the staff involved would be no more than a photo-op.

"So you do agree it's a good idea."

"Well no I don't think constituents have any business interfering with internal Parliamentary affairs."

"Interfering with Parliamentary affairs?"

"Golly!"—Barratt was intentionally appropriating the dull, cliché upper class mannerisms he used when meeting foreign dignitaries in order to arouse him further. "What affair? Nothing happened, and all of our security instructions and policies are in black and white everywhere you turn."

"OK fine Sam. Do what you think is best." Winchester's sigh of resignation was music to Barratt's ears.

"Grand. Well thanks for clearing that up." Barratt offered him a smile as she left, but Winchester wasn't willing to barter with no more than a pokerfaced nod.

After her departure, Winchester took a key out from the inside pocket of his blazer and unlocked the top drawer beside him. He rummaged through the draw until he came across a bound document, inside a green sleeve. It was marked 'Private and Confidential'.

"Samuel!—in here please." Samuel darted into the room.

"Everything OK?"

"I was due to attend the Disability Institute bash this evening. But there's been a change of plan. I won't be able to attend. One of the others will have to go in my place."

"OK then. Do I need to go accompany anyone?"

"No, no it's fine… I'm sure whoever goes will be all right. Anyway I need you to do something for me…"

"Go on…"

"This is a report. I need you to drop it off at Samantha Barratt's office."

"Sure, I'll go right now…"

"No Samuel, not now—this evening. She'll be at the DI thing so you'll be able to pop in and drop it off... Here's a key to her office..." Winchester put his hand into the drawer and shuffled around without looking and then produced a large bunch of keys. "Let's see, which one is for Barratt's office? Ah, here we go!"

"Oh...you mean you want me to *drop it off*. What is it anyway?"

"It's a market sensitive report about Mortimer Brothers. Legally speaking it shouldn't be in the public domain. Well to be frank it shouldn't be in any vicinity other than on the computers of the Financial Regulation Association."

"So then why do you have...never mind."

"You'll need to go quite late, but not too late, say a peep after ten. No pissing around. You'll be expected."

"*I'll be expected?*"

"Yes, Ryan from Security will meet you at the door. He's the main CCTV chap for the evening. He's one of ours if you know what I mean."

"Relieved to hear it!"

"At her desk, you'll see a lamp on one side, put it in the bottom drawer on the OPPOSTE side to the lamp. Got that?"

"Got it. Are you sure about this Terrance?" Bertrand didn't seem hesitant, but he was surprised.

"Well, we knew we had to take her out at some point. So this is just the beginning."

"Perhaps we can ask Sir Henry Jacob to have a word with her? Slow her down maybe?"

"No. Sir Henry has got other things to take care of. Anyway I was speaking to him today and he said that girl he's working with has made contact with Barratt—she and her friends. Let's try and avoid getting him too involved. They all think he's a blithering idiot. Let's keep it that way for now."

***

The Disability Institute / Future Leaders Annual Gala was an event held by the Disability Institute in association with Future Leaders, a network of entrepreneurs looking to promote employment best practice in a business friendly environment. In recent years, the event had reduced in scale due to less sponsorship coming in. It was still popular among media hacks and politicians as it provided an opportunity to mingle. A number of celebrities would also be paid exorbitant sums of money in order to present awards. Amber, Marcus, Tom and Isabelle saw such events as one of the special perks of working in an MP's office. Such events gave them the chance to network, as well as blow off some steam. Amber was seated at Guy Freedman's table, four rows from the front. Being located to one side of the enormous hall where the event was taking place gave Amber the chance to screen the crowd without looking too obvious. She was trying to spot Henrietta Barnes, but she wasn't sure which table she was sitting at—either the *British Tribune* table or the *Jemima Centre* table. Both were regular sponsors of the Gala, with the *Tribune* understandably forking out a larger amount than the *Jemima Centre*. Amber eventually spotted Barnes sitting at the *Jemima Centre* table. The actual awards ceremony was running to schedule, and finally, the award that warranted Amber and the team's presence came up. It was actually one of the awards reserved for a politician—best political spokesman for disabled people. In essence, it was a competition between the Shadow Employment and Welfare Secretaries, along with a couple of well-meaning Peers. Guy Freedman was on the shortlist—despite having moved portfolios, but on this occasion the award was *scheduled* to go to Lady Carlyle, one of Victoria Hanley's former associates who had done an admiral job of keeping her legacy intact by supporting and founding a number of schemes and charitable foundations. So when the winner was announced as Guy Freedman, Amber and the team had to instantaneously transform the looks on their faces from one of shock to one of unbridled joy. Amber was the only one who was struggling to conceal her frustration. Freedman's winning speech wanted to make her trash the table, run on to the stage and punch him.

"Well ladies and gentleman, I won't give all the tosh about how unexpected this is as I'm not a man of clichés... And in fact this isn't the place for a party political piece. What I do want to do is extend my gratitude to Sir Henry Jacob for giving me a platform not just in Political Engagement but... allowing me an opportunity to engage with a wider disability orientated field. Sometimes it can be frustrating when politicians aren't taken seriously when discussing some of the more sensitive matters in life. But what I think I've shown is that politicians are indeed capable of speaking in the common interest and not just in the interests of a few, as we're regularly accused of. But anyway I shan't bleat on any longer, I wish you all the best in the various contributions you're making to the cause of disable people and I hope to meet some of you soon."

It was difficult to determine the intended tone of Freedman's comments. At any rate, it was a woeful attempt to sound either grateful or thankful. For someone as slick as Freedman it just came across as robotic and emotionless. Clearly the last minute switch to give him the award wasn't properly thought through on his part. He was used to having his army of communications advisors prepare him for even the smallest media engagement. It was clear that the change in recipient was a hastily arranged affair, and it wasn't obvious who exactly knew. Those on the awards shortlist were usually informed of the winners beforehand in order to make the event run as smoothly as possible. There was a slight delay in the audience's applause so it was clear that the last minute change hadn't filtered through to anyone on the floor. Amber didn't want to end up smashing her glass on the table. She looked around to see where Henrietta Barnes was sitting and began to discreetly move to her table. There were a couple of empty seats so Amber was sure nobody would mind. Henrietta Barnes saw her as she approached and smiled. Amber mouthed the words "May I sit there?" pointing to a seat; Barnes nodded. The awards' half-time interval soon arrived, and the audience were treated to some quick fire stand-up comedy. The interval allowed Amber to start talking to Henrietta Barnes in a more decisive manner.

"Are you enjoying yourself Henrietta?"

"I was until your bastard manager was given that award. Don't know what's going on there."

"You and me both. None of us definitely knew anything about it."

"Really?"

"Yeah honestly. Day light robbery as far as I'm concerned. Don't tell Guy I said that though."

"Well that's interesting. Bloody outrageous to shaft Lady Carlyle like that. Someone has obviously had a word with somebody else."

"Who do you think?"

"I'm not sure but I'll find out. But anyway, how are things in the wonderful unpaid world of Parliamentary internships?"

"Oh you know—stressful. Things have been interesting since Giles stepped down, more work and so on. But nothing too dramatic unfortunately."

"I suppose you need to start thinking about something more permanent sooner or later."

"I suppose so. There was something I wanted to ask you about Henrietta…" Amber was anxious to cut straight to the chase.

"Oh? What's that then?" Barnes poured two glasses of orange juice and passed one to Amber. Amber pulled her chair closer to Barnes so that she wouldn't have to shout. The others on the table had gone for a stroll during the interval so it was an ideal moment to get some of Barnes' time.

"Well, it was something that happened the other week…that demonstration…did you hear about it?"

"Yes, I gather there was an altercation of some sort. I've heard so many things about it; it's hard to determine what's what…"

"Well, I was there so you can hear it straight from the horse's mouth now."

"Oh right, well go on then." Barnes seemed strangely distant, constantly turning her head, as if she was looking out for someone, but Amber didn't say anything about it.

"So there was a demonstration going on—call it unauthorised—call it whatever. And I knew one of the people taking part."

"So what happened?"

"Well, at the end, my mate was trying to unfurl a banner for some people to see. And then, for no reason, she was basically…beaten up by the security people." Barnes took on a tortured appearance.

"How bad was it?"

"Well she had to go hospital and stay overnight…concussion. And she's already unwell as it is. They dragged her OUT of her wheelchair. Animals."

"Damn it girl! Why didn't you come to me earlier?" Barnes was now with the programme.

"Well I was going to but it's been tricky. We've tried talking to Samantha Barratt about it. You might recall she asked some questions at PMQs." Amber was frustrated with Barnes implying that she had not done anything about the situation up to now.

"Has Samantha told you anything of interest?"

"No, not really. She just said she would raise it at PMQs and have a word with Terrance Winchester. But other than that, she just told us to locate a witness and if we can't, then to just let it die."

"And how is that going?" Barnes was now burning with interest.

"How do you think it's going? It's impossible. The thing is, where they were, we were visible to a section of Parliament House. But then, when I looked up at the window all the shutters were closed and nobody was there…"

"Keep your voice down…"

"Oh… Sorry, but yea, it was ridiculous. You know when you have a major security issue near the building as part of the drill they tell all staff to stay away from the windows. I'm certain that's what happened this time. But WHY? This wasn't a bomb threat or anything like that. They just use anything to shut people up."

"Yes, well, don't expect things to get any better… Listen, do as Samantha says, but I just want to double check exactly what you remember…"

"How do you mean…?"

"I mean, do you remember anything else? Anything! Think girl think!"

A flustered Amber rubbed her forehead.

"No, I don't know…" The comedian was in the middle of making a few wisecracks about the amount of jargon and acronyms used by ministers and civil servants. Then it hit Amber, like a water balloon thrown from the top floor.

"Actually wait… I completely forgot about it… I was in such a daze I…"

"Forgot what?" Other guests began to return to the table, so Amber pulled up as closely as she could to Henrietta Barnes' ear.

"When I tried to intervene I also got tackled to the ground. When I was on the floor, I'm certain one of the guards said something like, as he was walking away… L… LGW that's it," whispered Amber, doing remarkably well not to let others hear.

"Are you sure?"

"Yes, of course I'm sure! It would be an odd thing to remember, don't you think? A random set of letters?"

"It only just came to you now?"

"It came to me when the guy on stage was banging on about initials and acronyms. Why? Does it mean something to you?"

"Yes. It does. Listen, can you meet me in Samantha Barratt's office tomorrow please? In the morning sometime?"

"Erm, sure. Her parliamentary office isn't too far from Guy's. You'll have to bear with me though. Guy won't appreciate me just walking out randomly. I think he has a meeting at half ten away from the office. Would that be OK for you?"

"Yes, that's fine. I'll let Samantha know but in the meantime, not a word to anyone."

"Yes, of course." Amber was shivering. Her usually unreliable memory had finally come up trumps, and with Henrietta Barnes on board, things seemed to be moving in the right direction.

Chapter Ten

The Carrington Group, so-called because of the hotel its members would meet at, had arranged one of its unofficial get-togethers for its 'special' backers. Carrington was an association of medical laboratories, research labs and private pharmaceutical companies. The aim of the impromptu meetings was rarely to discuss the latest lab breakthroughs. They were actually carefully staged opportunities to secure backing for certain upcoming drugs. On the surface, there didn't seem to be anything particularly unholy in the scenario. Most firms were unable to seek public investment due to the stratospheric costs involved. Private capital was the only way some medicines would apparently see the light of day. Considering the sensitivity of what was being discussed, once past security, procedures for the event were relaxed. The event was spread across a number of rooms, decked out in fancy chairs, fancy food and fancy IT. Financial backers would roll from room to room, dropping in on presentations and popping questions to the manufactures. Discussions that seemed to have promise would then leave the prying eyes of the presentation rooms and would retire to private facilities that promised total anonymity. It was in one of these rooms where Hayes, Freedman and others were discussing the intricacies of a potential business deal. They weren't actually there to provide financial backing, but were instead being promised a slice of the action in the event a future Unity government was able to protect the interests of the firm and put in place a compliant regulatory framework.

"So gentleman, we've met a few times now so I hope we can clear up any lingering issues. I hope you don't mind us meeting under the auspices of Carrington, I'm sure you agree meeting here looks better for you than meeting in our private offices or somewhere like that."

"Yes, that's all fine. Guy and I just wanted us all to get together one final time before we sign things off if you know what I mean."

"Well Alex, there isn't much else to say that hasn't been said really. Each of you will get one off payment to begin with and then 0.5% for five years thereafter. Leaving you handsomely remunerated."

"I don't want you to think we're not fully invested in this, because we are. But I'm sure you're aware we can't just snap our fingers and expect the entire machinery of government to fall into line. I mean, we'll always encounter opposition, after all—this is a democracy!"

"We're not expecting you to change the world. You just need to keep the chains oiled sufficiently so we can get on with what we want to do."

"OK fine, well, Alex you're on the case on your side of things, right?"

"Yes. Clinical trials have always been a soft touch for government. I mean drugs need to be trialled, don't they? I've had a company set up…you know…we've…shall I say…won…a few low key trial contracts for less controversial drugs. We're using that as the backdrop to recruit for this. Sir Henry has been very useful in that department actually." Alexander Hayes looked at James Jacob, who was also in the room, but Jacob didn't even flinch.

"Just tell Alex and me again, how powerful is this drug again?"

"It has the mental stimulation of LSD and the sexual stimulation of Viagra without half the drawbacks."

"So there are still some drawbacks then? I can't give you a never ending supply of people."

"Come now Alex there are always drawbacks. That's why we need to crack on with the trials. Look, it's worth the risk. The regulations won't let us commence human trials because the side effects on our lab rats were too strong. We don't have time to adjust things for the rats, find a solution and then commence human trials. You know what this industry is like. Word gets out you're on to something big and that's it—everyone wants a piece of the action. Remember—we're paying you to take the risk. So are we all OK with that? You've been involved in this for ages now. We're this close."

"No, no that's all fine. I think we're agreed."

"What about everything else? Do you have sufficient control of things? We won't be seeing any dramas on TV that ruins everything, will we?"

"You may see dramas but nothing we can't handle."

"We'll just keep on top of things. You're definitely sure you can get people through our doors?"

"Absolutely. People will do anything when they are desperate and depressed, and we've made sure there's a long line of people that fall into those categories. Actually we're expecting one such wretched person at this meeting. For some crazy reason Sir Henry has arranged for..." The door then jolted open, and a security guard stood there, with Hayes' guest in close proximity. "Ah, hello there. Were you all right getting through security and all."

"Sir Henry said if I came here tonight you'd give me an advance on my payment."

"Ah yes, here you go." Hayes reached into his pocket and pulled out a bundle of notes, held together with an elastic band. He threw it, but it didn't reach its intended target, falling short by a few inches. The others in the room laughed at his incompetence. "So I take it you won't be joining us for some late night entertainment?" The others in the room continued to bellow. Hayes pointed at the security guard. "Can you kindly escort our friend off the premises?" And the two then left.

***

Two private taxis waited for Hayes and Freedman outside as they went their separate ways after the meeting. Hayes headed towards the fringe of the financial district. It was late at night—coming up to eleven. An associate was with him as, under the cover of darkness, he approached a house. He needed to ring the doorbell more than once. The lights were on but nobody initially approached to open the door.

"Mr Hayes! This is a bit late, isn't it?"

"Hello Mrs Thomas. How are you? I'm sorry for the lateness of my visit. Is it OK if I come in? I was coming back from a meeting and Samantha Barratt has been insisting I drop in on one of her more engaged constituents. My colleague here also reminded me of a letter you sent to Unity Party members about your daughter."

"Erm, yes sure, Clare is asleep."

"No, I thought as much, that's why I'm here late. I wanted to talk to you actually, without the pressure of Clare being around."

"OK well, you better come in then."

Hayes and his associate took up seats on the sofa while Clare's mother sat separately near the coffee table.

"So what did you want to talk about?" It was late and Mrs Thomas wasn't in the frame of mind to be making cups of tea or coffee.

"Well you wrote to Guy Freedman, Giles Gibbs and I, didn't you? Following the publication of the article you read—in Political Engagement I believe?"

"Yes, that's right."

"Well, we do try to help where we can. I know you're probably thinking I'm a frontbench MP and just looking for a good story. But to be fair to myself, I always mark out letters sent from people such as yourself; people who are dealing with the challenges of raising someone with special needs."

"That's really nice but where is all this going?" Mrs Thomas was increasingly tired and wanted Hayes to get straight to the point.

"Well, in the past few months I've been working with some colleagues in the medical profession. Being a politician you see I sometimes get to hear about new medical initiatives before others. You know—they try to reach out to the so-called 'Government of Tomorrow'. Anyway, there is a new experimental drug that's being developed—and to get to the jist of it—it may be of potential interest to Clare."

"Pardon?"

"I'm sorry Mrs Thomas this is all probably a bit random. A senior MP turning up at your door unannounced without any cameras or reporters. But don't forget even the Prime Minister Holds constituency surgeries. My colleague and I had this flashbulb moment and we thought let's get over there and show just one of our supporters that we're not all a bunch of money grabbing schemers. Some of us do actually care and want to help where we can. Do you remember Harry Christopher?"

"The boy that's gone AWOL or something?"

"No, not at all. After what happened to him I got in touch with his family to express my discontent with the way he'd been treated. I actually suggested to him what I've suggested to you. Without freaking you out—the reason why he's been so silent is because the medical firm behind the trials is as you'd expect engaged in extreme competition with rival drug firms and so privacy has been paramount. So, is this something you'd be interested in?"

"I'm not sure, I'd have to think about it."

"Well, take all the time you need. Here is the number of my private secretary. If you call him, you'll get straight through to me. Let me know whenever you're ready, and if you want to go ahead, I'll put you in touch with the relevant people. But just to stress one thing. I've taken you into my confidence as Samantha Barratt speaks so highly of you as a constituent. Regardless of whether you decide to take part, I'd appreciate it if you didn't speak a word of this to anyone."

Chapter Eleven

Guy Freedman was repeatedly walking back and forth from his office to the meeting room. Amber was observing him, wondering when the heck he'd leave. *Of all the days to break from his usual routine.* He eventually left at around twenty past ten. Wherever he was going it couldn't be too far from the office. Amber gave it five minutes after Freedman's departure before making her own getaway. Samantha Barratt's office was on the far side of Portcullis House, and as it was a sunny day, Amber didn't mind the short walk. Barratt's office wasn't on one of the main landings, so Amber had to take a couple of twists and turns to reach her destination. Walking towards the door, she quickly realised that someone else was already waiting there; it was Henrietta Barnes. Amber sped up and nudged her by way of a hello. Amber opened her mouth, but before she could get a word out, Barnes signalled her not to speak. Barratt pointed to the door and then her ear. She was alerting Amber to the raised voices coming from inside. Barratt was clearly having an argument with someone. Amber pressed her ear on the door to get an idea of who Barratt was talking to. *That voice sounds familiar…shit! It was Guy Freedman!* Amber pulled away and was about to hotfoot it out of there, but Barratt caught her by the arm.

"Where are you going?" Barnes was speaking so quietly Amber just about made out what she was saying.

"She's talking to Guy Freedman."

"I know, why are you going?"

"Why do you think?" spouted Amber is a whispered screech. "They could stop talking at any time. If Guy sees me anywhere around here, he'll wanna know what I'm doing and probably get rid of me."

"No, he won't. Look." Barnes pointed to the ladies lavatory that was located close to Samantha Barratt's office. "When I say, just run in there and I'll give you a shout when the coast is clear."

Amber nodded and they both continued to listen to what was being said on the other side of the door.

"Look Sam, all I'm saying is Winchester and all those chaps, they can be quite territorial. If I thought there was something in all of this, then naturally by all means I would say pursue it to your heart's content. But there isn't, is there? I mean, not really? Are you really going to believe what a bunch of impetuous kids are going to say over the people who protect you, day in day out?"

"Why are you so obsessed with me not following this up? It's good for our image. Surely even you can see that?"

"There are lots of ways of enhancing our image. We have entire teams of advisors telling us what's what. If we need one of these bullshit 'stay in touch with the public' things, they'll tell us when, but until then, no."

"Why?"

"I'll tell you why. How long has it been since we were last in power? In all that time, these people have developed their way of doing things. It's how this house functions. Convention, tradition, manly handshakes. If they say something needs looking into, then it does, and if they say something doesn't need looking into, then it doesn't. We have to work with these people when we get into power. And I don't want that Winchester or those guys from Security antagonised."

"Is that it?"

"Don't do anything." Freedman stood up. "I'm sorry, I can't stay much longer. I had to sneak this meeting in among other things as I'm sure you appreciate."

"No, I'm sorry, I insist you stay and tell me more."

"LOOK," grunted Freedman. "I'm not telling you again. These people don't need their competence questioned. I really MUST leave now."

Outside, Henrietta Barnes went to whack Amber's arm but Amber was already racing to the ladies. Freedman came through the doorway while adjusting his tie and instantly recognised Henrietta Barnes.

"Ah, Henrietta Barnes. How art thou?" Freedman wanted to insert condescension into his greeting and Barnes had every intention of returning it, but she maintained her composure. Freedman didn't care for her, and in her eyes, he was more repulsive than the filth that surfaces when drains overflow.

"I'm fine Guy. And how are things on the opposition benches? Gearing up for a victory parade I assume?"

"We're not taking anything for granted." Freedman didn't even look at her, instead fiddling with his mobile as he spoke. As he got to the end of the corridor, he put his phone to his ear and disappeared around the corner. Barnes waited a couple of minutes and then went to fetch Amber from the ladies lavatory. Amber and Henrietta Barnes shuffled into Samantha Barratt's office.

"Were you expecting him, Sam?" enquired Amber. "It definitely isn't in his list of appointments, or else I wouldn't have run the risk of coming as you can imagine. Oh my days, imagine what we would have done if I'd bumped into him?"

"Don't worry about that now," reassured Barnes. "He's gone and you're here."

"So why did my LGW remark spark your interest then?"

"Have you heard of Longacre Green Waterside?" asked Barratt somewhat snappishly, clearly still buzzing from her encounter with Guy Freedman.

"Erm, yes, well…I…of course! I know, I know! And so you think they are involved in all this then?"

"Well, if you're certain that's what you heard then absolutely." Henrietta Barnes' instinct for justice had been roused.

"Yes, well, I'm positive. So I take it they shouldn't have been there then?"

"That's the biggest understatement of the decade," exclaimed Barratt. "They shouldn't be anywhere near any government building, never mind apparently taking on security duties in Parliament. It sounds like cronyism at its worst and at its most dangerous. I've no idea how they've been getting away with it and what else they've been doing."

No more than a hundred metres away, Guy Freedman was immersed in a phone call.

"The stupid woman isn't going to budge. She's going to cause us a lot of trouble. Do you know what you're doing? I want no messing around, make it look good and make it look professional. Tell your people not to go straight for the desk, she may well-suspect something is up so let's not give her any handouts…"

Samantha Barratt, realising she hadn't shown courtesy to her guests, asked if they wanted tea or coffee, to which Amber and Barnes responded positively. The set-up of her room was far homier than Guy Freedman's, with an area for making hot drinks directly behind her main desk. Barratt made one cup and passed it to Barnes. She turned around and began to finish making the second cup. She was stirring the tea as she began to turn for a second time in order to pass the cup to Amber. Barratt's office door was then permanently disfigured as it almost cleaved in two as a result of the lusty blow from the other side. Barratt dropped the cup on the floor in pure shock, the thud of the door being blasted open, accompanied by men screaming, "Police! Police! Stay where you are!"

Amber and Henrietta Barnes shot up from their seats, with looks of bewilderment on their faces. Barratt had regained her composure. There were nine officers now inside the room, all of them plain clothed. Barratt wasn't sure who to aim her anger at, so standing where she was, shouted, "WHAT THE HECK IS GOING ON?"

One of the officers approached Barratt, casually, but with intent.

"You are the Right Honourable Samantha Barratt?"

"Yes, that's right, what's this all about?" Barratt was incandescent.

"We have a warrant here to search these premises."

"On what grounds?"

"My name is Detective Inspector Chris Lakeland. We have reason to believe you are in illegal possession of market sensitive data, contrary to section ten of the Financial Regulation Act."

"Do me a favour!" interrupted Barnes, with gusto. "Where have you got this nonsense from?" The officer was standing in between Barratt, and Barnes and Amber. With his back to the two of them he asked, "Excuse me, and are these individuals here for a reason?"

Barratt grasped the explosive nature of the situation instantly and so before Barnes could jump in, gave a quick response.

"They're just constituents here discussing constituency matters."

"Oh I see, don't you talk to your constituents in your constituency office?"

"I talk to my constituents wherever I like, thank you very much!"

Lakeland finally turned around to face Barnes and Amber. He paused a few seconds so that he could weigh up his options. The instructions from Freedman were clear—find the report and nab Barratt, anything further would need clearing, and he wasn't about to pull his mobile out to ask.

"I'm sorry ladies, I'm going to have to ask the two of you to leave. These offices are being searched as part of an on-going investigation." He gestured to one of the officers, now in the midst of turning Barratt's office into a tip. "Constable, can you escort these ladies off the building please."

Barnes looked at Barratt, looking for some kind of signal. Barratt just nodded at her without saying a word, as if to say she could handle it and would catch up with her and Amber when able to. Amber and Barnes left the room, accompanied by the officer. Barratt didn't ask any further questions; she knew something was rotten about the entire situation and wasn't prepared to aggravate things further. The officers carrying out the search had clearly been given license to show no respect for the office or any of Barratt's possessions. Pictures were being taken out of their frames and then being thrown on the floor once it was clear nothing of note was inside. Barratt and Lakeland just stared at each other, neither of them blinking or feigning movement. Lakeland finally flinched when having disembowelled most of the room, one of his officers turned to Barratt's desk. He started with the drawers directly beneath her lamp. He paused at each folder he took out, ostensibly to read the title, but really just to build up to the final act. The officer then picked up the entire pile he had just scanned, barged the lamp out of the way and slammed the entire batch onto the desk. The aggression was beginning to unnerve Barratt; she thought the frustration had come from the officer's inability to find anything. He then moved to the drawers on the other side of the desk. The top two had no files in them, just some personal belongings. Opening the final drawer, a handful of folders could be detected. The officer could see the words "Market Sensitive" on one of them and so on this occasion didn't bother emptying out the drawer. He pulled it out, did a quick flick through and waived it in the air, in Lakeland's direction. Lakeland stepped over and took possession of the report. He flicked through, stopping at specific pages for a few seconds.

"Can you tell me what this is and why you have it in your possession?"

"I don't know; I don't recognise it. What is it?" Barratt was strangely relieved that the officers had concluded their search so that she could begin to piece together precisely what was happening.

"This is a market sensitive report into Mortimer Brothers. The only place it should be is within the confines of the Financial Regulation Association."

"This is total claptrap! I've never laid eyes on that report."

"Out of respect for cordial relations between the police and parliamentarians, I won't be arresting you…as yet…even though given your unique knowledge of the Financial Regulation Act, you're certainly aware that being in possession of such material means we've got you banged to rights. I would, however, request that you accompany me to Old Market Police Station for further questioning." Barratt was keeping her wits about her.

"Yes, fine." Barratt walked over to where her coat and scarf were once hanging up and picked them off the ground. She put them on. "What about all this?" she asked, pointing to the state of the room the officers had manufactured.

"Your door will be sealed and an officer will be present so there's no need to worry." The deceitful scoundrel's attempt at sympathy was galling.

***

Old Market Police Station was of three strategic stations attached to the core centre of the City. It was only a stone's throw from the private offices, which meant the journey time in the unmarked police car was over within a few minutes. The station may have been located at the heart of a bustling metropolis, but it was a fortress in itself and so totally at odds with the offices and markets nearby. There had been a gradual trend to enhance the capability of some stations to help compensate for the overflowing prison population. The station had buildings dedicated to its primary purpose and then additional buildings that were detached from the main complex, designed to process high-profile and dangerous individuals, as well as incarcerate those that had spilt over from some prisons. Barratt instantly realised that she was being taken for questioning to the high-security section. She had become familiar with the station complex as a result of repeated visits as part of her support to investigate the increasing number of deaths in custody. Driving past one armed officer after another, through a maze of security barriers, illustrated that she physically she was in London, but geographically this could easily be any military black site in some distant country. All signs of civilian life were now extinct. The car eventually pulled over to one side. Lakeland stepped out of the car and walked around to Barratt's side. He opened the door, and Barratt hesitantly stepped out. Lakeland gestured to her to walk ahead, with himself following behind. Lakeland called for the colossal door that they had arrived at to be opened. He again gestured Barratt to enter first. There was nothing gentlemanly about this; he wanted to ram home to her that she was being treated as a criminal, even though she hadn't been charged as one. The walls were grey and despondent. They were a far cry from the walls of a typical police station. There were no posters promoting community cohesion or the dangers of gun crime. They approached the processing desk, and an attendant was waiting. But Lakeland waived his hand, as if to say, "We don't need to process her." He quickly turned to Barratt and asked, "That's OK with you, right? We're only having a chat for now, aren't we? No need for formalities?"

"Yes, that's fine." Barratt had lost the confidence in her voice and was now fully conforming to the sequence of events. They swung around two more corners before entering a corridor that had a number of rooms. Lakeland stopped at the second door and opened it. He again gestured to Barratt to enter first. She entered the room, and the lights automatically came on. Lakeland pointed to the seat he wanted her to sit in. She took her coat and scarf off and then sat down.

"Would you like some water? Or maybe tea, perhaps?"

"No, thank you. Let's just get on with this, shall we?" Finally being able to sit down had taken some of the uneasiness away from Barratt.

"Very well. So, tell me, what's caused you to delve into the world of corporate finance?"

"I haven't been delving into anything."

"So why have I found this document in your office?" Lakeland placed the report in front of her. She went to grab it but he pulled it back.

"I've never seen it before. I don't know what it is."

"The irony of the situation is that, even though it's been found in your possession and you almost certainly have read it, you're denying any knowledge of it makes this a tricky conversation. So, we can either get to the bottom of this like mature adults, or we can go down the more formal route."

"Listen, you silly man. I don't know how that got into my office. So if we're going to do this, we might as well go down the formal route and you charge me for something so that I can defend myself against this nonsense." A delicate game of poker was presenting itself. Barratt knew all too well that it was irrelevant whether she could clear herself of any wrongdoing. This was the sort of mud that her enemies could make stick, as well as the sort of mud that hung around in the public's imagination. Lakeland didn't have any orders as to following through with a full-blown show trial—not yet anyway. His immediate task was clear: rattle the woman sufficiently enough to make her realise she had problems of her own, thus diverting herself from other matters.

* * *

As Lakeland was carrying out his inquisition of Samantha Barratt, Guy Freedman was conducting a meeting of his own. Freedman, through his own wealth and through personal connections, had built up a portfolio of private accommodation across London. He had one or two well-known residencies, but there were at least fifteen to twenty that nobody knew about and so essentially acted as safe houses for Freedman and his guests. Each property was tied-up in a labyrinth of investment vehicles that made it almost impossible to link most of the homes back to Freedman—unless one of his inner circle decided to turn their backs on him. His position allowed him to avoid tens of thousands of pounds in taxes. He was now sitting on a couch at Number 6, New Hannover Street. Also present were Alexander Hayes, James and Sir Henry Jacob and a small assortment of some of their closest associates. Samuel Bertrand was on drinks duty. Everyone refused any hard stuff on account of it being an impromptu meeting and the need for all of them to go back to their various escapades afterwards. Water was the order of the day, and it was Samuel who poured the glasses. These men all aspired to be disciplined when it came to following routines.

"Come on Guy, tell us how badly your associates have screwed up." Hayes felt safe to take a stiff tone with Freedman knowing that this was as off the record as it gets. He also wanted to send as clear a signal as possible to the others without being pretentious, that this was no double act and it was he who was setting the agenda. Freedman gave Hayes a fierce look.

"They might be my associates but you were the one who insisted we keep Herron Tate in our pockets. So how exactly are they in our pockets? Look at the lengths we're going to, to sort this mess out. It was all going so smoothly. Nobody was any the wiser. And now we have to deal with this crap just to keep them happy."

"So which one of you two bastards are going to tell us what's going on here?" James Jacob's temper was delivered in short bursts of rage rather than drawn out bouts of anger.

"This thing with LGW and the demonstration the other day. That Barratt woman is getting too close for comfort, and I'm pretty certain the other woman Barnes has been sucked in as well now." Freedman's ancestors had managed to smuggle a number of artefacts into the country just before Britain began its global withdrawal following the end of the war. Freedman's personal favourite was a historic rug, now unfurled in his reception room. As he spoke, he was meticulous in walking around the rug and not on it.

"So what?" hissed James Jacob.

"Well for starters, LGW shouldn't have been there, as you well know."

"So what WERE they doing there then?"

"They may have had their contracts withdrawn but Herron Tate was desperate for them to carry on working there in some capacity. I agreed on the basis that us guys could use their people for our own benefit too. I wasn't counting on them starting a pitched battle with a bunch of wheelchair users. The instructions to all our people are clear—do your usual thing—don't get involved in things that don't concern you. I mean, by all means if you wanted to take out a few four-wheelers there are better ways of doing it—no offence Sir Henry."

"None taken."

"We can hush things up here and there. But if people found out LGW were working there we'd find it difficult to explain it away. And when it's a full on fist fight, people want answers. And to make things worse, that fool, Gregory or whatever his name is, was there."

"Ah, the boss' idiot offspring," confirmed Sir Henry.

"Yesterday evening, I had a quick chat with a couple of execs at LGW who made it crystal clear that Gregory's name cannot surface under any circumstances, or else they'll think twice about doing business with us."

"For goodness…LGW's ban will expire soon. When we win the election we can bring it forward even more. Why are we doing all this for? This is all a distraction. What will our real friends think if they see us tied up with this low level nonsense?" James Jacob was fairly exorcised by now.

"Exactly, you stupid fool. This stuff hasn't gone unnoticed by our friends. And they've made it clear they will make alternative plans if this isn't put to bed soon. I've told them not to worry and we've got it under control. But make no mistake. If it becomes a straight choice between Herron Tate and Pinnacle Lab, it's Pinnacle Lab all day long."

"What? They'd stop in their tracks over something as small as this?" James Jacob wasn't convinced.

"As far as they're concerned, they don't want ANY distractions. And frankly I agree. As far as I'm concerned, protecting LGW is just a means to an end. Surely you can see that? Considering the changes we're going to bring in and the amount of money we're bound to make, we can't have a sudden breakout of mass hysteria around disabled people this close to an election. It'll ruin everything."

"Oh come on. The public will go along with whatever." James Jacob was morphing into one of his flippant moods.

"You may well be right, but we can't risk anything. Just try and look at the bigger picture here."

"What about Barratt and Barnes?" asked Sir Henry.

"Barnes I'm not that fussed about. She's a ranting lunatic that nobody takes any real notice of. Always seeing conspiracies where there aren't any. As for Barratt, we just need to distract her for long enough. She clearly suspects something. And—to be frank—we've got the all clear from Terrance to sort her out as we see fit. He never liked that woman."

"Was stitching her up with that report wise? Surely that's playing into her hands." Sir Henry was the only person trying to air a note of caution. But Freedman seemed to have all the answers.

"We're almost in a position where any pursuing of this LGW protest story will lead to dead ends. We confiscated all phones. We obtained a lot of personal info from them so if any of the protesters say anything we can make their lives very messy. Gregory has said using his men in a potential public setting was an error on their part."

"Sorry Guy but just to be clear—how many LGW people are working around the Parliamentary Village? And has their remit changed since the last time we spoke?"

"No. It hasn't. And this is what pisses me off. There were only TWO LGW guys embedded with the security detail for the protest. We're not stupid. We've got about a hundred LGW satellites embedded across the Parliamentary Village and core departments. Nobody knows their designation apart from Alexander and I. Heck technically they're sub-contractors so if you follow the paper trail you wouldn't find anything untoward. You'd only ever know that certain people were LGW people if you KNEW them—or if one of them blurted it out by accident. This has all kicked off because that fool Gregory is embedded in Parliament for reasons I won't go into now—but you all know the fun and games he gets up to. He saw a chance to exercise his ego and that was that. If it was anybody else, well, frankly, we would have taken care of them. Permanently. And that would have been that. Can't accuse someone of something if they don't exist. But here we are."

"Can we not get Gregory out of there?" Sir Henry wanted a more coherent solution.

"No. He needs to be embedded in Parliament House. It's fine. He won't be making any more public appearances. I just need to convince our friends all is well."

"Yes, but what about Barratt?"

"What about Barratt? If it backfires, then we'll take care of it but until then we sit tight. Nobody can place us with Lakeland. That's one thing I'm sure of."

***

Back at Old Market Police Station Lakeland was dragging out the interrogation as much as he could while his colleagues debated the matter. Barratt was no longer in a timid mood and Lakeland wanted to cut her loose sooner rather than later. He had enough tricks up his sleeve to distract her a bit longer, however.

"So where were you last night?"

"At that Disability Institute thing."

"How long were you there for?"

"I stayed there for the whole event and then I left."

"And then you went back to your parliamentary office I assume?"

"No, don't be ridiculous. Why on earth would I go back there that late at night? I went straight home."

"Well, that's rather convenient, isn't it?"

"How so?"

"You see I had a quick word with the estates team and it turns out that the CCTV system for Portcullis House was down for about an hour due to what was described as emergency maintenance work."

"So what?"

"Well, let me spell it out to you. Here's you claiming you've never seen this report and you've no idea how it got in your bottom drawer. And there's you at some event. At the same time, the CCTVs are down for about an hour. And hey presto you've got your alibi. 'It wasn't me Your Honour! The bloke we can't find any trace of put it there'." Barratt was reaching the end of her tether and wanted Lakeland to make a decision one way or another.

"Well, it sounds like you've got all the answers. I suggest you put an end to this madness and charge me." Lakeland leaned back, smiling and then sat there motionless. He stood up and walked out of the room. He walked down to the far end of the corridor and walked into an empty room. He whipped his phone out and went to received calls.

"Hang on gents, this is Lakeland." Freedman was waiving his arm to tell the others to lower their voices. "Chris, how's it going?"

"I've got it as far as it can go before I have to charge her or let her go. We're about to start that 'going around in circles' nonsense otherwise and I don't have the patience for that."

"No, it's fine. Let her go."

"Are you sure Guy? She's obviously gonna be suspicious."

"Let her be suspicious. We just wanna drag her away from all the LGW stuff. Anyway we're not done with her. We'll get O'Hara to pump out some nonsense."

"OK—but don't go over the top."

"All right gentleman time to get back to our day jobs." All the men in the room laughed as their meeting was brought to a close.

Lakeland loitered for ten minutes before returning to where he'd left Barratt. Before he entered he went to the coffee machine and poured two cups.

"Here you are then," he exclaimed joyfully, as if he was bringing her a lucrative contract of employment. He placed it in front of her, but Barratt was now in an altogether different mode, not moving an inch. Lakeland wasn't fussed. He didn't say anything. He slowly drank his coffee; his slurps now the only noise that could be heard inside the room. After about fifteen minutes, he had finished the cup and cleared his throat to speak.

"Well, as you'd imagine I've discussed this with my superiors. We're not going to charge you, so you're free to go. But please can I ask that you remain contactable and not leave London for the next few days. We'll continue to look into this further and we'll be in touch again if need be." Barratt stood up without saying a word. Lakeland waited a few moments before getting out of his seat. Barratt had already gone towards the door. Lakeland came over and opened the door and again gestured to her to exit first. The path back to where they had entered the building was so far away Lakeland was having to constantly correct her direction along the way. The delay proved significant, however. At one point, Barratt could distinctly hear some sort of fracas—it sounded like someone was taking the beating of a lifetime—"When I tell you to stand there you bloody stand there!"—was the one sentence she could detect. Lakeland had maintained his swagger but when realising Barratt had heard the commotion he paced forward and shoved her in the back, "Come on! We don't have all day." They eventually reached the door they had initially entered. "Walk all the way down the railings and you'll eventually get to a cordon being staffed by a couple of officers. They'll escort you to the street level entrance." Upon reaching the realm of sanity, Barratt went and sat down at a bus stop, located just a few metres away from the station. It was difficult to imagine too many situations where someone would catch the bus in order to go to a police station. The bus stop was most likely there as part of attempts to increase routes to the shopping hotspots. Barratt was glad it was there. It was either the bus stop or falling flat on her face. She needed to gather her thoughts as quickly as she could. Sitting at the bus stop though, a somniferous mood seemed to overtake her...

Opening her eyes, Barratt found herself staring at Henrietta Barnes from inside a hospital ward cubical. Taking in her surroundings, she was able to sit up easily.

"What am I doing here Henrietta?" Barratt sounded angry rather than confused.

"Ah good, no lasting damage let's hope. Do you remember what happened?"

"I was at the bus stop near Old Market Police Station. I remember feeling a bit—unwell shall we say—and here I am!"

"You were found in a heap at the bus stop. You must have fainted or something. Hang on I'll get the doc…"

"No, wait; there will be time for that. Let me have a chat with you while I have the chance… Hang on… So how did you get here?"

"I was one of the 'in case of emergency' numbers on your mobile. The paramedic tried the others but nobody answered."

"Good. Under the circumstances I'm glad."

"What exactly happened at the station then?"

"It was nonsense. They spent hours accusing me of stealing some private financial info to do with Mortimer Bros. Never charged me. Just talked for ages. Based on what they're saying they could have charged me there and then. So why didn't they?"

"Let's hope nothing more comes of it." Barnes knew all too well, however, that Barratt wasn't about to let it go.

"No, no. This is it. This is insane. How the heck does something like that turn up in my desk? And they've made it impossible for me to prove otherwise. What's it all about?"

"You've been asking too many questions. You need to keep a low profile for the time being. Let things blow over. That fool Winchester probably has a hand in this. Whatever you do, make sure you stay on good terms with him. That guy has more informers than morals. This LGW stuff, that thing with the demonstration. Let's go off radar until we have more info."

The doctors gave Barratt a thorough examination and eventually concluded that her fainting had been caused by sudden stress. Barratt was kept overnight for observation and discharged the following morning.

Chapter Twelve

Amber was increasingly looking for excuses to spend more time in Parliament House. The nature of her role meant that she needed to attend there on a fairly regular basis, but that was always on official business. If she wanted the slimmest chance of finding a witness, she needed to build a far greater rapport with certain people—or else resort to outright walking around and asking people if they saw anything—not the most surreptitious way of going about things. On this particularly day endless delays on the underground meant Amber had to take an extortionate cab journey to Parliament House. Exiting the cab, she bent down to pay the driver. She handed him a twenty pound note.

"Here you go mate. Keep the change."

"Aww that's nice. It's twenty five quid."

Amber gave the driver the funniest look, before standing straight in order to get a five pound note from her back pocket. *That's tomorrow's lunch gone then.* The driver then gently waived his hand as if to say not to worry about it and sped off. Amber was grateful.

The parliamentary committee offices tended to be associated with the more intellectually astute employees of Parliament House. These were the people, who would spend ages working on documents, only for the relevant minister to invariably toss the outcome to one side in favour of something produced by the Thomas Foundation or some other organisation. Law and Order was still high on the political agenda, and so Amber had constructed herself the excuse of wanting to get greater exposure to the report writing side of things. She convinced herself this was actually punishment. The committees support staff were the nicest people in one sense, polite, approachable and honest. But the personality-deficit within some of them seemed to make time stand still. Outside the parliamentary chamber Amber had never seen so many

Cambridge educated individuals in such a small space. Although that was one of her own prejudices she had to get over. It wasn't their fault that the system was skewed in their favour, and they could all easily be doing something far more lucrative and immoral than writing parliamentary reports. Amber wasn't really allowed to contribute to any of the drafting. Her role was restricted to proofreading and providing admin support. This suited Amber down to the ground. It gave her plenty of opportunities to cultivate contacts and hopefully pinpoint someone who could help in her search for a witness. She was careful not to overtly desk hop from one team to the next asking random questions about whether people like looking out of the window. Amber narrowed her interest down to two individuals. Her de-facto supervisor while she was there, Alison Kane—by most accounts, an avid bird watcher and an intern whom she had no idea was working there until sometime after beginning her trips to the committee corridors—and Jermaine Baxter, a petit young man. Incredibly well-spoken but with an outrageous haircut that raised the eyebrows of security whenever he entered the building. Amber appreciated that about him. He didn't have the robotic persona of most of the others and was far more human than the majority of the people she spoke to there. Jermaine had the extra touch of common sense that the others lacked. Nobody had bothered to show Amber around when she began to attend Parliament House on a more regular basis. Jermaine took it upon himself to show Amber the various shortcuts that he used throughout the building as well as the extra exits that only staff were allowed to use. It wasn't until Jermaine showed her that Amber was fully aware of the canteen and the various kitchen spots. Discounted food was just the ticket for someone in Amber's position. She wouldn't have to go out every lunchtime and pick up an overly priced baguette that hurt her teeth every time she bit it. Jermaine and Amber were sitting in the canteen at lunchtime as the rain pummelled the streets outside.

"So how did you start here again? Was it through an MP's office or some other kind of internship?" Amber was trying her best not to speak with her mouth full.

"Oh no. It was actually through the Parliament House internship programme."

"Oh, I applied for that. But they make you do tests and stuff. I thought sod that—I'm not going through all that for an internship."

It was a strange mind-set considering Amber had always been handy with numbers and statistics.

"Ah well, this is paid—and it's for a year. But it's boring as crap though if I'm honest with you. You basically rotate around the various committees—it only gets interesting when it's one off stuff such as financial regulations or the one we had for the Public Advertising Bill. That was a laugh. Blackwood always cracks me up—for all the wrong reasons obviously. His shareholders must have too much money. They must have all got together one drunken night and said 'let's see what happens if we appoint this bozo'."

"Oh, were you in the committee room for that one? I was there too. I don't remember seeing you." A hint of excitement entered Amber's body.

"No, I wasn't in the committee room for that one. The setup is basically that they have a typist person. A techie comes in at the beginning to make sure everything is recording. The other people from our side are one or two policy experts. Sometimes I might join them or just stay in the office." Amber sensed this was the opening she was looking for. She hadn't had any sort of invitation from anyone she'd spoken to. Amber thought about whether she should just blurt out what she wanted to ask him or continue to gently scratch away at the surface. The sudden appearance of Samuel Bertrand, however, temporarily threw her off the scent and for some reason her instincts told her to raise her guard. Jermaine saw Amber look over his shoulder and adjusted himself ever so slightly to see what she was looking at. He turned back to face Amber, his face filled with displeasure.

"Oh not this guy…" Before Amber could ask what the problem was Bertrand had sat down beside them.

"Hi Amber, hey Jermaine. Been grounded by the rain, eh? Same here. So what are you two working on at the moment? Anything good?" Samuel Bertrand was never unafraid of interrupting the meetings of those he considered to be junior to him.

"No, not really, I'm just doing some shadowing and Jermaine is helping out the Justice Select Committee I think."

"Are you weighed down at the moment Jermaine? Do you think you can do some notes for me? The last set of notes you gave went down well with Alexander Hayes. Any chance of doing another job for me?"

"Erm, no, not at the moment mate. My next rotation starts in a bit and they've already sent me a few things I need to get started with."

"Fair enough. Well, give me a shout if you do end up having some spare time."

"Will do. Who exactly are you with Samuel? Alexander Hayes or Terrance Winchester?"

"On paper, just Hayes, in practice, both."

"How have you managed that?"

"Well Hayes is the boss, so you know how it is. They want Rein, some of the others and I, to basically be a mobile resource pool. It's good fun though. I've been doing quite a bit of stuff with Terrance as his office hours have changed."

"Do you have a favourite?" Baxter wasn't afraid to ask awkward questions, but always made sure he asked in a curious and polite way.

"How do you mean?" Bertrand sounded defensive.

"Of all of them who do you like working with the most?"

"No, no favourites. I'm obviously most familiar with Hayes but that's about it. OK I better be off—Terrance Winchester has been nice to his PA and has decided to eat with us commoners in the canteen." They all looked over to see Winchester talking to some colleagues; Bertrand went over and joined them.

"Did you see his face when you asked him that? Ha! Why don't you like him?"

"Thinks he runs the place that's why. Always asking people on the internship programme to do this or that for him—as if it's his personal programme—and then he takes all the credit for the work. He's also a bit of a control freak as well."

"How do you mean?"

"Just every now and then, he'll issue some random instruction asking us all not to do something, and he'll justify it by saying Hayes or someone has requested it. They're opposition MPs. Sometimes it's as if they have more say around here than the actual ministers—not surprising you might say considering the state of the front bench but still."

"What sort of things does he ask you to do?"

"Just random stuff—not answering the phone at certain times—don't ask!—Levels of noise in the office—they ain't even in the same building as us! How the heck would they know how much noise we're making? And in any case these are the committee rooms so we can't exactly have a rave can we. Oh, staying away from windows—that was a good one."

"Pardon?"

"Yea—EVERY SINGLE TIME there is any kind of demo or event in the area he'll send an email around telling people to stay away from the windows. And they're getting more regimented about it too. I remember during the Public Advertising Bill they literally had security officers up here making sure nobody looked out the window. It was a demo by disability campaigners. What did they think was gonna happen?" Amber felt the wind taken out of her, sensing that the lead she was looking for was about to be snatched away.

"So you didn't see anything then?"

"No, not from the window anyway."

"But some other way?" Amber's heart rate began to speed up again.

"Oh yea—you know Alison Kane is a nutcase birdwatcher. Well she set up a camera on the ledge outside one of the windows. No idea how she managed that. She must know more people in security than Samuel Bertrand! But anyway one evening I was pestering her about it and convinced her to take a look."

"Really? Oh my days!"

"Why? What's the big deal?"

"What's the big deal? What exactly did the thing record?"

"Oh, nothing from that one."

"You mean she has more than one camera?" Amber was starting to get irritated.

"On the floor above the committee rooms."

"Did you see the fight?" Amber was tired of taking the cautious approach and was now going to ask what she wanted to know. But she didn't initially lower her voice, causing Bertrand and one or two others to look over at her and Jermaine.

"Shoosh woman!"

"Sorry! Can we go to one of those private pods over there?" Jermaine agreed and the two picked up what remained of their lunches and went to one of the private pods in the canteen. Samuel Bertrand followed them with his eyes without moving his body. Amber sat down and wasted no time in getting straight to the point.

"Look. At that demo, a mate of mine basically got assaulted and since then things have been crazy. In the aftermath, they took everyone's phone to make sure nobody had recorded anything. And it's been impossible to find anyone who saw anything. It happened in broad daylight but it was in that enclosed part of the estate where tourists don't bother going to. And none of the press are bothering with it because apparently Parliament House only authorises official photography—whatever that means!"

"Fortunately for you, the camera on the floor above the committee rooms was just about high enough to capture what happened."

"You mean you've seen it?"

"Of course!"

"Flippin' 'eck man!"

"That's not the sort of thing I'd like to make public. A man can make a lot of enemies disclosing that sort of information."

"Can you actually see what happens?"

"Well, a few things happened but I assume you're talking about that girl being dragged out of her wheelchair?"

"YES!" Amber wanted to bang the table in celebration but managed to restrain herself.

"Keep your voice down!"

"Sorry. Do you still have it?"

"Yea—but Samuel doesn't know."

"Why should he know?"

"I think he suspects. I was watching it on my phone and he was sneaking around. He asked me what it was and I straight out said 'none of your business'—but I'm pretty sure he thinks something is up. The other day I was coming back from lunch and I saw him hovering around my desk. I'm telling you there is something about him. There's no way he's just an intern."

"How often is he here exactly?"

"Too often!"

"All I need is a clip of the main bloke, that's it! Nothing else! Please can I see it?" The desperation in Amber's voice was chronic.

"If that's all you want, you don't need to see it. I can tell you who he is right now. He's the only one I recognised. His name is Gregory Hector."

"How do you know that?"

"Because he used to work around Parliament House. Up until that demo anyway. Since then I don't think I've seen him. They must have moved him on a bit quickly. I think his father is well-known in the upper echelons but I can't remember exactly what he's in to."

"You legend. At least I have a name now. Please please please don't destroy that recording. Let Samuel sniff around as much as he wants. He doesn't have anything on you, does he?"

"No, well not yet anyway. I don't trust that guy. He seems to know so many people it's ridiculous."

"I've been keeping in touch with Samantha Barratt and Henrietta Barnes since all this kicked off. They should be able to do something now."

"I think you should stay away from Barratt. Not after she was picked up by the police. She's lost a lot of credibility."

"But she hasn't done anything—hang on—how do you know she was arrested? You got a camera outside her window too?"

"No. I heard Terrance Winchester talking to Samuel about it yesterday evening in one of the committee rooms. I was sorting out some of the cables at the back. I don't think they knew I was there to be honest until I walked passed them."

"I was under the impression it was all being kept hush hush. I haven't seen it mentioned anywhere—though if Winchester knows it's bound to come out."

"Well as an MP he's one of the most senior on all things security so I assume someone must have told him. It may even have been Samantha Barratt herself. So you already knew she'd been arrested? So how do you know?"

"I was in her office when it happened. Keep that to yourself though. I better run. Thanks Jermaine. You're a star. I'll catch up with you later."

Jermaine continued to sit at the pod for a further few minutes, trying to finish his lunch within the allotted forty-five minutes. He then threw his leftovers in the bin and began to walk towards the exit. He felt his arm being yanked behind him, almost causing him to lose balance. It was Samuel Bertrand. Bertrand gestured to him to escort him back to one of the pods. He didn't waste any time once they got there.

"Jermaine, what were you and Amber talking about just now?" Bertrand was stone faced.

"Nothing."

"It didn't seem like nothing. She seemed to be getting very excited for a second there."

"We were just talking about random stuff. No offence but what we talk about in private doesn't have anything to do with you, does it? What are you so bothered for?"

"It's for your own good. That girl is trouble. She's caused Guy Freedman all sorts of problems recently." Bertrand's impression of a wise uncle wasn't about to dupe Baxter.

"Well I wouldn't know about that."

"No, well I'm telling you now. If she's told you something she shouldn't have, it's best you tell me now so that I can help you. Or else later it might come back to bite you."

"No. As I said, it was nothing."

"Fine, just be careful."

Bertrand hurried away to one of the private telephone pods on the ground floor. But instead of using the phone already there he took his mobile out and dialled.

"Mr Winchester are you still in the building or have you left…? I think we may have an issue with one of the guys—one of the interns. We better give him the shivers… No I don't have hard proof but I'm certain. He's been acting funny and talking to the wrong people. Maybe we can search his area or something…? No, he's a nobody. He doesn't have any contacts so I don't see anyone making a fuss. He'll keep his mouth shut to avoid any public embarrassment… No, nothing is getting out of hand, trust me on this one."

Chapter Thirteen

Veronica and Amber sat on the sofa in Clare's house. They had both received news that Clare's condition had deteriorated once again and had come over to see how she was doing. Clare's mother jogged down the stairs and entered the room.

"Hey ladies, you can go up now. I just needed to sort a couple of things out. The stair lift has been a bit dodgy today so be careful as you walk up. There are bits sticking out."

"How is she?" asked Amber.

"She's seen better days. To be honest I think a lot of it is down to stress rather than her actual condition getting worse. She's a bit weak, but I think seeing the two of you will cheer her up no end."

"We're going to order a pizza from her favourite place so please don't cook anything Mrs T."

"Are you sure? Will you be ok?"

"We'll be fine," nodded Amber. "I've fed her before, the last time she had a bad spell. I know the rules and stuff, no worries." Amber felt compelled to give Clare's mum a quick hug, before she and Veronica went upstairs.

"All right babe!" blurted Amber as she and Veronica entered the room. The sight of Clare laying flat rather than sitting up, with several bottles of medication next to her, took them both aback. They were grateful to see her turn her head towards them and give them a trademark cheeky smile.

"You two all right?" Clare's voice was ever so delicate, like the defiant leaves on a train track about to be blown away by the oncoming locomotive.

"We are absolutely dandy. Though we were somewhat concerned to hear of your latest shenanigans. Any more of this falling sick stuff and we shall have to grab you by the legs and throw you out the window." Amber always had the ability to insert humour in the most tragic of circumstances.

"I don't mind being thrown out the window actually. I could do with being swept off my feet for a while rather than being cooped up in here."

"Have no fear; we'll get you out of here in no time." Veronica looked around for the stash of takeout menus they'd built up over the years. "Half chicken and half veg with a Barbeque base sound good?" Clare took her hand from under the blanket so that she could gesture a thumbs up to Veronica. Amber sat down on the bed next to Clare while Veronica made the call to the pizza delivery people.

"So what have you been doing up here then? I know you. You'd go mad if you weren't doing something active. So what is it? Crosswords? Up to no good on your smartphone? Painting?"

Clare lay back down and turned her head to the right, as if to point with her nose. Amber spotted the pad and walked around to pick it up.

"It's just some things I thought we could do with Blind spot and the website…"

"And some pretty good sketches as well I see."

"Well as you say I like to be doing something."

Veronica skilfully got off her wheelchair and parked herself on one of Clare's gigantic bean bags.

"Right ladies. We've got this guy Gregory Hector. We know who he is. We're not entirely sure what his business is in Parliament House. But forget that for now. What do we do about him? We can't do anything unless Jermaine gives us a copy of that tape. Is he going to Amber?"

"Yes, I think so. He's obviously a bit nervous. But I think he's a good lad. He's seen it and he's outraged like all of us."

"OK. We get the tape off him. Then what? Do we call some sort of press conference or something?" Veronica was eager to push things along in a calm but determined manner.

"No, of course not. We're nobodies. Nobodies can't call press conferences I'm afraid. Nobody would turn up. We don't have to do anything as grand as that anyway. We've got a ready-made way to nail him."

"How?" enquired Veronica.

"Henrietta Barnes obviously. We'll show her. Once she's confident it's legit—which in this case is easy to verify—she'll write about it in the paper. The police will HAVE to get their sorry arses involved then, at which point we give them the tape." Amber seemed assured about the situation, but deep down she was more nervous about Jermaine Baxter.

Clare gently nudged Amber.

"Do you think that will be enough?"

"It's hard to say these days. The guy is meant to be well-connected so he's bound to have all sorts of legal people going over it. But I reckon with that recording we've nailed him."

"Yea but what about Jermaine. He'll get the boot if that tape comes out, won't he?" Veronica's appreciation of Jermaine's predicament eased some of the awkwardness Amber was feeling.

"No, I don't think so to be honest. He has the higher ground. If something does happen to him, it's more of a sign that something dodgy was going on behind the scenes. I think if people are sufficiently outraged he should be OK."

"But there isn't really a guarantee of that is there? I mean let's face it…" Veronica sensed that the odds were still stacked against them.

"True, but I think we should be ok. In any case, I think it's the best route we have at our disposal."

Amber, Veronica and Clare weren't content to leave things at obtaining retribution for the attack on Clare. With organisations such as DI increasingly taking the official line on all things disability-related, a small space was opening for them and similarly-minded organisations to step into. With all the unique advantages that online campaigning and social media had delivered, news of the possible capture of Gregory Hector simply reinforced their desires to go further and make a greater impact on the issues that were so dear to them. They had regularly discussed the philosophical spider's web that was political participation. They were aware of the cynicism and political realism that underpinned the mind-set of organisations such as DI. Their minds were plugged-in enough to realise that such a mind-set held wide currency and favour. This was the kind of pickle that Amber had begun to think about more regularly. It was more a reflection of how her thoughts had evolved during her time at university and how things were now. At university, Amber was certainly engrossed by the political mass hysteria that many countries seemed to go through. But Amber quickly concluded that any attempts to instigate something better were futile. She definitely hadn't succumbed to the levels of apathy that had trapped large swatches of the population. But she was somebody who had a clear set of priorities as to what could and couldn't be changed in society. Successive governments had made sure that people had enough concerns of their own to take care of and not get involved in the plight of others. Whether the issue was employment or housing or education, the individualistic nature of policy making meant that most people saw everything as a zero-sum game. Amber couldn't remember the last time a government had even attempted to re-draw a policy for the long-term benefit of the general public. There wasn't really any malice on the part of Amber or anybody else that began to think in these terms. The malice came from successive governments that worked diligently to set in motion processes and procedures that were divorced from any coherent set of values beyond enhancing the power of the state or big business. That being the case, Amber had always thought that getting her own house in order was the most important thing, as there was nobody else to help her and her family if things were to go wrong. The situation with Clare and Veronica was forcing Amber to go down avenues that were never on her radar. Amber had to force herself to believe the online activism and demonstrations they were planning actually meant something and could have an impact. That it wasn't a case of simply playing into the hands of the people they were targeting—surely the biggest smack in the face has to be when the people you're targeting actively encourage you to do what you do. Such people needed to end up with egg on their faces, or else it could all be dismissed as a waste of time.

"I'm getting much better at this, aren't I?" Amber was delighted with her hand eye co-ordination as she fed Clare a slice of pizza. Clare smiled in sisterly adoration.

"Yes. I'm looking around and I don't see any stains anywhere. Big improvement on the last time." Clare had perked up more than compared to how she was when Amber and Veronica first entered. She gently turned so that she could see Veronica sitting on the bean bag.

"So what are we doing Roni? Action wise I mean? Most of my doodles are to do with the website."

"Well there were a few things I was thinking about. At first, I thought we could do one of those…you know…chain ourselves to a bastard retail outlet that's never improved its access even though disability access laws have been in place for years. But then, I

146

figured that's too cliché. Plus we'd all end up getting battered most likely."

"So what else were you thinking about?"

"Well. This might sound a bit wild…"

"No, no. We like wild…"

"Yes, well, I was thinking having a mass blindfold inspired March. I don't know where we'd start. But could go to Parliament House."

"Sorry. What do you mean mass blindfold?" A strangeness of the suggestion caused Amber to interrupt.

"We'd need to get a lot of people to take part, but what I'm saying is basically we go as a mass group blindfolded all the way to Parliament House or somewhere."

Amber looked bemused.

"How would we get there if nobody can see where they're going?" Veronica and Clare burst out laughing. Clare's asthmatic laugh sounded strangely uplifting, like the cheers of onlookers applauding the rescue of someone on the verge of drowning out at sea.

"Well Amber!" exclaimed Veronica. "We'd all collectively stop people in the street and ask for directions!"

"No, we'd book ten thousand cabs Amber. The blindfolds are purely metaphorical. We're too lazy to go that far—no wait actually we wouldn't be able to get enough accessible taxis!"

"No, listen silly Billy. It's straightforward. It's basically no different from a blind or partially sighted person doing it in one sense. And that's part of what I was thinking. Obviously, for a lot of people being deprived of one of their senses for a couple of hours will be too much for them. So we'd be getting some guys who are blind to sort of—lead." Veronica was overjoyed with her idea.

"And we'd all be following?" queried Amber.

"In a sense, yes. We'd be sort of arm in arm if you see what I mean."

"That seems like a good idea actually," said Amber, with Clare nodding in agreement.

"Right. Now for the difficult bit of getting enough people to take part. Trying to get people to take part. I've got some guys from a few visual impairment charities on board, but obviously the main thing is to get enough members of the public to take part."

"So I guess we need to switch into hard-core advertising mode," stated Clare.

"Yep. I think we can get a couple of thousand without too much difficulty. I think we can get that many just via the free spirited people who'd do anything at least once. But I want at least ten thousand. Make it a proper spectacle."

"Well then I suggest we get cracking with passing on the details to as many people as we can via social media. I'm sure Henrietta Barnes would be more than happy to put something either in the Tribune or via the Jemima Centre magazine. Shall we tell Bob O'Hara as well, just for a laugh? He'd probably arrange a drive-by or something." Clare and Veronica chuckled at Amber's contempt for Bob O'Hara.

"Veronica when were you planning for us to do this then? Will I need to get Freedman to give me a few days off?"

"It depends how long you're planning to work for the guy! I was thinking doing it in the run up to the elections. Maybe a week or two beforehand?"

"If you want to get people thinking about it as a proper political issue, don't you think we should do it a bit earlier? I mean I can't imagine it causing people to change their minds on any issue where disability or stuff has an impact." Clare wasn't suffering from any mental exhaustion.

"Well, to be honest I don't think it will change the way people think. Well not immediately anyway. We need to play the long game I'm afraid. I'm going for the impact aspect of it to be honest." Amber pulled out her smartphone to take a look at the calendar.

"If we assume the election will be Thursday, 5 May, the previous Thursday is 28 April. I'd say let's go for that date. Let's avoid Friday because people will probably be wanting to be getting home for the bank holiday weekend." Veronica and Clare signalled their contentment with Amber's suggestion.

"One last thing. Where is the meet point for the beginning?" Clare gently shoved Amber once more.

"I'd say Parliament Bridge Station. It's central enough but not too central that we'd be clashing with theatre land and stuff. Let's go with that for now, and we'll confirm it once we've got a route finalised."

Amber also agreed to try and push things with Jermaine so that they could get the recording from him and tie up Hector Gregory as quickly as possible.

"I'm just popping to the little girl's room." In a couple of swift adjustments, Veronica was on her wheelchair and exiting the room.

"That girl's upper body strength is ridiculous. If I ever become famous, I'm gonna hire her as my bodyguard!" Amber walked around to the other side of the bed where the lamp was on and sat down next to Clare.

"What's going on Clare? I don't think I've seen you this lethargic before—and we've known each other for a long time now missy."

"I know I was thinking about that the other day actually. Meeting you for the first time in Dublin, having that race with those two numbskulls we met. Those were the days, eh? And now look at me. I feel like someone's stuck a knife in my shoulder blade and is permanently twisting it."

"Recently I've appreciated why people get annoyed when people like me hand out empty platitudes about how everything is fine and dandy. I haven't walked in your shoes—I haven't ridden in your wheelchair…"

"But you're gonna hand me an empty platitude now, aren't you?" smirked Clare.

"No. I'm not."

"So you're going to tell me I'm going to die?"

"No. I'm not. I'm going to tell you that you have a job to do."

"And what's that?"

"Educating all the stupid people out there like me. It's tough but if people like you don't, then who will?"

"Sorry what are you on about?"

"Look there are three types of people these days. One type is the sort of person who starts crying when one of their fake eyelashes falls out. The second are people like you. The grafters, the visionaries. The people who know exactly what the problem is but get thrown in rubbish tips every time they point it out. Even worse than that—people who won't ever get a proper hearing just because they don't match-up to some sort of social eugenicist's picture of what a social reformer or commentator should look like. Sorry—bit of a rant. But you know what I mean?"

"And who is group number three?"

149

"I told you! Uneducated people like me who will listen to whatever just because we're either scared or lazy or stupid. These days it's the fake lashes that get all the attention—they're the nimbys, the tax-dodgers, the scumbags. The celebs that seem to take all the drugs in the world but never get arrested for it."

"But what's the point?" Clare's voice was breaking, as if she was about to burst into a fit of tears.

"The point is that you have to believe life will get better eventually—or else we all might as well just live in a cave somewhere."

"Why do I have to believe life will get better? Why can't people just accept that things are a bit shit and that's just the way it is. Manage expectations…"

"Yea you got that right—manage expectations. Don't you see? When old people say 'it wasn't like this back in our day' most people just think 'oh here we go racist patriotic rant coming up'. But I think what people who say that are getting at is that basically, nothing works anymore. Things used to… work before…seeing a doctor was easy, finding a place to live was easy. Finding a school was easy. Now most people *think* that everything has turned into a mess. Nobody trusts each other, so now people are just in it for themselves. You can join that group if you want but don't expect to find any answers. You need to do this thing with Roni and the others. It's not about making a mark or making a difference or any of that claptrap. It's about… not wasting all that good stuff inside you." Amber stood up and kissed Clare on the forehead, before giving her a gentle cuddle. "It's about showing sick freaks like Hayes and the rest that you've got the audacity to live—despite how much they want to wish you away." Clare looked staggered from Amber's outburst. She had never seen her friend so animated on the subject. Amber took a moment to settle herself, and she had a befuddled look on her face as if to say, 'did I just come out with all *that*?' Amber was desperate to change the tone of the conversation, even though as far as she was concerned she hadn't said anything wrong. "Where the heck has Veronica got to?" She stood up and walked to the door. She theatrically stuck her head around the corner. "I think she's on the phone in the bathroom. I can hear her muffled voice."

"All right, all right, don't eavesdrop on the girl!"

Amber came back to join Clare on the bed, and a few moments later, Veronica re-joined them.

"I better catch up on some sleep ladies. The doc said to build my energy and so on. I'll catch up with you soon for an update?" Amber and Veronica came round to give their friend a final hearty cuddle before leaving her to get some rest. Amber was two steps behind Veronica, and just as she exited the room, she glanced back at Clare and gave her a cheeky wink. Clare smiled and turned to her side. Downstairs, Amber and Veronica were putting their scarves on, getting prepared for the howling wind outside. Just as Amber was following Veronica out, she stopped and asked,

"Veronica, if I hang around for a couple of minutes to talk to Mrs T you should be OK to get to the station and stuff, right?"

"Absolutely. Nothing too serious? No secrets now remember..."

"No, no, nothing like that, I just want to ask about boring housing stuff."

"All right then I'll see you when I see you." Veronica smiled and left the house.

Back inside, Clare's mum offered Amber her fifth cup of tea of the evening but Amber refused.

"Sorry Mrs T. I don't want to freak you out or anything but when I was upstairs with Clare just now she didn't seem herself. I know that might be stating the obvious but that girl is solid as a rock. She was talking and so on, but she looked so distant. Like she was *waiting* for something to happen. Do you know what I mean?"

Clare's mum had a sorrowful look on her face.

"I just... I think it's a few too many setbacks. I... she might start to just go through the motions. What do you expect? On the one hand, you have these arseholes who bang on about getting more disabled people into work, and at the exact same time, you have a guy who probably works in the same building as that arsehole thinking of ways to make it easier for employers to stop employing disabled people. Then you have documentaries talking about how people like her are lazy sods and then she goes and gets her head smashed in when she tries to make a difference." Within seconds, Clare's mum had become incensed and Amber quickly gave her a cuddle to ease her discomfort. Amber's plump physique meant that people enjoyed hugging her, and she knew it. Amber took it as a compliment and was more than happy to dish them out. "But it's this housing thing that's really buried her."

"But she can stay here!"

"It's not that anymore. We need to get some equipment to help her. As she gets more fragile, this place gets less and less suitable."

"Won't the council do anything to help?"

"We're on the list and everything, and to be fair, we're quite high up. But this housing crisis will be the death of her at this rate. Do you have any idea how difficult it is to find anything that's suitable? I mean the population is meant to be getting older, isn't it? Every year there are more disable people, aren't there? So why the heck is housing going in the opposite direction? Is there going to be some kind of mass cull of disable people or something?"

"What do you think you'll have to do?"

"I'm not sure right now. Having to go far away would tear Clare apart. It's nothing to do with us being comfortable here. But you know—we have everything here. Friends, family…the doc knows Clare's condition inside out. She's isolated enough as it is with the backward attitudes she gets when she tries to go out or get a job. It's like they wanna finish her off by putting her in a bungalow in the middle of a field in the middle of nowhere."

Clare's mother would get annoyed when those around her would trot out the standard clichés about her being a powerful and inspirational woman. She was simply doing her best as a mother who had been abandoned by a conceited husband who fled the scene upon realising the significance of Clare's condition shortly after her birth. On one hand, Amber could see why she might feel annoyed. She wasn't asking for special treatment or some kind of best mum award. Clare's mother was simply pleading for someone in power with a drop of morality to understand that the predicament she and her daughter were in wasn't of their own making and that all they needed was someone to assess their situation in a fair and thoughtful way and assist with providing a humane solution—rather than an economic one. Amber used to appreciate this, but with the authorities continuing to engineer a 'Me First' generation, Clare's mothers only chance was really to scream as loud as she could until someone decided to intervene. If people on the underground weren't going to give up their fold-up seat for Clare on the tube, as far as Amber was concerned Clare's mother *had* to take a battering ram to them and get them to move. And if people wouldn't make space for her on the bus, as far as Amber was concerned she had to reverse into them. The problem with the 'Me' generation that the authorities were cultivating was that you had to act like an egomaniac in order to get your slice of the cake. But in Clare's case that wasn't happening. People looked at her as if she was some sort of stain on humanity. So for Amber, singling out Clare's mother wasn't about highlighting her super-human qualities—it was really about gaining recognition from the deviant minds around her that she and Clare were always human to begin with.

Amber eventually reached the train station around half an hour after Veronica, yet oddly, Veronica was still there, waiting at the platform.

"Hello stranger. I thought you would have been long gone?" Amber sounded cheerful enough, but Veronica seemed distant and slightly confused.

"Erm, no well, erm, the trains are a bit crap this evening. Thankfully it's quite late or else the platform would have been packed." Veronica was shivering, but Amber got the impression it wasn't because of the cold.

"Are you all right Roni? Is your condition flaring up again? I know you care about Clare but you need to look after yourself as well you know…"

"Yes, thank you!" shrilled Veronica. "I'm perfectly aware I've got to look after myself and my mum, that's what I've been trying to do all this time."

Amber wasn't sure what to say, but just then the train began to pull into the platform. Veronica was about to wheel away, but Amber stuck her hand out instinctively.

"Please, let me." Without any objection she took Veronica's handles and they both boarded the train.

Chapter Fourteen

The assisted dying debate always managed to stir the passions of anyone who claimed to have an interest—which after consideration was essentially everyone on earth. Amber, Clare and Veronica made sure they recorded the speeches of anyone who talked about the subject in the Commons. They kept cutouts of newspaper articles, but soon abandoned the practice as it was stone obvious to them that everything was available online. Amber and Veronica didn't like discussing the matter with Clare for one simple reason: many of the public cases of individuals who had gone abroad to end their lives had the exact same condition as Clare. Veronica and Amber didn't actually know where Clare stood on the topic—they used to know—but weren't sure anymore. As Clare's condition deteriorated, for some reason they assumed her thoughts on the idea would change too. It was a monumentally difficult subject to deal with. Although dead set against any notions of assisted suicide, Amber was acutely aware that there were people out there who regarded themselves as being in untenable positions that only had one remedy. What was bothering Amber was the changing environment that the debate was taking place in. Initially, it was a subject that all sections of society could contribute to. But Amber had noticed that in the last few years, people were being hounded out of the debate. Thoughtful and caring folk of a religious persuasion had mobs set loose on them every time they dared utter a word. The handful of well-intentioned politicians were dismissed as being out of touch on the topic. A case in point was that of Giles Gibbs. He was elected by party members on the basis that the public identified some kind of human element within him that wasn't present in any of the other leadership candidates. A significant part of this was attributed to his daughter. She had extensive special needs that required attended to. Gibbs spoke poignantly about looking after his daughter and the trials and tribulations that came with it. Far more moving though was Gibbs' comments about the joy and happiness that she brought him and the family. Gibbs often protested at the 'quality of life' argument put forward by those in support of assisted dying. Gibbs always said that one could see his daughter Jessica was happy. She regularly had a smile on her face. She would smile over the simplest thing. She was alive in that moment to the same extent a racing driver was when he took a bend at over one hundred and fifty miles an hour. The racing driver has his scale and Jessica has hers. There were many ways to enjoy life. It always riled him that the same cohort of people who supported the legalisation of drugs were the same group of people who were at the front of the queue when it came to questioning Jessica's worth. Her happiness didn't add up to their hedonistic ideal. The people who could really talk about the subject with a sense of understanding were obviously those who found themselves in that position. So who were all these other people and what was their real basis for supporting assisted dying? Was this really a topic that required input from those unfit or unqualified to speak? Surely, the sanctity of life was a topic that couldn't be detached from morality and ethics? But for Amber, that's exactly what seemed to be happening. A lot of the leading figures that were now contributing to the debate were from one institute or other, claiming some kind of moral authority to talk on the subject. Upon closer inspection, the vast majority were no more than think tanks with a unique policy bent. They all had the same shady financial backers and the same disreputable links to politicians and business. For these people, the real issue wasn't actually about whether assisted dying was right or wrong. There was something wider at stake. The debate about assisted suicide fed into wider discussions about human worth. Amber saw that many of the organisations that were taking a stand in support of assisted suicide were actually making covert points about what was acceptable and not acceptable in terms of supporting one's fellow man. It was for this reason that Amber took an interest in the subject more personally. The situation with Clare always hung at the back of her head like a puppy hanging on at the edge of a cliff. For Amber, the events since the demonstration were making her constantly question the value of togetherness. Amber was always someone who wanted to give people the benefit of the doubt. Everyone has so much to deal with, that when it came to serious issues, disengagement was the best course of action. But when it came to something as serious as assisted dying, Amber wasn't so sure. Perhaps the malaise was down to the fact that, these days, people just didn't care anymore. Perhaps what Amber once took as apathy was something more altogether disheartening. Amber always felt blessed that she had her mum, Clare and increasingly Veronica to support her. These were people that genuinely cared when push came to shove. Amber was slowly concluding that people just *didn't care* anymore, and that was a bad atmosphere to have a discussion about assisted suicide in. Hayes and Freedman probably felt the same and took it as confirmation that their political instincts were in tune. Giles Gibbs' ascension to leadership of the party was an excellent political manoeuvre. Samantha Barratt was spot on in her assessment of their devious motives. With Gibbs pouring his heart out, nobody was ever going to accuse the party of acting in an improper manner when dealing with the disadvantaged. Hayes and Freedman were experts at the 'packaging' approach to politics. They knew exactly how to come at a debate from different angles, strategically offering support when their friends needed it and writing in magazines like *Political Engagement* when opposition duty called. They were really a pair of Russian dolls. Nobody could really say how many layers they had or where their true convictions lay—if they had any true convictions. On the issue of assisted suicide, they rarely spoke in public on the subject. In private, their friends were anxious that they never took an ideological stance on the topic. There were a number of political and economic benefits that could be delivered if a libertarian stance was maintained on the issue.

Chapter Fifteen

The cameras that had been placed by the window ledges were of the up-to-date digital variety, meaning Jermaine roughly knew what he was doing. He was able to retrieve the recording without too much hassle. The old window was so far passed its sellby date that Jermaine almost cut his fingers on it. Amber and the girls were fortunate that it was these particular windows. Being part of the older complex meant that the windows could still actually be opened, as opposed to the new buildings that were totally locked out for security reasons. In actual fact, the committee room windows were soon to be fitted with some kind of contraption that wouldn't interfere with their listed status but would make it impossible to open them. Had the old buildings not been so spacious, summers would have been hideously hot. Jermaine was a diligent worker who often stayed considerably later than his colleagues in order to get work completed. With the weather showing no signs of calming, it seemed like a good opportunity to stay in the warmth of the committee corridors for as long as possible before having to make the unforgiving trek back across London. It had just gone past seven in the evening as Jermaine went through his usual routine of checking the weather and transport. Jermaine uploaded the video footage to his phone. He didn't have time to find the precise location he needed to confirm what he had seen previously. He was desperate to go to the loo, and so quickly hopped out of his chair and was about to rush down the corridor. He had realised that he'd left his phone on the table, and so quickly turned back to pick it up before hastening to the loo. The emptiness of the committee corridors, however, had caused him to let his guard down in one other area—he forgot to lock his computer before he left. It was something that he was usually fastidious about.

Samuel Bertrand briskly entered the room and sat down at the computer. The open plan office meant that there was nothing for him to search other than Jermaine's bag which was by the chair on the floor. A quick fiddle told Bertrand that there wasn't anything of interest there. Jermaine's small victory of taking his phone with him was about to be voided by Samuel Bertrand having temporary access to his computer. Bertrand had no more than a couple of minutes to put Jermaine in an untenable position that he could then use as leverage at a later time. He phoned a colleague.

"The silly bugger has left his screen unlocked. Quickly! Remotely log-in for me and let me go to a few dodgy websites and get them logged on his usage profile." Within a few moments, Bertrand had visited a number of offending websites. He wanted to download a low-profile virus but his accomplice from IT advised against it. Seeing that he had already been there for almost three minutes, Bertrand levered himself away from the desk, jumped out of the chair and made for the exit. Jermaine came back into the room, feeling relieved. Approaching his desk, he paused. He saw that the screen was still open. On the one hand, he realised that he'd forgotten to lock his computer, but at the same time he was aware that as a safety mechanism the screens lock after ninety seconds of inactivity. Jermaine's attention was then drawn to his chair, which seemed to be a lot further away from the desk than where he left it. The papers sticking out of his bag were the final giveaway. Jermaine began to panic. Someone had been here while he was away and now he had to figure out what they were doing and quick. He bent down to lock his computer screen and waltzed out of the room. There were a couple of people still working in one of the rooms at the end of the corridor.

"I'm sorry guys but have you two seen anyone come down here in the last few minutes?" Jermaine got a shake of the head from both and ran back to his desk. The contents of the bag seemed to be in order. If Bertrand was looking for the digital camera, Jermaine had put it in his blazer jacket and had taken it with him when he went to the loo. Sitting back at his desk, he began to undertake an inventory of his computer to see if he could find anything untoward, but the frustration of not knowing what he was looking for was causing him to tear his hair out. He opened all of his most recent documents and all were as they should be. It was then time to check the internet history in the event that someone had been doing something they shouldn't have been. Bertrand and his IT comrade had been thinking along the same lines and had made sure they deleted the anomalous entries. Jermaine leaned back in his chair for a few moments. He was understandably anxious and frightened. His gut feeling told him that this was something to do with Amber and the video footage they wanted from the camera. Amber's animated demeanour when they spoke in the canteen got the unwanted attention of Samuel Bertrand, and ever since, Bertrand had been floating around the area with increased frequency. But in any event, Jermaine had no plans of taking this sort of intimidation lying down. He may not have been as well-connected as Bertrand but he had enough common sense to look after himself. He just needed to decide whether handing over what he had to Amber and the others was worth it. As Jermaine left the building, he felt a hand tap him on the shoulder.

"Hey Jermaine!" Jermaine jumped. "Relax it's only me." Jermaine turned to see that it was Samuel Bertrand.

"Oh sorry Samuel. You know what's it's like this time of night."

"Do you always work this late Jermaine?"

"Not every day but when I need to. I'm quite keen not to let work drag on if you know what I mean. Why do you ask?"

"Oh no nothing. It's good to see someone as focused as you that's all. Do you want to go grab some dinner? My treat?" Bertrand seemed to be in a euphoric mood, full of jolly and all smiles.

"No, that's all right Sam. I need to do a few things at home. Perhaps I'll take you up on your offer another time, eh?" Bertrand smiled as they got to the underground station and went their separate ways.

***

Nothing had happened in the few days since Jermaine's computer was violated, and the weekend had come where he'd agreed to meet Amber outside of work for the first time. Jermaine had invited Amber along to one of his favourite steak houses in South London. He wasn't aware that Veronica was also coming along, and there was almost an incident to begin with. Jermaine had booked one of the private booths in the restaurant's lower ground floor, but the only way to get down was by the stairs, making it impossible for Veronica to get down. After a quick discussion with the head waiter the three of them decided to sit at one of the tables on the ground floor. As it was a late lunch, the venue was largely empty, allowing them to talk with relative freedom. Veronica wasn't impressed with the inability to go downstairs, and as she made her way to the table, she made her feelings clear to a group of staff. "I'm entitled to privacy as well you know." They smiled and nodded in response; their now mechanical customer service skills on full display.

"I'm sorry for inviting myself along like this Jermaine. I know Amber is your mate really—I appreciate this is the first time we've met."

"No, that's absolutely fine. I don't mind that at all. But in hindsight it would have made sense to tell me so that I could have picked a more suitable venue. I know a lot of great places to eat. A lot of the places in Central have been toned down to suit customer tastes—you know—people who aren't used to spicy food. The further out you go the more authentic the experience is."

"No, I'm sure this is a great place. It's not your fault Jermaine. There are lots of places like centrally or anywhere else that just pay token attention to access. It's not just people in wheelchairs you know. Just take a look at this stupid menu. I mean, even I'm struggling to read it. How the heck are old people or people with poor eyesight supposed to read it?"

"I don't know. I haven't really thought about it. I have a friend who has dodgy eyesight. When we come here I tend to just read the thing out to him."

Amber was anxious for the purpose of their get together not to be lost and so carefully directed the conversation to the relevant topic.

"Erm, well, Jermaine. Have you had a proper chance to think about that thing I told you about?"

"Yes. I have. But before we get into that there's something you should know."

"What's that?" Amber sounded worried.

"Something happened at work the other evening. And—I'm not having a go or anything but I'm pretty sure it's got something to do with you Amber and all this."

"How do you mean? What exactly occurred?" Amber was flurried.

"I was at my desk the other night—quite late—sevenish. I went to the loo and I'd forgotten to lock my computer—YES, I KNOW

SILLY ERROR. But, when I got back, I could tell that my desk had definitely been disturbed."

"How do you know it's got something to do with all this?" Amber wasn't trying to deflect blame; she asked more out of hope. She knew full well it was likely related to the recent goings on.

"It's Samuel Bertrand. He's freaking me out. After we had lunch the other day, he warned me to stay away from you, and ever since then, he's just been hanging around. Honestly, I'm a nobody at that place. I just come in, do my work and leave. If someone has gone through my things, then they must suspect something. I've no idea what though."

"What's it like working there?" Veronica wanted to know what he really meant by being a nobody.

"It's fine. Really. But at the end of the day we all know how it is in some of these places. Unless your white or tan you can't really expect to get where you want to be. Throw in a token brown person fine but everyone knows how it is."

A distressed Amber was now frightful of losing the one piece of good news they had.

"Does that mean you can't help us then?"

"No—I'll give you what you want. The way I see it, if I give you that footage I can use it as some kind of insurance or leverage if something happens to me." Jermaine reached into his pocket and took out a flash drive. He stretched over the table to hand it to Amber. Amber lifted her arm to take it, but Veronica grabbed her arm.

"Hang on Amber. What if something bad happens to Jermaine? I'm not sure I could deal with that…" The three of them sat in silence for a few moments, none of them knowing how to break the impasse.

"Take it. It's fine. Honestly. If something does happen, I'm not planning on sitting there and taking it. But what I would ask is some help from you guys if I need it. Are you OK with that?"

"Absolutely!" stated Veronica. With the matter settled, the next thing to sort out was what exactly they were going to do with the evidence. Amber was clear as to what needed to be done.

"We HAVE to show Henrietta Barnes. We know for a fact she'll publish something on it. She won't give a toss about any nonsense security implications or anything like that."

"Yes, but what about what comes after? I don't mean me but you know—Gregory Hector knows people. He won't take kindly to being publicly humiliated." Jermaine tried to focus their minds on the volatile aftermath. Veronica seemed to be optimistic about any possible repercussions.

"Actually I think it should be OK. Surely this is a black and white case, right? Anyone who sees the tape will know instantly that Hector is a complete twat. In any case, I think they'd be stupid to come after people. They'd be making it even worse for themselves." Jermaine flicked his nose out of nervousness. He didn't think what would happen next was going to be as rosy as Veronica thought. At the end of the day, a rich and powerful person was going to be publicly ostracised—and surely that would carry consequences.

**

Jermaine didn't even have time to unpack his things when he returned to work the following week when he was promptly dragged into a private meeting room by a member of security. He was silently pleased that they hadn't made a bigger deal out of it. He knew that by not causing a scene they weren't looking to hang him out to dry—not yet anyway. Walking into the meeting room, one of the Estate Managers was waiting there—along with Samuel Bertrand. This didn't bother Jermaine. Samuel was voted in as a Liaison Officer on behalf of the interns working across the parliamentary estate. How this happened was anyone's guess. Jermaine preferred to see Samuel there rather than some random person from human resources who would just go through a tonne of red tape before releasing him from the internship programme.

"Ah, hello Jermaine. We're sorry to drag you away from your desk but this is quite serious I'm afraid so rather than book a formal meeting with HR we thought it might be best if we just sat round a table ASAP and get it sorted if we can." Bertrand seemed hospitable enough.

"All right but I have no idea what this is about so you'll have to explain to me what I'm doing here." Jermaine remained calm and kept an excellent poker face. He always knew this was inevitable; he was just surprised as to how quickly it was happening.

"Think Jermaine. Are you sure you don't know what this is about? Has anything strange happened recently?" Bertrand was doing a good job of sounding like he cared.

"No, not that I can think of. No wait, actually yes, something strange did happen last week."

"What was that?"

"Well I'm certain someone was getting up to no good with my PC while I was away."

"What happened exactly?" Bertrand was doing all the questioning, with the representative from Estates just taking notes.

"Well it was that same evening I bumped into you actually. As you know I was finishing late, and erm, I went to the loo before I packed my things away. And when I got back things just seemed to be out of place. I'm certain that someone had gone through my stuff and that someone had gone on the PC."

The Estates Manager finally broke his silence.

"Aren't you aware of standard procedure? You must ALWAYS lock your PC if leaving the desk—no matter how short a period of time." He genuinely seemed irritated. And why not? Whenever anything like this happened, he would have to write a report and conduct an overview of protocol to make sure things were running smoothly.

"Yes, I know I'm sorry I'm usually really good with stuff like that but I was bursting. Surely security cameras and things can verify or not if someone was there."

"Well we're one step ahead of you Jermaine," assured Samuel. "Whenever something like this happens these guys always check the security cameras to make sure nothing untoward has happened."

"So what then? You didn't see anything then? So what else then? That's as far as it goes from where I'm sitting." Jermaine was keen to know what they had discovered.

"Well it doesn't end there for us," bit the Estates Manager.

"So go on Samuel, tell me."

"There was an alert on the night you were saying. Someone had accessed websites they shouldn't have been. They came to me first because I'm the Liaison Officer. And for the record, the first thing I said was 'he's a good lad, so let's check other options first'."

Jermaine looked at the walls to his right and then to his left. This was a sticky moment—and that was an understatement. In a split second, he had to decide whether to deny everything and take the flack or co-operate as much as he could. He knew he had the insurance with Amber and Veronica.

"Well. There isn't much I can say is there? I've told you my version of events. What do you want me to say?"

"I think…you'd be doing yourself a favour if you just came clean. It would only be a reprimand."

"If it meant keeping my job, I would own up to something I didn't do. Just to keep the peace. But I'm not owning up to THAT sort of thing. People will think I'm some sort of weirdo." Jermaine was sounding increasingly ardent.

"Well, why were you working so late that night?"

"Hang on Samuel forget all that. He's saying it wasn't him and there's no other explanation. I say we just notify HR formally and—"

"I don't think there's any need to get HR or anything like that involved is there Jermaine? You're a good lad. I don't want your career to be blighted by this." Bertrand stared at his colleague as if to tell him not to interrupt again.

"So what do you want from me?"

"An explanation of your erratic behaviour. I've been watching you recently and you've been all over the place. And—now I'm not one to pick people out for poor behaviour but you know Amber Watts?—She's a bit of a devious one to be frank. And if I was being honest, I've seen that ever since you've met her your behaviour has been a bit odd. Has she been harassing you about something?"

"Harassing? Ha! Definitely not." Jermaine let out a sarcastic laugh.

"But she wants something, right? I saw the two of you the other day. She was getting excited about something. REALLY excited. What was all that about? Tell me what she wants and maybe this internet business can go away." Bertrand finally got to the point of the entire meeting. He just had to get there slowly to minimise any suspicions Jermaine might have.

"Hang on Samuel shouldn't we get HR…"

"SHUT. UP! Well, go on Jermaine. I can tell she wants something."

"It's just something. You know. Her friend got injured in that demonstration. You know the one I'm talking about?"

"Yea." Bertrand folded his arms as he realised he was getting closer to what he wanted to hear.

"Yea. Well. Her mate got injured and they wanna prosecute the main security guy that assaulted her."

"And what does this have to do with you?"

"Nothing obviously. But I was telling them that we keep bird watching cameras in some parts of the building. And so Amber was asking if she could have a copy of the footage from the day of the demonstration because one of the cameras overlooks that part of the estate."

"Have you given them the footage?" In a split second, Bertrand became fraught.

"No! Of course not! That's why she's been bothering me. Asking if I'd give it to her."

"So you haven't passed it over then?"

"No."

"Are you sure?" Bertrand seemed to be turning red, but he was doing his best to keep his cool.

"Of course I'm sure. I ain't crazy. I took the footage from the camera but that's as far as it goes."

"So you were going to give it?"

"No. I was just curious that's all."

"Well would you mind fetching it and handing it over? You know you shouldn't be holding on to something like that, right? If it's got incriminating footage, it should go straight to the authorities here who will then liaise with the police in a right and proper fashion. Under no circumstances should these things be handed to some crazy bunch of activists looking to make quick headlines."

"Absolutely."

"Can you get it for me?" Bertrand sounded like he was asking for an overdue essay to be handed in.

"Yes, no worries." Jermaine darted out of the room and went over to his desk. He picked up his bag and rummaged around for a few seconds before pulling out the offending evidence. He calmly walked back into the room and sat back down.

"Here you go." He slipped it across the table for Samuel to pick up.

"Are you positive this is the only copy?"

"Yes." Jermaine had nerves of steel and wasn't about to give up his insurance any time soon. "So where does that leave us then? Are you satisfied? Are you still going to take it up with HR?"

"No. I told you. It's fine." Bertrand looked at his colleague to make sure he was in agreement. "I'm a man of my word Jermaine. I do think you're a good lad. I don't want to ruin things for you. Let me give you a small piece of advice though. If I were you, I'd stay well-clear of Amber. A girl like that can be serious trouble. I mean if you got on the wrong side of her she'd be able to go to Guy Freedman and make life a nuisance for you. On the other hand, who could you turn to? So take this on board. Stick to what you know. Once you have this internship under your belt, it will open up so many doors for you. You don't want to ruin that, do you?" Bertrand was now sounding like a careers adviser. But Jermaine could sense the dark, cryptic, sinister undertone behind everything he said.

"No, of course not."

"Well there you are."

Jermaine nodded. Bertrand offered him a smile as they concluded their business. Jermaine scuttled back to his desk and sat down. He didn't log on immediately. He went through his bag again but wasn't actually looking for anything. He just needed some time to think and didn't want to look like one of those idiots who just stare at their screen for ages. Having gathered his thoughts, he knew what he had to do first. He waited a few minutes before rushing to the toilets. Under the circumstances Jermaine felt it was crucial to do a quick survey of the cubicles to make sure they were all empty. Seeing that everything was clear, he pulled out his mobile and began to phone Amber. She didn't answer the first time, causing Jermaine to almost pull his hair out for a second time. His anxiety was eased when she finally answered.

"AMBER. It's me. Are you free to talk?"

"No hang on. One of the meeting rooms is free. Just a sec… OK go ahead."

"Bad news I'm afraid. I was pulled in today by Estates and Samuel. I've been set up. I'm sure of it."

"What's happened?"

"They're claiming I've gone on some dodgy website or something. They got me in a corner and basically said they'd keep it quiet if I told them what all the fuss was about with you the other day. I'm sorry Amber but I had to tell them that you were after the footage of the demonstration."

"OK, it's fine. They are conniving little arseholes. They were bound to find something out anyway. How much did you tell them?"

"Just that you were looking for footage of the demo and that I had some stuff from the cameras."

"Is that it?"

"Yea."

"So they don't know that you've actually handed it over already?"

"No! I think Samuel reckons he's nipped it in the bud. Assuming he believed me."

"Sorry, what was he doing there anyway?"

"Intern Liaison Officer."

"No, this is nonsense. I wanna know what that guy is up to. BUT for now they think they've got it covered?"

"Yes!"

"OK. Leave it with us. Next stop is Henrietta Barnes and Samantha Barratt. We need to get it out there quick."

"Just watch your back. This is getting serious. I'm telling you I was set up."

"It's all right, I believe you man. Calm down. I'll be in touch. Thanks again Jermaine. You're a legend."

Jermaine went back to his desk and dissolved into his char. All sorts of permutations were now going through his head. He had sacrificed himself so that someone else could get justice. This was how he was trying to make himself feel better. Nonetheless he thought, there was going to be a lot of upheaval after this. Samuel Bertrand and the others were bound to throw the book at him once Barnes began to publicise the footage. Jermaine didn't mind losing the internship per se. He knew he had it in him to find something else, maybe not as prestigious but certainly something more rewarding. The real concern was how far the parliamentary authorities wanted to take it. They now had the power to make his life a real mess if they wanted to. Using government computers to access naughty websites wasn't a criminal offence or anything like that. It did mean that if they wanted to, they could cancel his security clearance. That was a major headache. It would automatically rule him out of getting a job in any senior major public sector institution. Getting a job would always be tough no matter how good he was. Having so many avenues cut off in one sweep just made things more complicated and challenging. More concerning for Jermaine was all the gossip and rumours something like this could start. This was the sort of thing that could become very public, very quickly. That's the thing that was bothering Jermaine the most. He was the oldest of four siblings. He had always tried his best to be an adequate role model for his younger brothers and sisters. If it was to come out, he knew that his family would believe his version of events. He had never lied to them before and so why would he now? In any event, his family were always fearful of the type of job he was doing. They didn't see at as some sort of innocuous job that would lead to better things. Deep down them always fretted about something like this happening. They had read enough newspaper stories to know that it wasn't just in their imagination or the sort of thing only to be found in a crime novel. Jermaine had to sit down with them on more than one occasion and convince them that so long as he kept himself to himself all would be well. And yet here he was, trying to think of ways to mitigate any damage. Was it worth going back to Amber and begging her not do anything? Jermaine was sure he could convince her. There's no way she'd be able to hand the footage to Henrietta Barnes and get it published all in one day. There was time to rectify the situation. No! He was being selfish! It wasn't like Jermaine to lose his cool but he was now panicking. He hadn't realised but he'd now become one of those lunatics who stared at a blank computer screen while just sitting there. He hadn't moved. A colleague came by and jokingly asked if he knew where the 'on' button was. Jermaine didn't respond. He then thought about doing something he just really didn't want to do. Was it worth going back to Bertrand and coming clean about the entire thing? Jermaine was sure he could strike some kind of deal with Bertrand. At the end of the day, it obviously wasn't him that Bertrand was interested in—it was Amber and what was on that recording. He'd initially be annoyed that the full story wasn't disclosed first time around. If he was given what he wanted, then maybe all would be well? But thoughts of Amber came swirling into Jermaine's head. Even though he hadn't done anything wrong in all of this, he couldn't help but feel that if Amber was hung out to dry then it would be his fault. He didn't believe the nonsense about Amber running to Guy Freedman. He knew they didn't have that kind of relationship. But

Amber was becoming an increasingly good friend, and a friend in a dungeon full of snakes was something that was worth holding on to.

Chapter Sixteen

Samantha Barratt had been keeping a low profile since her run in
with the law. She had never been formally arrested or charged. But
that didn't matter. It had now become common knowledge that her
office had been visited by 'plain clothed' officers but nobody knew
the reason why. Some debates on TV thankfully stuck to the more
mundane task of deciding what the constitution said about the
powers of the police to search an MP's office. Everyone agreed
there must have been sufficient evidence, and this is where the
tricky questions started for Barratt. Lakeland had stuck to his
promise of not disclosing anything to the press. That in itself was a
miracle. Many politicians had complained that when it came to
reporting an incident, a member of the press would somehow turn
up before an actual police officer. But the very fact that Lakeland
had kept quiet was causing Barratt to worry even more. For some
reason he had cause to keep quiet. He could have made thousands
by tipping off O'Hara or someone of that persuasion. Barratt wasn't
as egotistical as some of her colleagues. But that was a good enough
reason for the likes of O'Hara to try and bring her down. In the eyes
of some parts of the press, the public liked nothing more than a do-
gooder being put in their place. Barratt tried to convince herself that
this entire thing really was part of some sort of financial
misdemeanour. There were always suspicions about Mortimer
Brothers. Perhaps the authorities were finally closing in? And she'd
been dragged into the mess by way of a warning to keep her hands
off anything to do with the investigation? Was there any sense in
going after Mortimer Brothers with everything she had? At this
moment in time, there didn't seem to be anything to lose. There was
a definite preference for going down in a noble cause rather than
being buried alive through a mass character assassination. As the
days passed, that had to be the inevitable end. There were already
three online petitions calling for her to be de-selected from her

parliamentary seat, though these were set up by known adversaries that were taking advantage of an opportune moment. Thinking intensely about what her enemies might want from deposing her almost caused her to have a nose bleed. It was difficult to accept that even her bitterest opponents would resort to this level of deception. It was worth thinking about the level of risk involved trying to falsely implicate a serving member of parliament in some kind of racket. It was difficult to think of anyone with that level of hatred for her. Thinking back to her many successful battles, there was only a handful that even remotely caught her attention. As an opposition MP, she was on the frontline during the battle over the Financial Regulation Act. When the legislation first reached MPs there was disquiet from both sides of the house over some of its provisions. It wasn't even the big banks or financial institutions that were being obstructive. Barratt wanted greater safeguards in place in the realm of conflict of interests. She knew that the public was sick to death of senior figures from the private sector enjoying a revolving door policy when it came to senior public service postings. Barratt was always frustrated with the incestuous nature of some large contracts that came about as a result of the relationship. Barratt was somehow able to secure enough supporters for her amendments to be accepted. In the process, a number of powerful enemies were made, but Barratt always knew this would be the case. But there were far easier ways to get back at her. So for Barratt it came back to the same question: who would be willing to take the sort of risks that had been taken in order to compromise her? No reassurance was required. It had to be someone a lot closer to home. Barratt's head had now turned to fudge. Barratt wasn't one for conspiracy theories. Whoever did this must have some sort of personal vendetta against her. She stopped thinking about people with political motivations to harm her and began to think more about who might have a personal grudge to settle. Within seconds, Barratt's attention was settled on one name: Giles Gibbs. The two had suffered more than one falling out over the years, and some were more serious than others. Barratt had never backed Gibbs to be leader of the party and had voiced her discontent publicly during the leadership campaign. Barratt never thought Gibbs was leadership material and made her reservations known. Had things worked out differently, she may well have been inclined towards frontline politics. But now with the likes of Hayes and Freedman calling the shots, any aspirations about making a pitch for the front benches were far from the front of her mind. Most observers assumed this was always the main source of animosity between them. Giles Gibbs' real gripe with Barratt actually concerned his first attempt to enter Parliament. Barratt and Gibbs were both on the shortlist to be the Union Party candidate for Caledonian Park. At the time, it was a hotly contested marginal seat. The resignation of the incumbent provided a golden opportunity for the Union Party to seize a coveted London seat. The job required someone with grit and fight. For all his qualities, Gibbs was never up to such a task, but Barratt was. She received the nomination comfortably, leaving Gibbs to wait another two years before entering Parliament via a safe seat—the only way he could enter successfully.

Henrietta Barnes had asked Amber, Samantha Barratt and the others to settle themselves down in her living room. Clare wasn't well enough to attend, and Jermaine had decided to keep his distance for the time being. One of Amber's favourite sketch shows was on the TV. It was a repeat of an old favourite, a combination of pure slapstick and sophisticated humour. *Doctor I seem to be unable to go to the loo standing up. Try lying down and see if that solves the problem... Darling I'm just going out shopping with my mum— Triceratops—I know you don't get along with her but there's no need to call her a dinosaur!—What? No! I said try Sarah's Tops— it's a new place on the high street aimed at older women.* Amber took an interest in the layout of Barnes' living room. Pieces of art were dotted around the corners of the room, with strange fabric, collages streaming down from two of the walls. It was clear Barnes' creative talents extended beyond her writing skills. Amber was certain these were pieces Barnes had made herself. Barnes detested the world of traded art and couldn't imagine her bringing such things into her home - unless they were from a market stall or something of that variety. Barnes came back into the room with hot drinks for everyone.

"So tell me Amber, what exactly are we going to see when we plug this thing in?"

"Plug it in and I'll show you. I've taken the liberty of putting it in the right place so we won't have to go searching for it. It took me ages. There are literally hours of nonsense on there." Amber passed the flash drive to Barnes, who promptly inserted it into her laptop and then launched the video when prompted. Amber knelt down beside Barnes.

"Sorry can you guys see? I hope my big head isn't in the way." Veronica and Samantha Barratt gave her the thumps up. "OK so at this point the demo has been going on for a while. You can't actually see me properly but I've arrived a few minutes earlier… There you see Clare leaving the main group and going nearer the building…then she tries to get the banner unfurled…and there you go." Everyone gasped as they began to appreciate the full force of the attack. "I was panicking at first as you can't see the guy properly. But as you see they begin to move to a better position and there look. You can see his face relatively clearly. I'm reliably informed that guy's name is Gregory Hector."

"Yes! Well-done Amber. You're absolutely right. And we've got him!" Samantha Barratt was ecstatic.

"Hang on Henrietta just one step at a time. Jermaine told me his dad is a high roller of some sort but he couldn't remember how." Amber wanted to make sure Barnes wasn't losing sight of her vigilance.

"His father is Olivier Hector. A nasty piece of work. He's a private investor type of guy. He's a non-exec on the board of Mortimer Brothers but his main thing is private security. This is going front page either tomorrow or the day after no problem!" Barnes put her arm around Amber. "You know Amber eventually people will want to talk to you about this. You won't be able to keep your nose out of it forever. Do you think you can deal with that?" Barnes' motherly touch seemed to be breaking through.

"Absolutely!" exclaimed Amber. "This isn't about me. This is about Clare. That girl has done so much for Roni and I. In more ways than you can imagine. This is the least we can do. Let's get the crapbag! Eh Roni?" For a moment it looked like Amber was about to shed a tear.

"Definitely!" Veronica rolled up next to Amber so she could hold her hand.

"Do you think I should tell Guy Freedman Samantha?"

"No, I don't think so. Let things run their course. We'll see what happens." Samantha Barratt was in an increasing state of anxiety when it came to Guy Freedman. His stonewall opposition to pursuing matters with parliamentary security seemed increasingly contrived.

"What exactly do you think will happen Henrietta?" asked Amber.

"Well if all goes to plan we should be able to get exactly what you want. If we can't get an apology from the guy himself—which we probably won't—we'll almost certainly get an apology from the government. It will be interesting to see the opposition's reaction too."

"In what sense?"

"Well Olivier and Gregory are two of theirs—excluding you obviously Samantha! People like Hayes have stronger links to them than anyone in the government. I suspect Hayes will be wincing."

Alexander Hayes almost had as many private flats as Guy Freedman. In Hayes' case, the benefits didn't fully come from inheriting the hard work of his father and grandfather—though this was obviously useful and not really begrudged. Instead, the extraordinary influx of foreign wealth provided the perfect opportunity for Hayes to maximise his commercial and business interests. Policymakers didn't seem to have any intention of derailing the hazardous boom and bust property cycle, particularly in the capital. Much of the foreign capital was supposedly being directed towards infrastructure investment, yet year after year the taxpayer's bill for such projects seemed to increase exponentially. London was seen as a safe haven not just for securing assets but also as a place where assets could be kept from the prying eyes of foreign governments and international investigators. Because in reality, much of the property wealth that was being acquired was merely one part of an enormous money-laundering jigsaw that often stretched across the world. London was cultured, full of friendly politicians that exhibited tremendous animosity to anyone who questioned the pre-eminence of the capital's property empire. Many of the capital's assets were purchased during financial swindles that took place when some sorry second or third world state was headed for trouble. Other assets were the result of oligarchs looking to add a façade of credibility to their dubious financial accounts. In such an environment, people like Hayes and their allies were in perfect positions to offer support. When the Alliance administration was working on a piece of legislation to liberalise overseas property investment, Hayes & Co worked overtime to make sure that the clauses of the Act were as conducive as possible to maximum investment and minimal oversight. Hayes was one of several public figureheads that portrayed themselves as the true friends of would-be property investors. The relationship allowed Hayes to form several lucrative business interests with far-flung individuals. But it wasn't just shady property investors that wanted to take advantage of London's banana republic property market. A number of international firms that wished to expand their horizons wanted to snap up key corporate real estate in order to get themselves on the European map. Hayes once met such a businessman—the head of a new pharmaceutical company headquartered in Belgium—Pinnacle Lab. The firm had developed a problematic reputation in Belgium due to the laboratory testing regime it had developed. Recent relaxations in the UK around drug manufacturing and testing had led the firm to establish a base on Carlton Docks in the capital. Hayes had done much of the groundwork to help make sure the expansion of the firm was smooth and took place with minimal fanfare. He used one of his own ghost companies to assist with the acquisition of buildings and put the company in touch with trusted accountants to process relevant paperwork. Hayes' real handiwork came when it came to passing the relevant pharmaceutical regulatory checks. The National Pharmaceutical Agency (NPA) was, at one point, a notorious and highly praised beacon for high standards in ethics in the field. Its predecessor was wound up by the then government following the atrocities at Kershall Wood. Hayes' father sat on the board of the NPA's predecessor almost as a front for his real activities at Kershall Wood. He was smart enough to keep his ethical public face divorced from his wily personal interests. Alexander Hayes didn't have the medical background to infiltrate the NPA's power structure on a personal basis, but that wasn't really needed. It would actually have been counter-productive in any event. The NPA was better taken care of the traditional way. Hayes and Freedman had made ventures into the NPA as soon as it became apparent that technology breakthroughs would lead to ethical dilemmas for future administrations. Hayes wanted to settle such debates before anybody had a chance to discuss them. Members of the NPA's Compliance Board had served in government under the previous Unity administration. It was enough of a way in for Hayes. As the regulator, Hayes didn't need to go through parliamentary channels; he could go straight to his comrades sitting on the Compliance Board. The Board was supported by advisers that had spent their careers flip-flopping between the private medical industry and the public sector. Hayes and his associates were well-placed to ensure that Pinnacle Lab's compliance hearings went through without major hiccups.

Hayes had asked his associates to meet him at one of his high-brow, and highly-secure, addresses in West London. Samuel Bertrand thought he'd done his job by handing over the information provided by Jermaine, but it turned out that the news had already reached Hayes via another source—Sir Henry Jacob. Bertrand had absolutely no idea how Sir Henry could have gotten hold of such critical knowledge before he did. Who on earth could his informant be? Surely not Jermaine? It had made Bertrand look unreliable in the eyes of Hayes. Hayes now needed to gather his soldiers and plan his next move, but he'd made it clear to Bertrand that his presence wasn't required.

"Well, Olivier. I don't need to convey to you the seriousness of this, do I?" Hayes took it upon himself to lead the discussions. "I have absolutely no idea why the silly fool insists on working around Parliament House. He can do his business at arm's length but he let his ego get the better of him. And now look. What are we supposed to do?"

"We can't let this interfere with our interests." Freedman's tone was sharp and to the point. "I say we give the rabble what they want."

"Are you saying I give up my boy to the scum? You know exactly what he's been doing with your parliamentary chums." barked Olivier Hector. "All those favours he runs for them. They come at a price."

"Look Olivier, you know he's a liability. At worst, what can happen? He'll have to take a back seat in your business interests and be the pantomime villain. Surely you can see that's a small price to pay considering how much you'll make with the Pinnacle Lab venture." Most people wouldn't use someone's son as a bargaining chip, but Freedman knew the amount of money at stake, money that Olivier wouldn't turn down.

"Gentleman. You need to re-engage your sense of perspective. We're on the cusp of something special here. A legacy that nobody will mess with if we play our cards right. So let's give the world one big news story. LGW aren't in healthy financial form Olivier. We don't need them anymore. You'll make a loss now but you'll make a killing with Pinnacle Lab. So, let's give Barratt and that lot what they want. Agreed? It will be an opportunity to show we're on the side of disabled people." Hayes was in a raucous mood as he explained the significance of the situation.

"If Gregory has to go down for something, then he'll want one of your lot to go with him or else he'll cause even more trouble. He's bloody minded. I can't do anything about that." Olivier Hector was stuck in between sounding paternalistic and feeling personally aggrieved. Guy Freedman looked at Hayes for a brief moment before fidgeting with his tie and then his mobile phone.

"Olivier you know he won't be going anywhere. You know we've got agreements with the right people. But in any case— you're right. We need to make it look believable. I suppose Samuel has been of use to us but if Gregory isn't going to play ball we can offer up Samuel to him. Would that be acceptable?"

"It makes sense I suppose," concurred Hayes. "Yes, I suppose it would sort out this issue with Samantha Barratt as well. Bugger. I really wanted to put that cow down once and for all. But, oh well. It's for the greater good I suppose."

"What about Gregory's interests with our fellow parliamentarians? Is there any way we can hand the reins over to someone else? I don't want people getting squirmish." Freedman wanted to ease the blow of losing Gregory Hector in the face of his father's agitation.

"Just a second gentleman. If we're hanging someone out to dry, then I need to know the full details. Also I want a larger cut."

"You what Lakeland? On what grounds?" Hayes was irate at the suggestion.

"The thing with Barratt was one thing—I knew you weren't going to make too much of it. But this is serious. If we're putting away an innocent guy, then I want a bigger cut."

"But he's not innocent! You know what he's been doing! All right. Fine. Five per cent. Is that sufficient?"

"I can agree to that I think." Lakeland smiled as he poured a drink.

"Right well, this is the lowdown Bob so pay attention." Freedman looked at Bob O'Hara in the corner, silent up to this point. "Hector Gregory and some of his old associates from LGW were sub-contracted by the current Parliamentary security team to work across the estate. Now obviously, they didn't realise it was really an LGW Trojan horse so to speak because we'd done a lot of work to get the paperwork in order—you catch my drift, don't you? The situation worked for everyone. I needed trustworthy people based around the estate to be our eyes and ears. Nobody is going to question a uniformed security guard, are they?"

"And what exactly was Gregory getting out of it?" O'Hara was finding it impossible to sit comfortably, ruining one of Hayes' favourite couches in the process.

"Ah well, this is the bit you have to play up. Oh, gents we're not handing the reins over. We give the game up. So basically Bob, Gregory was offering his old security benefits if you know what I mean." Freedman winked at O'Hara.

"No, I don't know what you mean…"

"Do you have a wire on you or are you intentionally being stupid? WELL! He got to know all about how to get dodgy passports and that sort of thing. More importantly working at immigration he was able to collect a list of workers."

"Do you mean workers with iffy credentials or iffy jobs?"

"You know. As they were processing people, he made deals with people. Usually with young women. Nothing too seedy—well some seedy stuff, but we won't go there. He basically got them cleared, and in exchange, they worked for him. He would send them out to work—as cleaners and the like—to our friends. The workers get paid whatever they're told and Gregory was charging clients a premium for the service. So that's the story. Everyone—Barratt included—will think that's the big story that has been hidden. BUT—make sure you make it clear that it was Unity people who went to Lakeland with the info and that it was Alliance people who were taking advantage of the situation. You can say that Samuel was a part of it—taking orders and so on." Freedman was now sitting in front of O'Hara, making sure he understood what needed to be disclosed.

"Guy—actually Bob—when can you get this out there?"

"Tomorrow I think."

"Good. I'll tell Samuel that we've been found out. I'll tell him to co-operate with Lakeland and that I'll get a deal with him. Guy you go and see Samantha Barratt tonight. Tell her you have a full explanation for everything and that you and Terrance are working with Lakeland and the police in order to get things sorted." Hayes seemed pleased that they had broken what looked to be a tricky impasse.

"And what you're arguing is that—while all this is going on—people will be so absorbed in it that we can get on with what we want to do?" Olivier seemed to be acquiescing.

"Precisely!" exclaimed Hayes. "It's my version of burying bad news."

"How is business going Alex? Are we going to schedule?" Olivier was now focussed on their main goal, totally forgetting the trouble he was about to land his son in.

"Oh quite good." Hayes seemed to have ants in his pants and he twitched around on his seat. "Recruitment is going well. Testing is as per expectations. We've had a few drop-outs if you know what I mean but hey ho. It's all for the greater good gentleman."

***

Alexander Hayes wasn't averse to calling in his interns late in the day—or night. He had instructed Bertrand to meet him and Terrence Winchester in Winchester's private office. His mindset was beginning to change ever so slightly. He didn't feel vulnerable, but he was uneasy about the unknown factor of having the recording somewhere out there. He knew he had to move quickly. Hayes told Winchester he didn't want it to look like an ambush, and so made sure he arrived around five minutes after Bertrnad.

"It's quite late gentleman so I take it this is serious." While Winchester and Hayes took their seats, Bertrand felt comfortable enough to poor himself a glass of orange juice.

"I've always looked after you Samuel, so I'm going to be honest with you now." Despite his best efforts Hayes was failing to sound paternalistic. But the look on his face caused Bertrand to leave his drink where it was and come and join the others.

"It's this rubbish with that recording, isn't it?" snapped Bertrand.

"Yes, and we need to protect our interests. Your interests," Winchester said calmly.

"We need to give you and Hector up…" Bertrand was about to start screaming his head off but Hayes stuck his hand up and gestured so that he could finish. "It won't be how you think Sam. Just listen carefully. We're setting a trap for Barratt and all that lot. We want to give the public the impression that the police have discovered something. This thing with Hector couldn't go on forever."

"So what am I supposed to sit in jail while you lot lap it up?" yelled Bertrand.

"I told you it won't be like that. We're going to agree something with Lakeland. From the outside it will look like they're throwing the book at you but you'll be fine. Trust me. Have I let you down so far?" Bertrand was visibly scared. "Does one million sound good to you? I'm raising your share." Bertrand stood up. He was moving his hands as if he wanted to hit something but he was keeping a lid on things.

"Fine. Excuse me you'll forgive me for going to the loo." Bertrand walked off to Winchester's private lavatory.

"Alex…"

"Yes, Terrence I know what you're going to say. He's not got the bottle for it, has he?"

"No. He hasn't."

"Fine. Lakeland and I will take care of it."

Guy Freedman was hovering on Samantha Barratt's porch, waiting for the right time to ring. He saw the light go off and didn't want to miss her so rang the bell quite enthusiastically.

"Ah Samantha. Sorry to drop in like this at such a late hour." Freedman was trying to sound warm.

"Guy. What on earth do you want at this hour?"

"I've got some important news. Can I come in?" Freedman stepped forward, assuming he would be invited in without question.

"Well I guess you better." Barratt wasn't actually dressed for bed. She had turned the lights out because she was about to watch a film. She led Freedman to her kitchen. "Can I get you something to drink?"

"Oh, a glass of water will be fine actually. I'm driving so can't risk it."

"I was actually offering you a cup of tea or coffee but water it is then."

"Oh I see, well yes, water is fine."

"Now what on earth is so important that you have to bother me at home?"

"Well Sam, I've got some good news, to do with your recent incarceration."

"OK then spit it out man!" Barratt didn't seem as excited as Freedman hoped.

"I've been working with Terrance to get to the bottom of what happened. After some sleuthing, we now know, and we've got the people responsible."

"Go on." Barratt perked up.

"Not to go into too much detail, but that file in your room. I know you claimed you had no knowledge of it. And now we can confirm that you were telling the truth. It was put there by Samuel Bertrand."

"SAMUEL BERTRAND?" growled Barratt.

"Yes. I believe he may even be confessing everything to Detective Lakeland as we speak."

"Why the heck is an intern breaking into my office and trying to incriminate me?"

"He'd been under the wing of a corrupt security officer—Gregory Hector. Hector has been running some kind of scam with the help of Bertrand to the benefit of a handful of backbench MPs. After you began asking questions about that demonstration he thought you were on to him and tried to shut you up. I believe Lakeland will brief you fully tomorrow but he said I could tell you now—strictly off the record." Freedman sounded like a doctor giving the wrong patient the all clear.

"I look forward to hearing what he has to say. The tosser!"

"This is a big win for us Sam. We can wrap up the election victory with this—and this will also push us to a strong majority. Unity MPs help to uncover sleaze of government backbenchers. Oh—I'm going to ask Amber and her friend for a photo shoot—no hard feelings and all that jazz." Forever attempting to be the great performer, Freedman was doing a standout job of delivering the news.

"Right...erm..."

"One more thing—Lakeland tells me that some sections of the press have got hold of it. I believe ministers are preparing for a media bloodbath tomorrow."

"Tomorrow?"

"Yes, of course. You know how these tabloids are. You seem more reserved than I had anticipated Samantha. Everything all right?"

"No, I'm fine. Just taking it all." Barratt cracked a smile and let out a soft laugh to divert Freedman's suspicious mind.

"Excellent, well, see you first thing in the morning in the briefing room then."

Barratt walked Freedman to the front door; he smiled, nodded and then exited.

Barratt ran to the phone like a person who'd just discovered their pizza didn't come with the toppings they'd asked for. Dialling furiously, Henrietta Barnes wasn't answering. Finally, on the fifth attempt, Barnes answered.

"Henri you'll never guess what's happened!" The emotion that Barratt had kept concealed was now oozing out.

"What?"

"GUY FREEDMAN has just paid me a visit. He said they've found out what was behind that dodgy file and that assault on Clare Thomas."

"What did he say?—Sorry I've just dropped my mug… Sorry go on, what did he say?"

"Apparently, one of the security people… Gregory…has been up to no good…and he even roped in Samuel Bertrand…one of the interns…to help! Apparently, the media have got hold of it and are running with the story TOMORROW!"

"TOMORROW? But that means—sorry I'm not buying it—where has all this come from?"

"Freedman was over the moon. He said the thing implicates the government but not the opposition. Can we still go with our story?"

"No. Not anymore."

Samantha Barratt sat down to see if she could make sense of what was going on. It was difficult to accept that no senior politician was involved in any of it, but the bottom line was that she didn't have any evidence to prove otherwise. Samuel Bertrand worked for Hayes and Winchester. Perhaps that was the tact she should now take? On the one hand, she couldn't hold them liable for Bertrand's misdemeanours. But surely, if it was proven that he was guilty, it suggested a shocking failure in judgement on their part? In the grand scheme of things, accusing politicians of lapses in judgment didn't count as much of a criticism. It made more sense to go after Winchester. At the end of the day, it was a security issue. Winchester held himself up as the guardian of parliamentary security, but as far as Barratt was concerned, he was just an old fool who had passed his sell by date. Barratt was sure that the allegiance many of her colleagues gave him was superficial, almost as if to not offend his feelings.

Henrietta Barnes was also engaged in a bout of soul searching. Like Barratt, she sensed that there was something more profound going on, but she didn't hold any of the cards to force the issue. Right now though, her caring instincts meant that Clare and Amber were at the forefront of her mind. If there was some greasy politician behind what had been going on, she was sure it would come out eventually; it normally did. She had the patience to wait for the possible eventuality. For now, she was preoccupied with ensuring that Clare achieved a level of contentment. Barnes then did something she hadn't done in a long time. She picked up her mobile and looked for a number in her address book. She looked at it agonisingly before pressing 'call'.

"Hello. Is that Bob?" she semi-whispered.

"Yes, this is Bob. And who might you be?" Came a blunt response.

"It's me, Henrietta Barnes."

"Ah my second favourite, Henri. You could have been first had you played your cards right. What can I do for you Henrietta?" O'Hara seemed jovial but no more flippant than his usual self.

"I've just heard some news?"

"What news is that then?"

"That you have a major story you're running tomorrow."

"You work quickly don't you Henrietta?" laughed O'Hara. "I've only just been given the details literally in the last few minutes."

"Well not as quickly as you or else I would have ran with it myself." Barnes was trying her best to sound cordial.

"Well thankfully our nice friends at the Yard dropped us a few tit bits. Had you been more welcoming of press-police relations they may have given you some info too." O'Hara sounded delighted with himself.

"That's fine but it's just that, well I was hoping you might include a few comments that I've collected from Clare Thomas, one of the main victims of all this? The girl that was dragged from her wheelchair."

"Erm no thanks. The public don't care what some cripple in a wheelchair thinks." O'Hara then put the phone down.

Chapter Seventeen

It was lunacy in the Parliamentary village the following morning. Reporters were running left, right and centre trying to get interviews from politicians and special advisers. *The National* was instigator with cheerleader Bob O'Hara playing his part to perfection. He had given snippets to some of his rivals to ensure there was blanket coverage. One of the major breakfast news shows was carrying an interview with Guy Freedman.

"When will these scandals end Mr Freedman?"

"If I said to you they'd only end when Unity are returned to government, you'd say I was political point scoring when the public want answers…"

"Well you are though, aren't you?"

"No, I'm telling it as it is. What the public want is a guarantee that this nonsense is nipped in the bud once and for all."

"And you can do that, can you?"

"Do you see any Unity politicians involved in this scandal? And who exactly has helped the police with their enquiries? As soon as this palaver came to light, it was Unity that took immediate steps to bring an end to the situation. For the first time, a British political party can't be accused of covering up for its friends." Freedman sounded more statesman-like in his responses than Hayes ever could.

Henrietta Barnes and Samantha Barratt were looking on their smartphones, having breakfast together at a café some distance away from the Parliamentary village.

"What's going on here Henri?" The breakfast atmosphere made Barratt's question sound more casual than what she intended.

"I've no idea. I'd love to get five minutes with Samuel Bertrand. Do you think they'd allow you to do that? Just see what he has to say for himself?"

"No way. I hear they're holding him under the Counter-Terrorism Act. They're justifying it on security grounds." Barratt looked over her shoulder every time a new customer entered the café.

"And what about Hector Gregory?"

"I haven't heard a word about him. Not a peep. I know both were arrested." Barratt looked at her watch. "Lakeland is meant to be briefing me this morning but he hasn't been in touch yet."

"What about these MPs then? Four have stepped down today. Aren't they going to be prosecuted?"

"I honestly don't know."

Lakeland had been temporarily detained by Hayes and Freedman. It was important for them to agree as much of the show trial as possible. They were well-aware that now that the story was all over the media, it was more difficult for them to control the output, regardless of whether the likes of O'Hara kept up their end of the bargain. It would be foolish of them to attempt to clear up all traces of complicity. They just needed to erase any evidence pointing to the more illicit activities that Gregory had provided for. Hayes knew exactly where to start. With Alliance reduced to its knees, now was the time to pressurise some of its more vulnerable members. Hayes picked up his mobile. In actual fact, Alexander Hayes had a number of secure mobile phones, a tactic he must have picked up from watching or liaising with high-level drug dealers or people traffickers.

"Home Secretary!" he bleated joyfully.

"What do you want you little…!" It was the voice of a wounded animal, hanging on desperately for survival, but seeing its herd disappearing into the horizon, and now abandoned, vulnerable to one final killer blow.

"Now now Home Secretary. You knew the risks of what you were getting yourself into. But don't worry. I have an offer for you that will make it all go away."

"What?"

"We have friends in the telecommunications industry, who I'm sure would be willing to dispose themselves of certain call logs and other bits that might be looked upon unfavourably."

"All right so what do you want in return?" It was a squealed response.

"I want you to bin the new safeguards to the Counter-Terrorism Act that people are going mad over. I don't care how you do it. Just work with whoever you need in order to get the implementation scrapped."

"But that's political suicide!" came another booming reply.

"Home Secretary. Hasn't the penny dropped? You're already going down. I'm just giving you an easy way out. How would you rather bow out? Do you want the likes of Bob O'Hara spreading your filthy laundry all over the front pages?"

There was silence for a few moments. "Fine! I want proof you're going to keep your side of the bargain. By 3pm today!" He then put the phone down.

None of the politicians that had been using Hector Gregory's services were going to be prosecuted. Freedman had met with the relevant individuals the previous evening after having left Samantha Barratt's place in order to confirm exactly what their defences were going to be. A combination of blissful ignorance and claims of deceit on the part of Gregory would prove enough to dissuade the public prosecutor from taking the cases all the way. That would mean more outrage from the public aimed at the Alliance Administration, and that would give Unity even further cause for joy.

Amber couldn't get hold of Clare or Samantha Barratt. The last she had heard was that the story was going to be broken that day. Upon seeing the front page of *The National* Amber was totally scatterbrained. The outcome was what she wanted but she instantly knew that there was a lot more going on here.

"Amber who are you trying to phone exactly?" Amber's fussy behaviour in the office had caught the attention of Marcus. She didn't bother responding. Instead she rushed to the cloakroom to collect her jacket.

"Sorry I need to go home for a little bit. I'll be back soon."

"Is everything O…" Amber was already out the door before Marcus could finish his enquiry. Amber went straight to the committee building so that she could speak to Jermaine. She knew it would be ridiculous if she just stormed up there so instead she sent him a text asking him if he could meet her in one of the local cafés. It wasn't too far from midday so Jermaine agreed.

"You're definitely sure you didn't tell them that we had evidence of the demonstration?"

"For the final time yes! As far as they're concerned, you were bugging me, and that's it. I told them I didn't share anything."

"Well then that leaves an interesting question, doesn't it?"

"What's that then?" Jermaine was tucking into a very late vegetarian English breakfast.

"What are they hiding? There's no way they'd just publish something like this without a good reason. I mean what's going on? Have you heard anything up in the committee rooms? Lots of MPs go up and down there all the time? Have you heard anything?" Amber didn't want to come across like a pest but that's how Jermaine was probably interpreting her constant questions.

"No. Not anything out of the ordinary. The atmosphere is quite feverish but other than that the others tell me this is pretty much what it's like when a major scandal breaks. Press Officers are all over the place. Journalists running around parliamentary village. People glued to the television screens and radio to see who is doing the next interview. This is all par the course apparently."

"Nah, this is bollocks. We're missing something man. I don't know what it could be though. These guys, they don't just give up one of their own without a good reason." Amber flung her head back and untied the knot in her hair before tying it up again.

"What do you mean by 'these guys'—are you talking about your boss?"

"I don't know!" Amber's voice was crippled and depleted.

"Well if I hear anything out the ordinary I'll let you know."

Amber left the committee building and began the short walk back to the private offices. Although it was now lunchtime, Amber thought it best she show her face quickly rather than be absent for a further hour. It was unusually mild so she decided to take the longer route back. Amber quickly detected a commotion coming from somewhere close to Parliament House. Amber spun round the corner to see a small demonstration taking place near one of the main entrances of the complex. None of these demonstrators were in wheelchairs. There weren't actually too many of them. They weren't young people either. Most of the participants seemed to be quite mature in age. A number of chants relating to clean government could be heard. Just a few feet away, a number of Parliamentary security personnel were standing around. There couldn't have been no more than six or seven. Television cameras had been set up early that morning across the Parliamentary estate.

The group were receiving plenty of exposure. Away from the main crowd, a couple of the demonstrators had pulled away so that they could give interviews to reporters that were standing by.

Amber's phone began to buzz in her jacket so she took a few paces in order to move away from the noise.

"Amber it's Henrietta."

"Henrietta! Where on earth have you been? I've been trying to get hold of you and Samantha Barratt but it's been impossible."

"Sorry Amber we've been trying to run around to see if we can get a word with Samuel Bertrand but he's being kept strictly under wraps."

"Have you heard anything then? Do we know why this story has been published in the way it has?" Amber was in an odd position. On one level the front pages should have put a massive grin on her face, but now she was looking for something that undermined the story in some way.

"Right now it's difficult to say. But Bertrand obviously works for Hayes so he's clearly involved somewhere. I don't buy this bullshit that Unity MPs have uncovered all this. I don't care if people accuse me of being a conspiracy theorist." The wind was blowing hard as Barnes was talking.

"I don't understand what's gone on here. Jermaine tells Samuel about some iffy video footage, Samuel does his job by telling his boss and then Samuel himself gets done. Has he taken one for the team then? Or is Hayes punishing him for something else? Because whatever the case I don't think any of this has come out for the greater good if you know what I mean."

"Samuel DEFINITELY wasn't on that footage, was he?" Barnes was now shouting because of the wind.

"No, definitely not."

"Then he wouldn't have incriminated himself. He's not stupid. Maybe he and Hector Gregory REALLY ARE working together. BUT I DON'T GET IT!" Barnes was exasperated; she sounded like her eyeballs were about to explode.

"He was seriously bugging Jermaine."

"So are we saying Samuel got the footage, and knowing it would implicate him, he panicked and then went to Hayes for protection? Hayes is smart. He probably rightly estimated that it wasn't the only version, or else I can't imagine them feeding their chaps to the sharks. It's made them look really good it has to be said. They've taken a massive gamble and it's working for them. Amber do you know where Clare is?"

"No, I've no idea. I can't get hold of her or Mrs Thomas. Why?"

"Samantha Barratt told me that they were going to get her and some of the other demonstrators down to Parliament for an apology of some kind."

"I'll let you know if I hear anything." Amber hung up and ran back to Portcullis House.

***

The reason why Amber was unable to get hold of Clare was because Clare had managed to get herself booked on a pre-recorded show for the First Broadcasting Service. The broadcast was part of a book launch by Carl Kelly from the Grove Chambers Institute. He had written a book supposedly providing evidence of how receiving or not receiving benefit money had a direct impact on personality and social development. Kelly's presence had been protested at a handful of university campuses but beyond that the book had received little attention. It was about to get a major boost through this interview to be broadcast on national television. Clare was on a consultation panel for the broadcaster. She was one of a number of individuals who had applied to be participants in debates that impacted certain sections of society. There was no payment. First Broadcasting Service put more of an effort than most to make sure where possible it engaged regular members of the public. Their first choice on this occasion had pulled out, so Clare got the call.

"Carl Kelly, we often hear about the idea of entitlement but what does it mean?"

"I think when the British public hear the word entitlement, they want it to be synonymous with fairness. I feel there is a perception that such a link has been broken."

"But fairness is a moral concept, and your book seems to evade that little bugger quite well, doesn't it?" Sir Richard Willis was going to try his best to test Kelly.

"Well my book tackles the matter at an economic and social level I never had any intention of venturing into."

"What. Nonsense..." blasted Clare.

"Clare Thomas you don't sound like you're impressed."

"No. I… I'm. Not. I'm not saying…he's going to intentionally." Clare had spent days saving her remaining energy to take part in the interview but it was still a struggle "But whether he likes it or not…he's passing judgment on people like me."

"How exactly am I doing that? The book is backed up by research that's difficult to argue against."

"But there are lots of pieces of research in this area that are, shall we say, more humane than yours?" Sir Richard sensed what Clare wanted to say and decided to ask rather than wait for her to follow up.

"Sir Richard I think the public will take my conclusions for what they are: a confirmation of what they've been thinking but too scared to say in public for fear of being shot down."

"Oh. Here… We. Go. Do you not read…newspapers? Do you…not listen to the radio?" Clare's breathing was quite heavy but she was soldiering on in good manner. "Do you…not read the internet? There are loads of people…that harp on about this sort of thing… What you're saying is…anyone…who wants to challenge you…is somehow a threat…in reality you want to…say what you have to say…without being challenged."

"I'm sorry, that's crazy. As you say, these debates are happening in many spheres and people of opposing views are the ones that are having them." Kelly was unyielding.

"So this idea of certain people being shot down is nonsense then? We seem to have a new documentary or reality show about this subject every week, don't we?"

"Yes but…" Kelly began to respond but Sir Richard came back with a trademark interruption.

"Carl Kelly, tell us then in layman's terms what is the jist of your book's argument? What do you think is happening and what do you want to see happen?"

Kelly at one point seemed to be getting just a tad visibly flustered with how slow Clare was answering questions but straightened his back and cleaned his glasses now that Willis had given him an invitation to do so.

"What we're saying is, Sir Richard and Clare, that being in receipt of state support can, when approaching certain levels and for certain lengths of time, have a detrimental impact on society and personal development. It essentially creates a mindset, with a set of associated behaviours, that I personally think, leaves us a number of challenges to overcome."

"I.e. the benefit bill and unemployment?"

"That's right Sir Richard."

"This is just…pure bandwagoning." Clare hurtled back into the debate.

"What do you mean by bandwagoning Clare?"

"Hypothetically speaking, if…the government…said today…that the entire…benefits system…was going…to be…abolished…would that be enough…to placate people like you?"

"That's absurd. Nobody is suggesting anything like that and to suggest it is pure fear-mongering."

"Fear-mongering? The only…people doing…that are…the politicians and media…drip…feeding…stories…about conniving…disabled people."

"Carl Kelly what sort of solutions are you suggesting the government follow?" Sir Richard saw that Clare was breathing increasingly heavy and thought that was a good moment to push the conversation along. But Clare wasn't having it.

"Carl…how does…science contribute to this debate…exactly?"

"I think it can show us where we're going wrong in some areas."

"But…what does…science have…to do…with it?" Clare was a lot calmer now. "Why are we…concentrating…on the scientific findings…related to benefit use only? Scientists and researchers highlight the human downside…of lots of…government policy and nobody listens. Better employment rights and more accessible…buildings or whatever. What makes these…findings so special?"

"Clare makes a good point doesn't she Mr Kelly? Governments seem to have a pick and mix attitude when it comes to using evidence to make policy, don't they?" Sir Richard was pleased with how Clare was doing. The danger with such engagements was that the expert would bombard their opponent with random statistics to put them off, but Clare was holding her own.

"No, I don't think so. I think, what it comes down to is willpower. In some areas, the willpower is greater than in others that's all."

"Is it…willpower…or is it…that you know…the public will let you get away with it…as we're seen as different?" Clare managed to nip in another question before Sir Richard was able to.

"There is a debate to be had there I admit. As in a government doing something perceived to be morally questionable. But to be frank, if the measure has the support of the public, can it still be regarded as immoral?"

"OF COURSE IT CAN! The public…can't be used…as a benchmark…of morality. Especially when you…consider the…freak show—let's gape at this person to make ourselves feel better—mentality that has developed in this country…"

"I'm sorry both but that's a discussion for the lecture theatres I think… Clare Thomas do you think the modern definition of entitlement has become detached from what it was from when the Welfare State was set up?" Sir Richard now put Clare on the spot.

"I think…we're going backwards. House prices, stagnant…pay, the gig…economy, stupidly high tuition fees. Normal people…are being asked…to stump up…increasing amounts of money at a time…when money is increasingly hard…to come by…and it's people like me suffering the brunt. I go to a Job Centre…and they offer…me a cleaning job. LOOK AT ME!" Clare growled ferociously. "Would you offer…me a cleaning…job Carl?"

"No, of course not that was a terrible mistake in my eyes."

"How much…have we really progressed…really? Since things like Kershall Wood? That was science…wasn't it? My own grandmother…was a victim of it…and because of what they did to her…here I am, a victim today." Clare's revelation caused Kelly and Sir Richard to stumble in their words, before taking a few seconds to gather themselves.

"Yes, but Clare everyone has acknowledged that was junk science and the perpetrators were totally discredited. We've come light years since then." Kelly attempted to sound earnest and sombre.

"Well, thank you both I'm afraid we're going to have to leave it there. Carl Kelly's book is out now, and if Clare had a book, I'd tell you when that was released as well, but for now, thank you Clare Thomas." Clare felt the need to smile following Sir Richard's closing remarks. It was the most natural smile she'd expressed in a long time.

***

Terrance Winchester had convened an emergency session of the Principal Security Committee in order to reassure Members and the public following the recent developments. Winchester knew how to sweet-talk even the most persistent of inquisitors. On paper he had a lot to answer for. Being Chair of the Security Committee wasn't like the chairmanship of other get-togethers. Winchester was privy to discussions in the most intimate parts of government. He knew everything from the contingency security arrangements of the Prime Minister to the dietary requirements of the most senior members of the security services. It was the cumulative advantage of being in a post for such a long time without challenge. There was no direct questioning of his competence during the entire session. Most of the talk was around Hector Gregory and Samuel Bertrand. Gregory was the subject of the majority of the inquisition. It had been disclosed that due to his links to an overseas government, rather than being prosecuted in the UK, he would be sent back without any chance of return. That's what Hayes and Freedman meant when they said he'd have to take a backseat. As for Samuel Bertrand, the story being conjured up by the likes of Bob O'Hara seemed to be filtering into the imaginations of the lay observer. A storm of questions was beginning to be asked. Who did Bertrand work for? Which foreign government had he signed up to? How much information had he managed to obtain? And what was he doing with it? The provisions of the Counter-Terrorism Act meant that officials didn't have to answer any of these questions for fear of jeopardising an investigation that was crucial to national security. A discussion show in the early evening largely reflected on the dangers of foreign powers and what could happen if someone had indeed infiltrated the heart of government. Watching on, Amber found it all phantasmagorical. How on earth had an act of dishonesty perpetrated by an Englishman turned into a debate about the defence of the realm and the dangers of crazy foreigners?

There was one last task for Hector Gregory to perform before he was banished from the land. Guy Freedman had arranged a photo opportunity so that the cameras could capture a public apology given to Clare. Freedman had first suggested that the apology take plan a few yards from the main chamber in Parliament House so that plenty of politicians could stand around and look good in the background. But getting there was so inaccessible Mrs Thomas insisted the meeting happen somewhere else. Clare demanded that the meeting take place at the exact same location as the original demonstration, and Freedman was in no position to argue. It was mid-afternoon and the sunshine made for a crisp and perky day. As Clare and her mother approached the area, a scrum of cameras swarmed all over them. Many of them were so engrossed they failed to detect they were creating an obstacle for mother and daughter to get passed.

"Can you get out the bloody way please!" screamed a member of the Parliamentary security team that had come to assist them. The team eventually formed a cordon around mother and daughter as they approached the meeting place. Guy Freedman and Terrance Winchester were waiting there to greet them both.

"Ah, wonderful! I'm so glad you agreed to come!" enthused Freedman. He bent down to shake Clare's hand. Seeing that she was struggling to form a hand in order to shake his, he warmly rubbed his hand on the back of hers and smiled joyfully. "Let me introduce you to Terrance Winchester, one of Parliament's senior MPs in the area of security." Winchester clicked into gear and approached Clare and her mother.

"Good afternoon Clare, Mrs Thomas. Thank you for coming out on this bright but chilly afternoon. I understand that this sort of cold can be an issue for you Clare. We'll get this done as quickly as we can. But before we get to Hector I'd like to formally apologise to you first. I take these sorts of security issues incredibly serious and I am SO sorry about what happened. I've seen the video and it's absolutely disgusting. Thanks to you we'll be making changes around here. I'm just so upset they had to come about in these circumstances." Grace and affection reverberated as he spoke. Winchester gestured to Mrs Thomas to push Clare along the path set by the security cordon. It was only around ten to fifteen metres before they reached their destination. Clare could make out Gregory standing with two of his representatives. The three of them stood forward, but Clare gestured to the two intruders to walk away so Gregory was left alone. Gregory stood there as Mrs Thomas pushed the wheelchair to within a few centimetres of him. The cameras had now made a second cordon around Clare, her mother and Gregory, which was the cue for him to begin his apology.

"Mrs Thomas, Clare… My name is Hector Gregory—but obviously you already know that." Gregory was doing an excellent job of stuttering right from the beginning. "I am the one responsible for inflicting those injuries upon you at the demonstration you attended. That behaviour was, well, I don't have the words. I've humiliated myself and my family, but above all, I've injured an inspirational young lady. I don't know what you've read about me in the papers but that really isn't me. I'm a businessman and sometimes I'm guilty of bad judgement. And I made probably…the worst decision of my life on that day. So today, I extend a hand of friendship to you and extend my apologies to you, sincerely and unreservedly." An exhausted Clare tried to speak but the energy had been zapped out of her. She simply looked up to her mother, who was standing over her, and made a circle gesture with her finger. Mrs Thomas retracted and turned the wheelchair and began to push Clare in the direction they had just come from. Hector Gregory stood where he was, not knowing whether to chase after them or simply go back to his representatives. He glanced at Freedman. Freedman had his arms folded and waived three of his fingers to indicate to Gregory to walk away. He then walked over to Clare and Mrs Thomas and began talking to them while escorting them back to the specially arranged transport that he had set up.

Chapter Eighteen

Jermaine had decided to join Amber and Veronica on their planned walk around as part of their preparations for the pre-election march. The town planners had done the best to make the outside of Parliament Bridge Station as annoying as possible by placing pot trees in the most ridiculous positions. They were merely a good place to leave leftovers from lunch or have a cigarette. They provided no aesthetic benefits whatsoever. The main benefits of using the station were the large concourses outside. They were able to hold several hundred people at the busiest times. The friends had discussed the idea of postponing the march at one point due to the revelations about Hector Gregory. It was Amber who pushed for things to go ahead. As far as she was concerned, the group had some momentum following the recent series of events and they needed to take advantage. Although she wasn't present at the dummy run, Clare had done an excellent job of mobilising online support for the march, and the figure was now reaching ten thousand participants. Henrietta Barnes and other progressive voices had talked about the march in their respective publications too. What was initially an intimate fight for justice had now become something much bigger, and Amber could only see the positives.

"This looks all right, doesn't it? I mean under the circumstances I think this was a good shout Amber. If we're gonna have lots of blindfolded people, we can't make it too much of a walk purely to be safe." Veronica whizzed around the pot trees with Jermaine and Amber on her shoulders.

"So ladies—the route itself is actually pretty straightforward. I'm just having a look at these things that the police liaison sent to you. Because they are closing a few more roads than what we expected it should be relatively straightforward."

"Veronica I'm going to be really cheeky mate! If I push you, would you be happy to jot down landmarks and that kind of thing that we walk passed. I want to send it out to everyone through our various online networks." Veronica happily took the pen and pad Amber was holding.

"How's Clare guys? Have you two heard anything?" Jermaine paused for a second as he put some headphones on.

"She's stable for now, Jay. She's on some new meds isn't she Amber?"

"That's right. They've changed her medication quite frequently in recent months so let's hope this one helps."

The trio had been moving along their intended route for the march at a relaxed pace. About ten minutes into their trek, a beautiful vintage blue Mercedes decided to join them. There was no way any of the three would notice. The roads were actually quite busy and they weren't taking too many twists or turns, trying to keep the route as straightforward as possible. Amber popped into a shop to buy some chewing gum. When she came out she saw the Mercedes pull up and put its hazard lights on. She didn't think anything of it until someone stuck their head out of the window.

"Amber!"

"GILES?" Amber walked to the curb of the road to make sure her eyes and ears weren't deceiving her. Jermaine and Veronica looked just as surprised.

"Without wanting to freak you out, do you have a few minutes?"

"Erm yea sure…" Giles Gibbs flicked his head to indicate to her to get in the back of the car.

"You two go on and finish the rec, I'll catch up with you this evening." And with that Amber hopped into the back of the Mercedes.

"This is a bit…strange Giles. Not that it isn't good to see you or anything…"

"Would you like a drink? No booze I'm afraid. Just orange juice… If you lift up the armrest, you'll find a couple of cans."

"Yea sure…" Amber gently lifted the arm to reveal a couple of warm bottles of orange juice.

"Darling could you just drive us around the Parliamentary village a few times."

"Hi Mrs Gibbs. Hope you're well." Giles' wife looked into the mirror and smiled but didn't say anything.

"So, err, how are things Giles? How can I help you?" Amber was more curious than nervous. If this was the back of Guy Freedman's car, she'd be terrified.

"It's nothing Amber. I had a chat with Samantha Barratt. She got me up to speed with some of the things that have been going on. Her arrest, your friend's demonstration, this thing with that lad who got arrested." Gibbs was totally frozen, looking straight ahead while talking to Amber.

"Well it looks like everyone believes the whole nonsense with Samuel."

"I take it then you don't believe it?" Gibbs took a sip from the bottle of mineral water he was holding in his hand.

"No, I don't actually. He may well have played a key role along with that Gregory bloke. There's got to be something more." Amber had no issue with letting her guard down with Gibbs. Whenever they'd met he'd always been pleasant and accommodating.

"You're not wrong Amber."

"How do you mean?" Amber suddenly felt her toes begin to twitch. She was more than happy to share her thoughts, but at no point was she expecting Gibbs to concur.

"Don't you see? You're absolutely right. These things don't just happen. It's every politician's dream to blame everything on the Civil Service or some administrative function or whatever. They've just announced a route and branch enquiry into Parliament House's procurement and contracting operations. Nobody cares about how Gregory or Bertrand got so close to the centre of government. The truth would be too much to handle. They just want to reinstall confidence in the system." Gibbs' volatile words weren't matched by his demeanour; he wasn't flinching or changing colour.

"So what are you trying to tell me Giles? If everyone is barking up the wrong tree, which tree should we be barking up?" The weightiness of Gibbs' words was dawning on Amber, and her voice had now lost any sense of casualness.

"I'd say it's more a question of which sewer you need to wade through. Samantha told me she's already given you an indication as to where your eyes should really be focussed."

"Has she? I don't recall…oh my days! Guy and Alexander Hayes? But I don't think she meant anything outrageously sinister—she was just saying they're a bit funny. But what is it exactly? What have they done?" Amber recalled her initial meeting with Samantha

Barratt, but, in all honesty, if she'd really thought Hayes and Freedman were an immediate threat, then surely she wouldn't have maintained cordial relations with them in the way she had?

"They haven't done anything. It's what they want to do. But people from the outside can never make anything stick. It's like dealing with never ending Russian dolls."

"But Giles—no offence or anything—but most people regard you as one of them. So why are you warning me about them? And why haven't you spoken out about it yourself?" Amber was now fearful, but all the while Gibbs continued to be passive. If something momentous was being disclosed, he wasn't making a big deal out of it.

"It's true. We've got too much invested in each other. But I don't appreciate someone using my disabled daughter as cover to gain political capital. That's them Amber. That's not me." At long last, a pinch of emotion could be heard from Gibbs. It was as if he was trying to restrain himself, but his paternal instincts were forcing him into action.

"So why the heck are you telling me all this? I'm a nobody. What do you want me to do? If this is some sort of confession, you've totally picked the wrong person. And if it's just a warning, I've had enough of those!" Amber wanted to bang her head on the window. Gibbs didn't answer her questions.

"I saw how you were with your friend Clare at the restaurant. Remember? How you feel about her doesn't even come close to how I feel about my daughter Jessica." Amber wasn't sure if she should be offended by the remark, but she didn't have time to think as Gibbs continued to talk. "You see that folder. Take it. It contains information about one of Hayes' interests. Get to the bottom of that and you'll see. But be careful. The guy Lakeland from the Met is in Hayes and Freedman's pocket. They've got a few."

"What? Do you have proof? Can't we go to the po…"

"Take this. As far as I know, this is the name of a clean officer."

"He…"

"SHOOSH! Don't say the name out loud!"

"Why?"

"Protect yourself at all times Amber. I don't know if this car is bugged. I have it scanned regularly enough. I don't want to get anybody else in trouble."

"But you've just told me! So if it is bugged I'll get into trouble too!" Amber was slowly becoming petrified. Gibbs then turned around for the one and only time and face Amber.

"You're already in trouble Amber. You don't take a knife and fork to a rib eating contest. If you get to the bottom of that paperwork, you'll be all right." Amber sat back in her seat and didn't say another word. Gibbs dropped Amber off close to where he had initially picked her up and then sped off. Amber couldn't decide if she should call Henrietta Barnes there and then or wait a while. *What had just actually happened?* On the face of it, it was the most unnatural thing. A recently retired politician having a heart to heart with a powerless intern? Amber didn't want to admit it, but for her own safety she had to. It was clear what was going on here. All those funny feelings about things not being right were crystallising into cold hard facts. She couldn't give Gibbs the benefit of the doubt any longer. She had clearly caused Freedman too much trouble, and Gibbs had just set her up in an enormous bear trap. He even had the audacity to tell her what was coming. She now had dynamite in her hands, and all that was required was for a police officer or knock on her door and do the formalities. Her knees were turning to custard as she thought about her predicament. *Screw it!* If she was about to be taken to the cleaners, she may as well do as much as she could while she had time. Her anger towards Gibbs was causing her to squeeze her hands together in fury. She wasn't going to trust a politician again.

***

Lakeland came bursting into Alexander Hayes' office. Hayes had a number of his aides there and instructed them to leave immediately. Lakeland made sure the door was firmly shut.

"What's wr…"

"One of our trackers began to tweak." Lakeland was jumpy.

"Which one?"

"The one in Giles Gibbs' car."

"What was he saying?" Hayes was chewing the end of his pen, not really showing a sense of fear or apprehension.

"Just telling that intern of Guy's…"

"Amber?"

"Yea—he didn't tell her enough—but he gave her something to look into. A file or something. Do you want me to take care of it?"

"Yes. But wait. Let me talk to him first." Hayes' response was scintillatingly cold. Using his fourth mobile of the day, he dialled Gibbs' number. "Giles Giles Giles."

Gibbs was silent for a few seconds while he evaluated Hayes' tone.

"So you were listening? You f..." exhilarated anger pierced every word.

"Well, of course. I'm a good friend. That's what good friends do. It's important to know what's troubling our loved ones. But you clearly haven't been a good to that lady-friend of yours. We'll catch up with her soon enough. You know we will." Hayes had a barbaric sense of cordiality as he spoke.

"She's a smart girl. She isn't scared..."

"Unlike the pathetic little toad you've turned out to be! Don't worry. We'll take care of it." Hayes sensed quickly Gibbs wasn't about to give anything up. After hanging up, he looked at Lakeland, who was still standing in front of him, and indicated with his fingers to get out the room and get on with things.

***

The death of Giles Gibbs was front page news for days. A number of documentaries and interviews were broadcast, featuring friend and foe. There was universal consensus that the imminent death of his daughter was more than he could handle. And it was now left to his wife to pick up the pieces and move on with her remaining children. Gibbs' suicide note was only disclosed a few days after the death. "Jessica. No one will ever believe how much your mother and I loved you. It's difficult to explain to people how much happiness you gave us. Your giggles. Your smiles. Your adorable little sneezes. When the world around us looked to make excuses for your non-existence all we ever had in our hearts was overwhelming joy. And now, you're about to leave us, and it's all too much for me, princess. People will ask why I never stood up for you or people like you. If you ever felt I wasn't there for you, then I'm utterly sorry. I don't care if anyone else doesn't understand, as long as you do. If I have failed you, then I deserve what's coming to me. I'll love you forever. Daddy."

Jessica had taken several turns for the worst, and the doctors had informed mother and father that the end was near, and for Giles Gibbs, that signalled his end too. Most of the debate afterwards revolved around the philosophical undertones of Gibbs writing a suicide note to his daughter—the one person who would never be able to read it. There was a defined arrogance to these mutterings. The discussions had the mark of people who never felt close to someone beyond artificial pleasantries. People who perceived the relationship of parent and offspring through a quid pro quo conundrum. Gibbs had been found shot in his car. His own private revolver, a memento from his army days, dangling from his hand. Lakeland was obviously irritated in the days that followed. Had he waited a day or so Gibbs would have done his job for him. But it was no skin off his nose. He had a job to do and he'd done it. Years of police work had given him precise knowledge of what a suicide looked like from a forensics perspective.

Amber had left her internship role at Guy Freedman's office after her encounter with Giles Gibbs. As an intern, she was fortunate that there was no need to serve out a notice period, and Isabelle had kindly agreed to give her a reference if she obtained a job. Most important of all, however, was that she didn't have to face Freedman to resign; she simply notified one of his aides. That didn't stop her from being at the forefront of Freedman's mind. Hayes had asked him to find out what Gibbs had given to Amber. The execution of Giles Gibbs only completed part of the job. Freedman assigned the task to Lakeland. For the time being Amber held all the cards. There was no way Lakeland could admit to the car being bugged, so he had to take a cautious approach to begin with. And with so much upheaval already having taken place, for the time being, there wasn't an appetite for any underhand tactics towards Amber. But Hayes' patience would only go so far. Sooner or later he'd want the matter settled. Lakeland and a uniformed officer knocked on Amber's door, and that's where Amber was intent on holding any conversation.

"Hello Amber. I believe you already know who I am. May I come in?" Lakeland was annoyed at having to go through these legal motions. For a police officer, he surprisingly lacked the strategic nous that could be found in someone like Alexander Hayes.

"No sorry, we're about to have a family get together. We'll have to talk here." Amber had a towel in her hand which was acting as a useful prop, but she was trembling. She couldn't believe Gibbs had killed himself. Yet from her perspective this left only one explanation, an explanation that left her terror-stricken and fearing for her safety. She was making sure the front door was only partially open, with Lakeland just about able to see her forehead and brown eyes. All this, while also suffering from the heavy weight of guilt. Gibbs had been truthful all along and had possibly given her something that could turn the tables on her pursuers.

"Very well. We're just clearing up some formalities regarding Giles Gibbs' death. Don't want anyone accusing us of conspiracy theories or anything like that. The GPS from his car indicated he stopped outside a shop a few days ago near Parliament Bridge. We went down there and the CCTV caught you jumping into his car. Is that right?" Lakeland was happy to reveal this information, as it was the kind of thing he'd disclose during a more normal investigation.

"Yep that's right. Mrs Gibbs was there too."

"That's fine I wanted to ask about his state of mind. How did he seem? Did he say anything out of the ordinary? To be honest I didn't realise you too were close." Lakeland was making light-hearted attempts to fish for information.

"Well oddly enough—although we always got along—we weren't close in that sense. But I always liked him though. I've no idea why he wanted to talk to me of all people."

"So what did you talk about?"

"Nothing. He just talked about his daughter. So yes—she was on his mind. But I could never have expected something like this."

"Yes, well, it was a shock to all of us." Lakeland was trying his best to sound forlorn. In his case, news that Gibbs had left a suicide note was the biggest shock. "If you remember anything else, here's my card." Lakeland and his colleague turned away and walked back to their car. They sat in the car, running over their next steps. Lakeland was jumping out of his skin to just get on with it, but Hayes had instructed him to hold fire momentarily. Hayes felt that at some point Amber would fully implicate the people that she relied on most. Using the security and surveillance at his disposal, if he could take everyone out in one swoop, it would make life easier in the long run.

In her living room, Amber was having a get-together—but not the family variety. She had invited Henrietta Barnes, Veronica, Samantha Barratt and Samantha's sister, Helen Barratt. Helen Barratt was a detective in the Metropolitan Police and it was her name that Giles Gibbs had given to Amber. They had all met up to discuss the file Gibbs had also passed over. Lakeland had yet to start twenty-four hour surveillance of Amber's house or else he may well have moved in right away. Nor had he managed to get Hayes' friends in the telecoms industry to intercept Amber's phone calls. As each new request went through, so the financial compensation increased to, and as a result, Lakeland was unable to proceed with further targets until Hayes had said so. As far as Hayes was concerned, Amber was just an inbred member of the public. There was no point in wasting valuable resources on someone so pathetic.

"So what are we looking at Helen?" Henrietta Barnes didn't really want a methodical breakdown. She wanted the essentials and more importantly if there was anything there to nail Hayes or Freedman.

"It's high level forensic accountancy. It's detailing information about ghost companies and that kind of thing. Much of it associated with Pinnacle Lab. It's a pharmaceutical firm." Detective Barratt was flicking back and forth through the documents.

"Yea I know them," snapped Amber. "As far as I'm aware, their boss is quite friendly with Alexander Hayes... Oh sorry, do you guys want anything else to drink?" Everyone smiled and shook their head.

"Well there is certainly enough here for Hayes to answer a few questions. Embarrass him a little." Detective Barratt was highlighting sections as if she was revising for an exam.

"Henrietta is there enough here for a front page article? Will your bosses go for it?" Veronica was animated, but Samantha Barratt attempted to note some caution.

"Are we sure we can go with this stuff? For all we know Gibbs was just trying to feed Amber nonsense in the hope of her taking this to the police and causing an embarrassment to the Met by making them chase geese."

"I sent a copy to Helen and she had one of her people take a look at it. As far as we can tell, it's all legit. That's right, isn't it Helen?" Amber didn't appreciate Samantha Barratt insinuating chronic gullibility on her part, but she didn't make anything of it.

"Yes, based on what my guys have, the numbers and the documents are all genuine. Hayes definitely has some questions to answer. It will definitely make him feel uncomfortable. He'll try his best to dismiss it as typical accounting practice and get a load of his mates in the industry to back him up and give interviews to people like Bob O'Hara." Detective Barratt seemed happy enough.

"Right, that's good enough for me," exclaimed Barnes. "And it's not like they're going to ask about the source—if they do—we'll tell them the truth. That'll shut them up for a while." Barnes seemed to be caught between delight and over-confidence.

"But Henrietta, what about the warning Giles gave me? What was he getting at?" Amber began to twitch nervously.

"To be honest I'm not sure. If he's talking about some of their immoral policy positions, I've been documenting all that for ages. None of that is new to people who've been following them for a long time."

"No, it's something more I... OH MY DAYS! OH MY DAYS!" Amber looked like she was about to have a fit.

"What's wrong Amber?" Veronica and the others were taken aback by Amber's outburst.

"I think I've overlooked something! Can you all wait here? I'll be back in half an hour!" Amber shot out of her chair quicker than a mouse trying to evade its captor and ran out the door without even bothering to put on a jacket.

Amber darted across a number of streets, somehow managing not to slip or trip over anything. Lakeland was still parked outside and began a calm pursuit, taking care not to get too close. Narrowly escaping being hit by a car, she finally slowed down when reaching a street of terraced houses. She approached the door at the end of the road and pressed the buzzer five times, not caring if it annoyed the inhabitants. It didn't take long for someone to come to the door.

"Flippin' 'eck Amber, are you all right? You look like you're about to have a heart attack! What on earth is wrong?"

"Sorry to bother you at home, Izzy. I really need your help with something." Amber put her arm on Isabelle's shoulder so she could get her breath back.

"Yea sure do you want to come in?"

"No sorry. I know this is ridiculous, me bothering you like this but I don't have time. Do you remember that meeting you had with

Guy Freedman and Sir Henry? The one Marcus and I dropped you in?"

"Yes, what about it?"

"Remember you said you recorded it on your phone? Could you send me the file? It's deadly important, Izzy." The oxygen was beginning to reinvigorate Amber.

Without questioning her any further, Isabelle dipped into her jeans pocket and pulled her phone out. She began to fidget with the buttons for a few moments.

"There. I've emailed it to you. So what's this all about?"

"How much did you listen to?"

"Just the meeting bit."

"This is just a punt. Izzy you better come with me." Amber was worked up like someone who'd been waiting at a cash point only to discover it had run out of money upon reaching the front of the queue.

"Where are we going?" Isabelle was remarkably calm considering the situation.

"To my place. You'll see when you get there."

Amber and Isabelle arrived back at Amber's house where the others were still present.

"Everyone, I'd like you to meet my mate and colleague Isabelle. Izzy would you like a drink?" Amber was flustered but focussed.

"I'll have an orange juice, thanks."

Amber obliged before clearing her throat as she sat down on the corner of the sofa, waiving her phone in the air.

"A while back Izzy attended a meeting with Guy Freedman and Sir Henry Jacob. She basically got bored and began to record the meeting on her phone. They didn't realise. Izzy left her phone by accident and it was still recording after the meeting was over. Well I hope it was anyway. This might be a long shot but I think we…"

"For goodness sakes girl play the thing already!" screamed Veronica.

Amber messed around on her phone to get the file playing. She skipped the bulk of it and hit the play button at around the ninety per cent mark.

"Does this sound familiar Izzy?" The device was on full blast so everyone could hear but Amber stuck it up to Isabelle's ear anyway.

"Yea they're just wrapping up here. I stopped listening and typing in a few minutes as they just say that's that and let me leave. Forward it about three minutes."

Amber did as instructed and pressed play. There was silence for a few minutes before a door could be heard closing, followed by a few more seconds of silence. Guy Freedman and Sir Henry Jacob began to talk.

"I'm still not pleased with Giles, Guy. I think he should have hung around a bit longer."

"Well the man is obsessed with his spasticated daughter. I don't think it makes any difference to our plans anyhow." Henrietta Barnes covered her mouth at the language used, as well as Sir Henry's apparent refusal to challenge it. Sir Henry's next comment would make her and the others gasp.

"If he'd just put the stupid bitch down. I know it's his daughter—but he's really off his game."

"OK you know well, let him deal with his shit. But anyway. Alex wanted me to double check how things were going with recruitment for the trials? Has everything been all right? Are your networks proving receptive?"

"Oh absolutely, there are enough dumb and deluded people out there."

"You're not telling them what Rimotim is, are you?"

"No, of course not you silly man."

"So what are you telling them?"

"Well for most of them I don't have to say anything. They're retarded and their parents tend to be either useless shits who don't care or people left in the gutter by government policy and desperate for money."

"How much are you offering them again?"

"Two grand."

"So test subjects get two grand and we get a few million. I can see the justification in that." Freedman and Sir Henry begin to laugh wildly before the door can be heard again and Isabelle's voice comes into ear shot.

"Sorry Guy and Sir Henry I left my phone here I'll just—"

Amber pressed stop on her phone. A sense of dizziness entered the room as everyone attempted to process what they had just heard. Nobody had noticed the horror that had enveloped Veronica's face. She threw up and began to try and speak but no words were coming out. Amber fetched a bin, but by the time Veronica had come to her senses, an irate Henrietta Barnes had stood up and begun pacing around for a few moments, not knowing whether to smash a glass against the wall or throw a chair through the window. But within seconds her senses returned to her. This wasn't the time to get emotional. This was a time for action—real action.

"Isabelle. Are you comfortable with us using this? It will obviously come back to you." Barnes somehow managed to sound soothing.

"Well I have no intention of going back to that scumbag after what we've just heard." Isabelle crossed her arms and flicked her hair, trying to display a sense of authority.

"I always thought Sir Henry was a bit of knob. But this is just…" Samantha Barratt seemed stuck between devastation and resignation.

"We can't hang around this time and let them get away with it. First editions have gone out but once Hayley sees this I can convince her to put out a second edition. I know Sir Henry. He'll go to his office first thing in the morning. That's what he always does when he's in a pickle. And we'll be waiting for him. Everybody go home. Do your usual thing. Isabelle go to my office tomorrow morning. You'll find a job waiting for you. Samantha, I'll meet you at Sir Henry's office first thing…half eight." And with that Henrietta Barnes concluded the meeting. As everyone began to leave, Samantha Barratt stopped and turned to face Amber.

"Amber I don't want to freak you out but I think you and your mother should come and stay with me tonight, just as a precaution." Barratt seemed sincere enough, so Amber nodded and said she'd explain things to her mother when she arrived home later.

For Barnes, what she had just heard was a brutal vindication of her writings and a shocking indictment of the political system, that senior policy makers could behave in such a manner suggested that they had long operated in a culture where malice and egoism had become bedfellows and where compassion had been evicted from the political compass. Outside, turbulence was rising in Lakeland's car as he was telling Hayes what had just happened. "Look I'm telling you something is going on!"

"Well unless you can put your finger on it stay put for the time being. If one more person turns up, then go in there and do your thing."

People were about to leave when Amber told everyone to stop. Instinct had told her to check outside the front door. She stepped out and walked forward a few paces. Although it was raining, as it was a fairly residential street, it was easy for her to spot cars that didn't belong there. A grey saloon was sat there but with the windows tinted. Samantha Barratt was almost about to join Amber but her sister pulled her back. Amber began to walk towards the car. Lakeland saw her coming; he put his hand inside his suit pocket. He paused for a moment before turning the keys and making a rapid getaway. Amber thought she was going to wet herself. She turned back and went inside.

Chapter Nineteen

Samantha Barratt had managed to convince the Head of Facilities Management at Media City to allow them into Sir Henry Jacob's office. In their eyes, it was a minor misdemeanour compared to what Sir Henry Jacob and his associates appeared to be up to. Barnes and Barratt looked around the office without touching anything until Barnes saw a framed picture of Sir Henry and Lady Victoria Hanley. Barnes paused for a moment, before picking up a glass and smashing it on the picture. After a few minutes Sir Henry arrived. He was on the phone as he came through the door and immediately stopped talking. He waited a couple of seconds before saying, "Something has come up James, I'll have to call you back." Barnes had taken a seat and sat down at Sir Henry's usual spot, leaving him to squander in the middle of the room. "So ladies, to what do I owe this pleasure? I'm generally relaxed about visitors but they don't tend to be waiting for me here before I actually get here." Barnes and Barratt waited there without saying anything. "Well, come on ladies, spit it out." Barnes simply began to play a copy of the recording she had taken from Amber and stopped after the offending speech had been broadcast. The second edition of the *Tribune* had chosen to attack Hayes and Freedman but without referencing the recording and so Sir Henry seemed genuinely curious at the presence of Barnes and Barratt. He now knew why they were here.

"I always knew you were a scumbag Sir Henry. And now we have the proof." announced Samantha Barratt with menace.

"Oh come now ladies, that was nothing. You all know Guy Freedman is a bit of a tearaway. You need to keep him happy or…"

"Don't give me that claptrap Henry." Barnes smacked the desk with her hand. The desk was one of Sir Henry's prized possessions, an antique passed down from his grandfather from his days serving overseas as a senior administrator in the Foreign Office. Barnes pulled out a scissor and began dragging it along the surface of the desk, leaving a long, white blemish. "What kind of nastiness have you and Guy and Hayes been up to?" Sir Henry was squirming more than an infant that had forgotten his potty training instructions. Sir Henry's mouth was moving but nothing was coming out. "Let me explain something to you Henry. This is it for you. We're going to devote every front page just for you until we get to the bottom of it or until you drop dead. You can kiss all this goodbye. After we're done, the only thing you'll have left is that poxy knighthood." Barnes' militant demeanour could lacerate a piece of steel twenty inches thick.

"It's just a way to make some money. It's not me. It's Alexander Hayes." Sir Henry just about managed to get the words out as his voice began to disintegrate.

"What about Hayes? What's he got going on?" demanded Barratt.

"This firm approached him a while back. Pinnacle Lab. They had this drug that they'd come up with. But it was too unstable and weren't given permission to trial it on humans until they sorted it out."

"Go on," snarled Barratt.

"They basically offered him a cut of the profits if he'd work with them to get it through various hoops, regulatory, political…and testing. It's like a really big deal. They'd stand to make billions from it." Sir Henry attempted to take his mobile out but Barratt stepped across and whipped it out of his hand. He even sounded excided as he described the scenario to them, as if by some ridiculous twist they would turn around and ask to be included in the deal in return for a share of the profits.

"So where the heck do you and Guy Freedman come in?" shouted Barratt.

"He got Guy involved because…well you know what those two are like together. He needed help to find what he called low profile volunteers for the trials. Disabled people, homeless people, that sort of thing. People that nobody cared about. But honestly I only put forward people I thought were no hopers. If you go to Carlton Dock, Hayes has set up a company to process the trials." Sir Henry was, to the astonishment of Barratt and Barnes, was now trying to sound distraught and magnanimous about the entire thing. The perverse nature of the operation was either lost on him, or more probably, like Hayes and Freedman, he didn't have the moral aptitude to discern why it was wrong. The heartless, care-free social and political atmosphere that had built up over the past years could regard Sir Henry as a perpetrator and a victim.

"So what's all this then Henry?" Barnes stretched her arms out to highlight the surroundings they were in and their various awards Sir Henry had won. "What's that?" she screamed—pointing at the now broken picture of Sir Henry and Lady Victoria Hanley. "Just a façade of lies and hypocrisy?"

Sir Henry was about to respond but he saw Barnes move from around the desk and approach him. She stood directly in front of him and bent down so that they were making eye contact. "I'm going to make sure every single day of the rest of your life is a total misery." Sir Henry wheeled around to his normal spot and played around with the draw. He pulled out a pile of papers and some photographs. He leaned forward and placed them all on the far side of the desk so that it was easy for Barnes and Barratt to pick them up. They did so and then turned around and headed for the door.

"You think you're all so perfect, I suggest you have a chat with one of your new chums, then you'll see!" Sir Henry was crestfallen but there was a dark flippancy to his words.

"What do you mean?" asked Barratt as she turned around to face him again. Sir Henry picked up his mobile and held it so that Barratt and Barnes could see the display. Both women stood there for an age. Sir Henry had a smile of pure evil written on his face. The smile transformed into a look of wrath as he threw the phone like a javelin in the direction of Barnes. Barnes stuck her hand up to divert the incoming missile on to the floor. She bent down, picked it up and turned back around to leave the room. Barratt turned the door knob and once the door was fully open, a vicious gunshot rung out. Screams could be heard from the corridor as people began to rush around in hysterical panic. Barnes and Barratt looked at each other, but at no point looked back. With expressionless faces, they walked out the door.

***

Hayes had done an excellent job of positioning his sycophants to suck up the pressure of the negative *Tribune* front page. The line he was taking was attempting to dismiss what had been written as standard accounting best practice, combined with crassly alluding to Barnes' questionable mental state. It was the accusations being levelled at Freedman that were causing Hayes a rare case of nervousness. The two of them had enough eyes and ears across the parliamentary village to know when a negative story was coming their way. There was no indication where the story had come from, and now Hayes was struggling to get in touch with his partner in crime. He'd left a number of voicemails but Freedman had failed to get back to him.

While Hayes was unable to get through to any of his allies, there were plenty who were trying to get through to him. Most of them were expected, apart from one—the Home Secretary. Hayes rejected the call a few times before finally answering.

"How can I help you Home…"

"All deals are off you slimy…!"

"I beg your pardon? You do realise what you're saying?" Hayes had had his stumps taken out and was no longer sure of himself.

"I know exactly what I'm saying. I've just had a very interesting tip off from one of your colleagues. News is that you're finished. You and Freedman. You never know who to trust in this game, do you?" The call was ended there and then. Hayes was apoplectic. His brain went into top gear, trying to pick apart the situation and attempting to identify the traitor. In reality, the Home Secretary had dropped him an enormous hint—had he analysed his words more carefully. That morning Samantha Barratt had decided to test the strength of his bird's nest by tipping off the Home Secretary. In one last dash for survival, he agreed to play ball. Barratt was Hayes' parliamentary colleague, but his arrogance would never let him make the connection. There was only one person who had the level of greed and power to betray them. Hayes was having difficulty getting through to Lakeland, so using one of his secure phones, he sent him a text, consisting of a skull and cross bones emoticon and the word 'O'Hara'.

Within a couple of hours, the death of Sir Henry Jacob had broken. The twenty-four hour news channels had begun to broadcast live from the scene. Samantha Barratt had phoned her sister to make sure either herself or another clean officer got to the scene first—anyone would do apart from Lakeland at this stage. Detective Barratt managed to get one of her trusted associates on the case

213

before Lakeland had an opportunity to stick his ore in—but only just. Lakeland eventually got word that something was about to happen at Carlton Dock. He went to his mobile in order to phone Hayes and saw the message that was left for him. He ploughed through the London traffic. He wasn't hearing any sirens but was unsure if that was a good thing or a bad thing. Taking the final corner, he realised he was minutes too late. He drifted past before speeding off. He now had other matters to attend to. The interlude provided the chance for Barnes and the sisters to exchange as much information as they could about Carlton Dock so that they could execute a blitz search. Detective Barratt had covertly put together an assortment of her most trusted officers and asked them to remain on standby. Sir Henry's words were not enough to enter the premises and Detective Barratt needed something, anything, from her colleagues in forensic accounts in order to make a decisive move on what Sir Henry had told them. During the agonising wait, if Detective Barratt was honest with herself, her main concern was one of the team tipping off Lakeland or Hayes from the very outset. The corruption hadn't spread to an uncontrollable number of officers, but Detective Barratt couldn't really know for sure who was on the straight and narrow and who wasn't. As it turned out, things had gone her way on this occasion, and she was determined to make it count.

Colleagues in forensics eventually gave the green light she was looking for to undertake a raid on the premises. The exchange at the front gate didn't last long, despite the fortified nature of the place. Detective Barratt entered the building escorted by her officers and was promptly greeted by a number of men in well-ironed shirts and beautifully tailored suits.

"Erm excuse me what on earth is going here?" yelled one of them. "This is a medical facility! I don't know what you're doing but…"

"Excuse me sir are you in charge here?" interrupted Detective Barratt.

"I'm head of facilities and—"

"Perfect. Can you two do the formalities with this gentleman?" She left two of her colleagues to brief the representative as she signalled to the rest of the team to break into units and search the various buildings that made up the complex. The Head of Facilities was calling his supervisors to update them on what was going on.

"Carl. Are you upstairs in your office? We've got a serious problem down here…!"

Nobody was aware of Carl Kelly's involvement in the activities of Pinnacle Lab. Hayes had obviously chosen him as a fellow Grove Chambers man and someone who could be relied upon. He also had the requisite medical background. Kelly didn't fail in his duty, relaying the imminent tale of catastrophe to Alexander Hayes.

"Who is it? Has Lakeland turned on us?" Hayes had finally succumbed to the paranoia that someone with so much on the line would inevitably fall victim to.

"I don't know! He's nowhere to be seen! It's Barratt!" Kelly was clearly frightened.

"Get out of there Carl. There are two helicopters on the roof. Take one of them. Alf can fly the thing! We'll have to re-group elsewhere." Hayes was blunt and tortuous.

"Yes but…" Kelly wanted further instructions but Hayes slammed the phone down.

Within a few minutes, Detective Barratt had reached Kelly's office, but he'd made a break for it out of the window. Barratt headed for the window and saw Kelly crawling up the pipes, despite being only two floors from ground level and officers not covering his side of the building sufficiently. Detective Barratt radioed her colleagues to inform them she was going to the roof. She had asked for all lifts to be shut off so it became a matter of invoking all her marathon training and running up sixteen flights of stairs. Barratt was conscious of a bullet or some other weapon welcoming her when she reached the roof. When she got to the top all she found was Kelly arguing with the colleague he had nabbed to fly the helicopter.

"LOOK WE DON'T HAVE A CHOICE! WE'RE ON THE WRONG UNIT! IF YOU WANNA GET IN THAT HELICOPTER THEN WE'RE GONNA HAVE TO JUMP THE DISTANCE. IT'S NOT THAT FAR. WE JUST NEED A GOOD RUN UP!"

"DON'T MOVE! STAY WHERE YOU ARE!"

Screamed Detective Barratt. But before she could approach, Kelly's colleague bolted like a horse that had won the Grand National. He landed on the roof of the adjacent unit with centimetres to spare and zoomed to the helicopter to get it started. Barratt and

Kelly stared at each other before Kelly looked back at the helicopter. Still recovering her breath, Barratt shouted one last time, "DON'T BE A FOOL, WE CAN…" Kelly began to pole vault across the roof before leaping once he got to the very edge. Fractions are everything in long jumping, and one isn't helped when carrying excess weight. Kelly missed the unit by no more than an inch and plummeted to the ground below. Barratt ran to the edge to glimpse the wretched mess that lay below. But she noticed the helicopter pilot hadn't got the contraption going. She began to scream at him, urging him to stay where he was. Witnessing the death of his boss had turned him into a trance like state and he simply stood there while she radioed for assistance.

Downstairs, she returned to one of the main wards where 'patients' were being attended to by police officers as well as medics that had been called for. Some patients were sitting up and talkative, others were moaning in pain and others were totally motionless. Detective Barratt pulled out some photos Sir Henry had passed to Samantha Barratt and Henrietta Barnes before his demise. Barratt robotically raised her eyebrows and looked around before returning her gaze to a new photo. She approached one of the beds where a girl was moaning in discomfort.

"Hi sweetie, is your name Clare? Clare Thomas?" asked Barratt ever so delicately.

"Mmm," came a muffled response.

"Do you know where you are honey…? Do you know how you got here?"

"Sir… Hen…treat me…help…to get better." Clare began to sob uncontrollably. "My stomach is kill…please…I…"

"Oh sweetie, it's OK! I need you to hold on a short while longer! You'll be all right!" Detective Barratt didn't want to move her. She squeezed Clare's hand and moved her hair from her line of sight so she could see better. A call came in on the radio ordering her to go to the basement. The team had discovered a number of post-mortem examination rooms. The police had the grim task of attempting to identify the bodies they had discovered. The photos provided by Sir Henry had been distributed in a desperate attempt to put names to faces. There was one body, however, that needed no family identification. Harry Christopher was found, apparently having been dissected and patched up on more than one occasion.

The police were trying their best to pin down Alexander Hayes' location but to no avail. A combination of documents provided by a summary search of Sir Henry's office and information collected by forensic accounts had managed to uncover a series of undeclared properties used by Hayes, but all searches returned empty results. It was information left by Giles Gibbs that proved to be most illuminating. He had left enough to pursue Hayes overseas, something that Detective Barratt and her colleagues would now have to do. Hayes was fully aware that his attempts to reinforce his secretive world with papier Mache were crumbling around him, but just as his father and grandfather, he always had a contingency plan up his sleeve. He phoned Guy Freedman from a secret location and finally managed to get through to him. Hayes' anger had now left him, and his mind had returned to the mode of cold calculation.

"Guy. Listen, they'll be coming for you." Hayes sounded cooler than a duck. Freedman on the other hand was hysterical.

"What the heck is going on Alex? What's happened to Sir Henry? And why are they raiding all your flats? Can we cover this up?" Staggeringly, the scale of what was happening hadn't quite dawned on Freedman, as he tried to hold on to the old certainties he and Hayes had spent years building up.

"Look. We'll have to reconvene another time. Just remember who your friends are and you'll be fine." Hayes promptly hung up and dialled a new number on the phone.

"Detective Barratt. I'm sorry I can't talk for long."

"Why don't you come down to the station and we can talk about it?" Detective Barratt knew that despite the weight of evidence building against Hayes, there was no way he'd phone her without having an appropriate exit strategy.

"Look!" Hayes sounded ferociously solemn. "You're looking in the wrong direction. I don't know what all this is about but I can answer all your queries in two words."

"And what words would those be?" Her ears were on fire.

"Guy Freedman. He's the one you want!" Hayes sounded increasingly frenzied. "I'll turn myself in, but only after I know Guy Freedman is at a safe distance." Hayes hung up the phone for the final time. Detective Barratt knew that for the time being at least, Hayes might as well be on the moon. The outcome of inquiries into police scandals such as cash for access had somehow led to a decrease in resources rather than an increase. Barratt also knew from the stockpile of information that had been revealed in the last twenty-four to forty-eight hours, Freedman had enough questions to answer of his own.

Freedman had arranged a press conference to announce his resignation as a Member of Parliament and as Deputy Leader of the Opposition. Extra security had to be brought in order to deal with the media scrum in attendance. The age of social media meant that despite only a few hours since Sir Henry's downfall, news had spread about an impending crisis in the Unity Party. Hayes' disappearance was having the temporary ironic impact of working to his favour due to there being no one to speak on his behalf, thus nobody was in a position to say anything concrete. He'd used every inch of his network to extract himself from the political furnace, leaving behind an assortment of confused special advisers and PR experts. Media and political commentators kept peddling the same lines—either that no one was able to contact Hayes or that he had also committed suicide due to some piece of horrific news that was about to be disclosed. Detective Barratt wanted to give Freedman as little traction as possible. She knew where the press conference had been planned and had issued a statement to say that she'd be updating the public on the events that had taken place and a press conference would start forty minutes before Freedman's at the Havering Centre, just a five-minute walk from Unity Party HQ.

"Good evening everyone and thank you for coming at such short notice. By now, I think you are all aware of the death of Sir Henry Jacob. I can formally confirm that his death was a suicide. I can also confirm that his death was in connection to what at this early stage looks like a corruption scandal that we have uncovered in the last forty-eight hours. The investigation centres on a series of financial and medical malpractices committed by firms who at this point shall remain un-named." She paused for a moment. How much should she make public? Was now the time to let everything out? If she publicly called out Hayes and Freedman, there might be a potential political meltdown. But maybe that's what the country needed? "At this stage, I would also like to formally confirm that we are seeking co-operation in this matter from Guy Freedman and Alexander Hayes, two individuals who you all obviously know. I would urge them to make contact with us so that we can resolve this issue in a professional manner. I'm now going to hand over to my colleague who will take questions and give you further details as to some of the developments that have happened today." The media mob began to shout out questions as Detective Barratt left the stage. She reached the exit where a number of officers joined her. Detective Barratt had become chief attraction in the media circus as she entered the building and headed for the conference area. As she entered the main room, the media scrum that had followed her had joined those present to create a vortex of flashes. Guy Freedman walked into the room flanked by two of his aides, but before he sat down he saw Detective Barratt standing at the far end of the conference room. The two were standing looking at each other. Freedman had his hands in his trouser pockets briefly before taking them out again. He then turned in the direction he had come from and returned to the private room where he was making the final touches to his resignation speech. Detective Barratt swooped into the room moments later.

"Out of courtesy, I'm not going to arrest you here in front of your friends and colleagues. I ask that you accompany me back out through that crowd without saying a word and then onto the police station." Freedman nodded and began to walk behind Detective Barratt as they left the room. A security cordon acted as a steel ring as the two headed outside towards a waiting police car. The cordon wasn't enough to neutralise the motorcycle that came rocketing by, firing multiple shots that took out Freedman, as well as Detective Barratt. Armed police took out the motorcycle within seconds. But it was really a suicide mission. Having so many connections to the downtrodden meant that Hector Gregory was able to convince someone to take on the task in exchange for a healthy sum of money for their family. Half a dozen paramedics attended to Freedman and Detective Barratt. It didn't look good for him, but Barratt had only been hit in the shoulder—though she felt like she'd had her liver torn out. She needed Freedman, and despite protests from paramedics, she jumped in the ambulance with him.

In the days that followed the monumental events of Guy Freedman and Alexander Hayes' downfall, a torrent of special shows attempted to dissect what had happened to the Unity Party and what could be done to protect the integrity of the British state in the future. Amber had managed to get herself into the audience for a panel show where the participants answer questions from audience members. Much of the talk seemed to be politically correct drivel in Amber's eyes. The nature of the discussion was that, despite the spectacular nature of the events that had taken place, a few rotten apples had infected what should still be regarded as a competent political system that could take care of the under-privileged and hold the powerful to account. Nobody seemed to want to address the level of manipulation that Hayes and Freedman were able to attain without challenge, how they were able to establish influence in every orifice of power without any form of scrutiny. It seemed to Amber that what people were saying was that what had gone wrong was not the level of power that had come to be vested in Hayes and Freedman, but rather these were two chaps that didn't appreciate the rules of the game and pursued their own personal agenda. British political power was apparently a labyrinth, where a combination of instinct and good fortune were the only tools that could be used for successful navigation. The same politicians and the same academics from the same institutions had spent so many years perpetuating this mirage that it was almost impossible to hold a public debate about what was going wrong and how to fix it. Amber had put her hand up several times before finally being picked to ask a question.

"I'm sorry panel but isn't this really all about control, how politicians and vested interests hold it and how the common man like all the people in this audience are at the mercy of these people."

A representative from the Alliance Party was asked to respond.

"I don't think we should be saying 'these people' as if there is some kind of shadowy club pulling the strings. I think everyone around this table wants what's best for this country. I think we need to work together more efficiently to deliver prosperity for…"

"Oh my days, are you insane!" interrupted Amber with gusto. "Whether it's obscene house prices, obscene tuition fees, waiting forever to get a doctor's appointment, an abysmal social care system—the bottom line is that you either sink or swim. Why is it that someone can have their benefit cut off with the click of a finger but it takes weeks to reinstate it again even though no wrongdoing is done?" The audience began to breakout into rapturous applause. "Why is it that all of these events have come about following the quite blatant targeting of disabled people but you can't be asked to invite a disabled person on to the panel? And if there aren't enough disabled politicians, perhaps we should ask ourselves why that is?" The audience continued to applaud but the chair of the panel simply thanked Amber for her contribution and moved on.

The show was recorded in the late afternoon, giving Amber enough time to make her way to the hospital. Lakeland's absence from recent events was partially contrived. He had reported back to his superiors that Isabelle appeared to be a key conspirator against them, and so was given orders to address the situation. He'd viciously attacked Isabelle in her home and was only interrupted by a neighbour who had heard the sound of items being smashed to pieces. He was told to take his time with her due to the apparent fatal blow she'd struck to everybody's plans. Amber sat by her bed, totally guilt-ridden. In hindsight, of all the people to suffer, she thought she'd be first in line, considering the amount of trouble her and her friends had caused. Isabelle had used her sophistication of thought to keep out of trouble, and yet here she was, battered and bruised, and all because Amber and Marcus didn't want to go to a meeting. By now, Lakeland had left such a trail of devastation he had stopped bothering to cover his tracks. He knew the current game was up. His knowledge of all things police and security made him a useful asset to Hayes, who in due course managed to smuggle him out of the country.

The doorbell was ringing incessantly.

"All right calm down, I'm coming"

"Hello Veronica." Barratt and Barnes didn't have the friendliest of faces. Barnes held up Sir Henry's phone so that Veronica could see her contact details. Veronica was shaking. She reversed, turned around and headed towards the kitchen, with Barnes and Barratt following her.

"We're not here to judge you Veronica. We just want an explanation." Samantha Barratt was almost pausing between every word, trying not to explode into a fireball of fury. Veronica was swivelling all over the place. She felt as if she was being sucked in by quicksand with only a helium balloon keeping her intact.

"Shit shit shit! You don't understand! You don't know! Sir Henry lied! I didn't know what he was doing!" Veronica knocked a vase over as the presence of Barnes and Barratt was slowly causing her to have a breakdown.

"What were you doing for Sir Henry?" Barnes seemed more irritated than angry.

"You know what I was doing!" screamed Veronica. "I was recruiting people for his stupid research! I'm telling you all he said was that it was experimental and confidential! I was desperate for the money and he knew it! I always thought he was useless! How was I meant to know he was some sort of eugenicist freak?"

"For crying out loud Veronica did you not stop to think just once?" barked Barratt.

"Of course I did. I thought to myself—no sod is gonna help me. I've been declined treatment on the National Health twice. It was this or a slow death!" Veronica was sobbing, screaming and waiving her arms around all at the same time.

"Did you get Clare involved?" asked a more settled Barratt.

"No, I did not thank you very much! I've no idea how she got there. I'd never betray Clare!"

"But you were all right betraying all those people you did recruit?" Barnes didn't mean to sound smug but that's how it came across.

"Oh shut up, Henrietta! I haven't betrayed anyone! I told you I didn't know what was going on there. At the end of the day, those people were as desperate as me. If the situation was reversed, they'd all have done the exact same thing!" Veronica was now emboldened following Barnes' haughty comments, but she tried not to sound too condescending. Samantha Barratt sat down and rattled her fingers on her knees.

"All right, fine," stated Barratt as she stood back up again.

"What do you mean fine? What are you going to do?" enquired Veronica nervously.

"We're not going to do anything," replied Barnes. "As for what you're going to say to Amber and Clare—assuming she makes it, that's entirely up to you." Neither said goodbye as they left. They were caught between disgust and disappointment and weren't really sure how to react. Henrietta Barnes had had enough excitement for one day and began to walk home rather than taking the tube. She regretted her decision towards the end of her journey as it began to pour with rain. The sudden onslaught made her rush across the road, and she was oblivious to the car speeding towards her. She was catapulted into the air. The car screened to a stop, but the driver didn't get out. He merely looked in his rear-view mirror. Bob O'Hara had been left to fend for himself. He could feel the walls closing in and all his venom had coalesced around Barnes. If he was soon to be terminated, he had to take out his chief adversary. He'd already messed up one attempt to run someone over in his life, and he wasn't to mess it up for a second time. He spun the car around and went for Barnes again.

Chapter Twenty

Samuel Bertrand wasn't about to be released any time soon, as at the end of the day, he had carried out much of Alexander Hayes and Hector Gregory's dirty work. But there was sufficient evidence to suggest that his actions paled into insignificance compared to some of the others involved. Bertrand wasn't being held in solitary confinement, despite Freedman previously leading a campaign to have him put there. Bertrand had got wind of what happened to Guy Freedman and was cognisant of the fact that he was probably next. At this stage, nobody had any information regarding Terrance Winchester's involvement. Winchester wasn't going to go lying down, and if it was up to him, he'd prefer it if no news came out at all. As far as Winchester was concerned, he needed to hang around in order to begin the nurturing process of the next generation. Freedman and Hayes were doing a stellar job, but they committed the cardinal error of getting too big for their boots and not understanding the precarious balance that needed to be struck between taking advantage of the system and maintaining the status quo. Freedman and Hayes had messed things up so badly it would be a while before Winchester would be able to oil the chains again and begin to get people in the places they needed to be. But he didn't have time on his side, and nothing would be possible if Bertrand spilled the beans on what he knew. Bertrand had kept quiet up to now for his own personal safety, but the treatment of Guy Freedman suggested that even keeping silent was no guarantee of staying alive. Detective Barratt was notified of a disturbance at Bertrand's prison and raced to the scene. Bertrand's cell was a blood-soaked mess, resembling an abattoir rather than a prison cell. An inspection of the cell that followed turned up a few personal possessions, as well as a hidden piece of paper stored behind a loose brick simply addressed to 'the police'. Bertrand was hoping Detective Barratt would be first on the scene and thankfully for him, she was. The paper contained an admission of guilt on his part, as well as critical information about Winchester's involvement in the things that had been going on. Bertrand declared he was unable to connect Winchester's activities with what had happened at Carlton Dock, but he provided information that implicated Winchester in a series of security breaches around parliament that had been attributed to rogue members of parliamentary security. Winchester was a wall of charisma. Much of his success came down to taking advantage of simple pleasantries he would offer. Agreeing a causal infraction of the rules at a dinner party to help a friend and not signing certain pieces of paper in the name of minimising bureaucracy were just two of the smaller ways Winchester got his work done. Only someone close to him would know the sort of underhanded actions he was capable of. Bertrand didn't explain how he was chosen to be one of the main shit-throwers in Winchester's inner circle. For now, that wasn't important. Bertrand had given sufficient times and dates of unauthorised activity that would take a lot of explaining. Bertrand also confirmed that it was Winchester who ordered for the file to be put in Samantha Barratt's desk. Detective Barratt shared the information with her sister, but they had no intention of bringing in Winchester with cameras and fanfare. Both knew Winchester, like Sir Henry, was a creature of habit and headed straight to his parliamentary office where they were sure they would find him.

"I'm sorry, I do prefer when people knock…" Winchester turned around to see the Barratt sisters enter his opulent office. They didn't say a word. There were two chairs conveniently placed, and the two sat down.

"What's it all about Terrance?" asked Samantha Barratt quietly.

"What's what about darling?"

"Putting folders in my desk, letting LGW work here, Alexander Hayes and Guy Freedman, Pinnacle Lab." Winchester knew playing the ignorance game was out of the question. He had the naïvety to think that taking care of Samuel Bertrand would cut all links back to him.

"Well…what can I say?" Winchester sat back, not even blinking.

"There must be something behind it all you little rat!" blasted Detective Barratt.

"You'll never understand." Winchester was shaking his head. He didn't appear to be in a charitable mood.

"Money? Drugs? Political power? What exactly do you want?" Samantha Barratt was getting angry. She wanted to smack Winchester in the face.

"What's best for us is also what's best for this country. You'll never see it. You'll realise one day, but by then, it will be too late." Winchester's cryptic, self-aggrandising remark was the final indication that he was sticking to his guns. But in reality, he didn't have to say anything. His aims and those of his associates had been concocted and implemented over a number of years, and only trained eyes like Henrietta Barnes knew what their modus operandi was. It had got to a stage where they were practising their dark arts in plain sight; yet no real challenge to their legitimacy was being made.

"Is that it? No grand Winchester speech?" Samantha Barratt was desperate for Winchester to say more. But for Winchester, the game was up, and he refused to utter another word. Having been apprehended, Winchester was in the same predicament as Bertrand. He had no intention of cooperating with the authorities, but he knew he was no longer of any use to Hayes and the others who had managed to slip through the net. But unlike Bertrand, his parliamentary background meant he was afforded levels of security far higher than anything given to his former favourite intern. There was no way anybody was going to get to him any time soon.

The day of the blindfold march had arrived with a lot more fanfare than had been anticipated. Veronica was keeping her secret for the time-being, intending to tell the others about her wrongdoing after the march. The event was rightfully benefiting from goodwill that had come their way following the disclosure of the ghastly events at Carlton Dock. It was a carnival atmosphere as around twenty-five thousand people lined up behind what Veronica called 'the professionals'—a number of blind and partially sighted individuals who had happily volunteered their services. One of the companies that Veronica had managed to get to sponsor the event was an accessible vehicle organisation that brought along accessible ice cream trucks. Many participants were managing to hold an ice cream in one hand while remaining attached to those near them— sometimes with hilarious consequences. A number of Members of Parliament had also signed up to take part in the event, so as a result, security was more intense than what would be the case for such an event. But it wasn't enough to stop the events that were about to follow. A flash followed by a dramatic explosion followed by haunting screams of panic. Alexander Hayes was thousands of miles away, watching events unfold on his smartphone. He passed the phone to James Jacob, who took the phone, glanced at the footage and passed it back to Hayes.

Amber didn't have time to process the news of the explosion as details came in on her phone. She was at Clare's house, along with Clare's mother, doctors and representatives from social services. A combination of Clare's existing illness and the drugs injected at Carlton Dock had left her in a semi-catatonic state. Changes brought in by the government meant that due to the severely impaired nature of the patient, a compulsory transfer of care was possible if two doctors agreed. As far as Amber was concerned, the phrase 'transfer of care' was a euphemism. Whenever such orders had been made for patients since the legislation was introduced, it seemed doctors only had one thing on their mind. Either that, or pressure from unknown sources was causing them to evaluate life and death situations in very different ways. The Assisted Dying Act had a preposterous clause claiming to make things easier on the patients by allowing doctors to administer the relevant drugs at the patient's home. Amber had spent a lot of time with Clare ever since the hospital had made their intentions clear. As far as she was concerned, Clare was full of life—the authorities just didn't want to see it. A flicker of a smile, a spontaneous grunt, an almost imperceptible laugh—it was all there. Despite the transfer of care having taken place, the doctors still needed Mrs Thomas' authorisation to proceed or delay matters by obtaining a court order. Amber was in a fit of tears as she repeatedly called out Clare's name.

"Clare Gwendoline Thomas!" she screamed with love and anguish. "If you don't give me a smile this very second, I'm going to take that painting of your garden and tear it to pieces!" Clare was motionless. Nobody in the room could really tell what was going on inside her head—if anything was going on at all. Mrs Thomas was a ghost, sitting at the end of the bed on the far side to Amber. Amber skidded around and began to ferociously rub her arms and cuddle her. "Mrs Thomas... I know this is... I mean...you don't need to do this now. There's a time for everyone Mrs Thomas! They don't know that this is Clare's…!"